Nakamura Reality

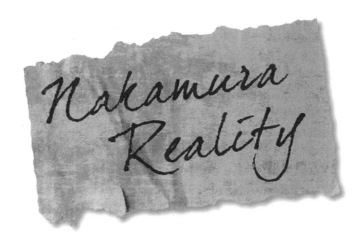

ALEX AUSTIN

THE PERMANENT PRESS
Sag Harbor, NY 11963

Excerpts from *Nakamura Reality* have been published in *carte blanche*, *Rose and Thorn Journal*, *Black Clock*, *Apeiron*, *This Literary Magazine*, *Heavy Feather Review* and *River & South Journal*.

For information, address:
  The Permanent Press
  4170 Noyac Road
  Sag Harbor, NY 11963
  www.thepermanentpress.com

Library of Congress Cataloging-in-Publication Data

  Austin, Alex—
    Nakamura reality / Alex Austin.
      pages ; cm
    ISBN 978-1-57962-409-5

  PS3601.U8544N35 2016
  813'.6—dc23   2015040870

Printed in the United States of America

This book is dedicated to my agent,
Claire Anderson-Wheeler.

Prologue

Oceanside, California

Hugh Mcpherson glanced at his watch. *Thirty minutes.* The waves weren't getting any smaller. Slabs of water, *rhinos* the surfers called them, which didn't stop dozens of thrill-seekers in black wet suits from stepping into their path. Kneeling on the sand, a short distance from Hugh, his sons, Takumi and Hitoshi, gazed mutely at the scene. Although there were surfers not much older or taller than the twins, none were quite as young as eleven, none with their slender builds, none with their narrow shoulders. If Setsuko had seen the surf, she wouldn't have considered letting their sons go in. But his wife had remained at their Oceanside time-share condo, feeling ill, attributing it to the take-out dinner they ate on the two-hour drive down from their Studio City home, where their suitcases were packed to take their real vacation, a month of summer at her father's house in Tokyo. A month of rain and humidity . . .

After Setsuko made known that she wasn't going to the beach, Hugh made the phone call, and then showered.

Leaning back on his beach towel, Hugh scanned the path of a seasoned surfer as he soared down the steep front of his wave, cutting white tracks, sending up sparkling jets. For such big surf, the water was beautiful—light green and transparent. A bright, warm day under baby blue skies. Hugh pried the lid off his coffee and sipped the flavorless 7-Eleven brew.

"They aren't that big," said Takumi, five minutes older than his twin and the more assertive of the two.

"What if we stay close to shore, Dad?" asked Hitoshi.

"Just catch the wash," added Takumi.

"Let's just wait," Hugh responded.

Hugh drew out a box of donuts from his gym bag, opened it and offered the jelly-filled cakes to his sons. Hitoshi took one, but Takumi declined. As Hugh chose one for himself, a seagull swooped down and settled a few yards away. Hugh closed the box, set it on the blanket and bit into his cake.

"Not like we're swimming. We've got the boards," insisted Takumi.

Hitoshi clapped his brother's shoulder. "We'll stay close together."

"We've surfed bigger waves at Topanga," added Takumi.

"Way crazier than this," said Hitoshi.

"I know, I know," Hugh admitted.

"What's so special about today then?" asked Takumi.

Yes, *what was so special* . . .

A cadre of surfers soared down a wave's slope like rocket streamers.

"Nothing," snapped Hugh.

"Why did we come here then?" asked Hitoshi.

"You're always telling us how good we are," said Takumi.

"You are good," Hugh said with conviction.

"Then why can't we go?"

Hugh set down his half-eaten donut on the box and pointed. "Look at the size of that wave."

"We wouldn't take that wave. We're not stupid."

"Of course not, but . . . it's not just one wave." Feeling a flutter of air, Hugh twisted to see the gull, Hugh's half-eaten donut in its beak, taking off.

"Hey!" said Hugh, reaching for the bird but catching only air. Sighing, he shoved the donut box in his gym bag. The boys seemed not to have noticed the theft.

"We'll stay close together."

"Let's give it time," said Hugh.

Groaning in disapproval, they worked their torsos out of their wet suits, revealing the smooth fair skin, identical down to the freckles on their shoulders.

Twenty minutes.

Sipping his coffee, Hugh leaned into his sons, thinking he would hear their whispers of consolation, but they were silent, staring at different horizons. His head felt heavy, feverish. He closed his eyes for a moment, hoping to slip an oncoming headache. The clap of a wave breaking close to shore sounded sharply like a gunshot, taking away his breath. He swallowed, drove his hand through his hair and laughed stupidly. *Relax. Relax.*

Hugh squeezed Takumi's shoulder. "How do cheesesteak sandwiches sound when we get home?" he asked. Even the mention of food usually got them out of their funk, but Takumi merely shrugged. Hugh grinned and kissed Hitoshi's cheek. "Cheese-steak sandwiches *and onion rings?*" Hugh asked. Hitoshi scrunched his nose, but nodded. Hugh turned to Takumi, who pulled away as Hugh mussed the long black hair.

"You're *excellent* surfers. My two little *rippers,*" said Takumi, mocking the words Hugh had said but a week ago.

Nearby, the marauding seagull mewed insistently. If Hugh told the twins he had to go back to the car and ordered them not to go into the water while he was absent, they would obey him. He was confident of that. But could he be sure that they wouldn't scurry back to the parking lot? Something might happen while they waited. Sand in Hitoshi's eye. A shard of glass rising from the beach to open Takumi's foot.

Fifteen minutes.

He gazed helplessly at the ocean, wishing he were Poseidon who might calm it with a flutter of his hand.

Carrying a surfboard, a boy in a wet suit walked by their towels, skirted a man with a tripod taking pictures, stepped into the surf and then turned back and waved. The twins stared jealously. The boy was a small girl.

"Dad?" said Takumi.

"Look," said Hitoshi, pointing at the line of surfers, "that wave is nothing!"

It was not nothing, but it was by far the smallest wave of the morning.

"The surf report was right," said Takumi.

"Can we go now?"

Hugh peered beyond the surfers to where a sleek cabin cruiser—the design strikingly futuristic—motored. The boat rose and fell on the swells that formed along its trajectory. But the waves were not so big that the boat vanished. The swells were flatter now. The sea was shaping itself to Hugh's desire.

He followed another set of diminishing waves. It was not an illusion. The sea had calmed. "I think we're OK. Go for it."

"Yes!"

Beaming, they slipped back into their wet suits and folded the Velcro leashes around their slender ankles. The leashes were made for thicker limbs and though wrapped their tightest still had play.

Carrying his coffee, he walked with his sons into the surf. He was hip deep, and the backwash was enough to knock him off balance. The chaotic waters reflected sunlight in a hundred directions, poking holes in his vision like a kaleidoscope. To Hugh's right a man stood in the water with a boom box on his shoulder, the crack of the waves breaking up an odd fragile cover of an old famed song.

Five minutes.

Takumi and Hitoshi threw themselves onto their surfboards and paddled into the wash.

"Catch one for me," Hugh said, though he wasn't sure they could hear him over the thundering waves. Through his eyes, compounded like a fly's, he followed their lithe bodies as they fought through the surf, paddling parallel, nosing down to penetrate the broken waves.

They faced a set that carried surfers. They broke through the base of the first wave, disappearing as the comber rose up to curl and collapse. Hugh saw them again, just as the second wave struck. They made it through the third and took their place among the dozens of other surfers on the flat water, waiting for the next set. Hugh watched all the surfers drift to the right. A wave formed, rising. The twins paddled side by side forcefully, belying their age and size. Together they turned, shooting forward as the wave lifted them until they were on the crest, held in suspension for an instant and then rocketing down, soaring the wave's infinite face. Crouched, they cut right and then left with dazzling synchronicity. As the wave folded and crashed, they rode parallel to the shore and then rolled off their boards, disappearing into the froth, above which a pelican shimmied as if caught in a crosswind.

When the twins reappeared, they turned their boards around and started paddling out again. He caught the fierce smiles. In their wet suits, they could stay in the water for hours, and they would stay until he returned. As Hugh backed toward the beach, he stumbled in the backwash and dropped his coffee cup, which seemed to bound joyfully atop the waves. Following the Styrofoam as it skipped seaward, Hugh had an inchoate urge to call back his sons, but the tick of his watch drowned the shout in his heart.

Time.

As Hugh approached the parking lot, with a view of the sun-bleached broken trestle that had given the surf spot its name, a vintage red Mustang roared down the access road. He pictured a woman at the wheel, unsettling green eyes, parted lips, body posed against naked red leather. As the car came closer, he glanced down at the New Jersey license plate that read CSNDRA. Momentarily confused, Hugh lifted his eyes to the driver, who smiled broadly.

By the time Hugh returned, most of the surfers had moved farther out, where the swells had regained their early morning size. He scanned the black wet suits, looking for the smallest. Beyond the surfers, the futuristic boat now roared with power as it motored west, showing its stern to the enormous waves. He walked to the water's edge and called their names. The ocean's roar drowned his voice. He would not have been able to reach them with a bullhorn. The surfers were fighting against a current that threatened to pull them off the break. The set came. The first was the largest he had seen all day.

A dozen surfers turned their boards toward the shore and paddled to get ahead of the wave. Hugh tried to pick out his sons from the other surfers being lifted on the swell like chips of wood, half failing to catch it. For a few seconds, the pack was invisible. The second wave rose. More surfers strove to take this one, arms windmilling, heads raised like beasts sniffing their prey. When the third wave came, it was enormous. The remaining surfers were determined to ride the monster. Hugh saw his two boys turn their boards to shore and paddle furiously.

Lodged ten feet high on the face, they stood up and shot sideways, moving fast. Spreading apart as the wave carried them shoreward, they cut trails, carved the rushing slope. Touched by their skill, Hugh breathed sharply and caught the scent of the Mustang's interior—*her* scent.

Fuck.

As they toppled off their boards, Hugh yelled for them to come in. They were close enough to have heard, but, ignoring him, they turned away and lay on their boards, stroking seaward. He strode through the backwash, knees pummeling the frothy shattered waves.

"Takumi! Hitoshi!" Hugh shouted. "Goddamn it, come in!" The next wave was the largest of all, a violent unforgiving watery claw. The air rushed from his lungs. *Come in! Come in!*

Hugh dove. He drew himself to the bottom and swam. Thirty seconds later he surfaced for a breath, coming up within the fury of a collapsed comber. He kicked to stay in place, bobbing like a cork as he strained to see his sons among the distant pack. "Takumi! Hitoshi!"

He dove again, remaining underwater until his lungs burned. As he surfaced, a current gripped him and ripped him seaward as if he were a weightless rubber inflatable. *Get beneath it. Get beneath it.* Diving, he fought his way down three feet, six feet, ten feet, until his fingers clawed the dark seabed. The riptide's grip relaxed. For twenty seconds, he swam perpendicular to the current and surfaced again. He was no more than twenty yards from the pack. He spotted the two small wet suits. His boys were flat on their boards, turning now to get in front of the rushing wave. He screamed their names, and in coming about for the wave, they showed their faces.

Not his sons' faces. Not *his* sons. Hugh bobbed on the water's surface, his heart forgetting to beat as he scanned the surfers for their familiar forms. Not there. Not there. Where then? A massive wave rolled toward him carrying a dozen surfers. Where then? He pressed his hands to the sides of his head as if to hold his skull together. He dove into the sea that hid his sons.

Chapter 1

Twelve Years Later

"Tonight at Huddle's Books, we are honored to have Kazuki Ono, who joins Dickens and Orwell, Kafka and Pynchon—and precious few others—as a novelist whose name has become an adjective."

The crowd that jammed Huddle's, a small, independent Pasadena bookstore, applauded. Many of the hundred or so fans raised copies of Kazuki's *Enrique the Freak* above their heads and banged them like tambourines, the sound echoing raucously off the store's high ceiling. Though almost giddy with excitement, the fans were careful not to drop the numbered tickets that would allow them to queue up and meet the author after he read from his latest work.

In the rear of the bookstore, Hugh drew ticket ninety-nine down his unshaven cheek. He had arrived late so as to be camouflaged by the crowd. Across the room his ex-father-in-law, Kazuki, whose sight was never good, wouldn't recognize him—more than ten years had passed—but should he happen to walk by and see Hugh, the author known as the Lion of Osaka would surely roar. With luck, the crowd would disperse by the time ninety-nine stepped up and asked for his favor.

Since his sons' deaths, Hugh had followed Kazuki's work like a fly on a window pane searching for a way out, for in his fiction Kazuki might forgive the most untenable of his characters. But in all eight novels since the tragedy, there had been nothing connected with Hugh or his sons or his wife, no character's mistake that paralleled Hugh's horrific mistake. No message, no pardon. He had bought *Enrique the Freak* earlier in the day but hadn't read a page. He no longer expected to find consoling words—only a simple favor.

Hugh glanced down at his book and turned up the back cover. The rainbow grid that overlay the blurbs and biography framed Kazuki's photograph, a head dominated by the mass of now mostly gray hair, though it had been freakishly blond in his youth, a rare pairing of rare genes. A face with the same bone structure as his daughter's, Setsuko's.

It was a resemblance that had struck Hugh wordless when he first met Kazuki nearly a quarter century ago in that quiet candlelit restaurant in Tokyo's Roppongi District. Then, as much as now, from photos, Hugh was familiar with the narrow, fine-featured face, but he was unprepared for its luminous beauty, a light that seemed only available in cinema close-ups.

It had been five years since Hugh had seen Kazuki in person. Kazuki had appeared at this same bookstore with *Sleepwalkspace*, his eleventh novel. Hugh attended that night, too, listening to Kazuki read in his hesitant English, a mark of typical Japanese modesty, for, in truth, Kazuki's English was perfect.

As on that night five years ago, Hugh had come tonight to ask Kazuki to take a letter to Setsuko, for since she'd returned to Japan, hardly a month after the tragedy, and the subsequent divorce having been decreed final, there had been no further communication between them. Hugh's phone calls had gone unanswered, his e-mails declared undeliverable, his letters stamped *return to sender*, unopened. That letter too had met no better fate for on that night as Kazuki read from his novel, Hugh heard the soul-shaking voices of his sons, as if they were perched at the author's feet, telling their story in counterpoint. Though its source a delusion, the guilt pressed Hugh's chest like a hundred fathoms of sea and he fled, letter in hand.

Now the bookstore's owner signaled for Kazuki, who stood at the rear of the platform, to come forward. The crowd erupted with applause as the author stepped on the stage, still looking trim and athletic at seventy. At his side, he held his novel.

Kazuki bowed several times, smiling. He closed his eyes and the applause tapered off as he stepped up to the microphone.

He began, "Thank you. During my promotional tours, I visit many large bookstores: vast bookstores, I might say. Most are part of chains, which is simply the nature of bookselling these days, and I have no complaints about the way my books are treated. But there remains something special about an independent bookstore like Huddle's, where can be found the obscure and the masterpieces, terms not mutually exclusive. This is a house of words."

The crowd applauded.

"Now in this house of words I would like to add a few more of my own." He lifted his book, set it on the podium and opened it. "*Enrique the Freak*, Chapter One.

"I leased an apartment in the Hatsudai District. The landlord explained that as a condition of the lease, the body would be kept in the living room as I—" Kazuki paused, and then repeated his last two words as if to reassure the audience that they were hearing correctly. "—as *I* had been kept by the previous tenant. He would be visible, floating in liquid nitrogen in a Plexiglas chamber, but the mechanisms for his maintenance would be silent. The building's electricity supplied power, but in the event of a power loss, an emergency generator would take over. There was no need to pay special attention to the chamber, as the dust and grit could be removed with a common household cleaner.

"Any attempt to hide or cover the body, for example when guests came over, would break the lease. The landlord advised against inviting children into the apartment—not that the children would be disturbed by the sight, but because even the best-behaved sometimes get into mischief, occasionally putting their own lives in danger . . ."

The floor shifted beneath Hugh's feet so that he had to grab the bookshelf to steady himself.

Kazuki went on: "Any damage to the chamber would be his responsibility. He—" Again Kazuki paused, and then repeated, "*He* agreed, knowing he constructed this arrangement or *had he* was . . ."

Kazuki looked up suddenly, as if someone in the audience had jeered. He tilted back his head. His eyes danced around and his mouth fell open. As the audience murmured around him, Hugh clasped the bookcase, bracing for the targeting finger and the terrible accusation: *You dare! Murderer of my grandsons!*

But Kazuki said nothing. The crowd, following Kazuki's gaze, turned their faces toward the high ceiling and a soft clapping. Above them, a seagull beat its wings as it calmly circled the assembled fans. The bird didn't seem to be seeking a way out, and there was no sign of how it had gotten in, but though all eyes were on it, the seagull vanished as mysteriously as it had appeared.

Offering the crowd a bemused smile, Kazuki returned to his reading, not noticing that one of the audience, too, had gone missing.

Chapter 2

As the car descended the 101 freeway's steep grade from Pasadena into Burbank, the lights of the San Fernando Valley spread uniformly across the basin to the distant shadowy face of the Santa Monica Mountains. As Kazuki gazed studiously, he searched the seat for the pill he had dropped. No bigger than a pencil point, the tablet eluded his normally sensitive fingertips. The bottle from which he had shaken the pill rested in the console and contained a month's worth of the drug, but Kazuki resisted the easy way out, hunting with as much diligence as he would an elusive word. Soft, soft, soft, ah, hard on the buttery leather. Nipping the tablet, he swallowed the damn thing. With luck, the drug would keep the abdominal pain at bay for a few hours.

A burst of hot white fire appeared to the south, as a rocket rose in the night sky, exploding into dozens of silver streamers, which in turn fragmented into ten thousand multicolored sparks.

"That was a big one," said his driver, Jack, as the boom of the primary explosion rattled the windows, followed by the small artillery of the streamers and the chattering of the final firecracker-like bursts.

Under the dying lights, Kazuki snatched the ivory envelope from the dashboard and turned it over. He traced the handwritten letters of his daughter's name. He glanced up as another explosion unsettled the night. Setsuko, Hugh and the twins had lived only a few blocks away from the theme park. Twice Kazuki had visited the house with the bright green front door, basketball hoop above the garage, the trough of neglected rose bushes. *Hitoshi and Takumi racing down the sidewalk on their Big Wheels.*

Kazuki sighed, "It was a good crowd."

"They're all good crowds, Kazuki. They love where you take them."

Kazuki smiled and studied the envelope again. "The woman who gave you this couldn't describe the man?"

"She was trying to keep her place in line. She said he seemed nervous," Jack responded.

"It's his handwriting," Kazuki said.

"I thought I might have seen him . . ."

The car raced past the Los Angeles River, channeled here in concrete. Kazuki fumbled with the controls on his door.

"Open the window?" asked Jack.

"Please."

The window slid down and the car dropped below the speed limit. A warm wind perfumed with jasmine and citrus whipped up Kazuki's hair and took his breath. Pinching the envelope at one corner, he thrust his hand into the rushing air. His hand vibrated and the envelope made a frightened whistling sound like a trapped bird.

Chapter 3

Pushing back an avalanche of soft drink bottles, Hugh grabbed his gym bag, packed with beach gear and topped with several paperback novels, slammed his trunk for the last time and set off for the beach.

As he passed a shabby trailer that had parked in the same spot for weeks—his rehearsal time—its door opened and a woman wearing a lip ring, black stud large as a marble, stepped out.

"You got a cigarette, babe?" she asked.

"I don't smoke," said Hugh, staring blankly at her, though he had seen the young woman a dozen times.

"You could carry a pack anyway, for the needy," she said with a grin. "Going swimming, huh?" she added, glancing back as if to see the Pacific, but the trailer, parked at an angle to the road, blocked any view of the ocean.

"Yes," said Hugh softly.

She licked the stud and pushed her hand through unkempt blue hair streaked with red like an arrow's fletching. "Your routine, right?"

"That's right," said Hugh, slowing a little, perhaps losing five seconds. He now resumed his quick pace. "Later."

"Have a nice day, Buddha," she laughed.

Hugh raised his hand above his shoulder and waved good-bye.

Hanna was the name of the woman at the trailer. Her boyfriend's name was . . . Kyle, yes, Kyle. They were a couple he'd heard arguing regularly at the Peace & Love Café three miles north. Once when Kyle went to the café's restroom, leaving Hanna and Hugh on the deck, he'd spoken to the young woman. Then she made an almost tearful apology for their loud and personal spat. Hugh lied and said he hadn't noticed. She accused him of being too polite, and then asked him what was the worst thing he had ever done in his life. The very worst thing. Before he had the chance to decline to answer, she declared that his worst was nothing compared to hers. But by then, Kyle had returned. With a *pleasure to talk to you,* she truncated the conversation. Hanna had noticed his beach "routine." So what? All the better.

On Pacific Coast Highway, the summer traffic stuttered. A few thousand feet above the sea, a small buzzing airplane pulled a banner: *I don't always drink beer, but when I do . . .* A homeless man, barefoot, bearded, ragged and stained, walked by, reviling invisible enemies.

At the crosswalk, Hugh pressed the yellow button that eventually would stop the traffic. He pressed it twice more for luck. Sometimes the walk sign would not appear for ten minutes, but today the lights changed almost immediately, clearing his path across the highway. He was almost through the crosswalk when a siren sounded behind him. He turned to see a boxy, red ambulance, lights flashing, barreling out of the canyon.

Hitoshi! Takumi!
Hitoshi! Takumi!
The ambulance maneuvered south through the frozen PCH traffic, the lights and sound gone so quickly—the twin rivers restored so swiftly to their flow—that it might never have been there.

Beyond the birds-of-paradise, trashed bougainvillea and ice plant, the Pacific spread as tight as a child's skin. A wave smacked the shore, growling as it rushed back over a million pebbles. At the break, fifty surfers sat frozen on their boards waiting for a set. Beyond the surfers, a kayaker paddled past a buoy, and then slowed against the vast sea. Reaching the steps that led down to the sand, Hugh smelled the tar of the dark brown logs bordering the stairway. When he left the beach, he would sit on the wood to wipe the sand off his feet, the timbers' heat radiating through his buttocks. In the wood someone had painstakingly carved the Wilde quotation that Hugh read a year ago, and now whispered in his ear as if by a ghost:

Death must be so beautiful. To lie in the soft brown earth, with the grasses waving above one's head and listen to silence. To have no yesterday and no tomorrow. To forget time, to forgive life, to be at peace.

Hugh glanced down to where the inscription should be, but wasn't. Someone had ripped out the seductive words.

Except for surfers, Topanga beach, strewn with flea-infested rotting kelp and innumerable rocks, drew few visitors—a handful of canyon residents, Europeans, Hispanic families, boys and girls bathing naked like flower children or in their drooping underwear. It was to this beach that Hugh had brought the boys to learn how to surf, and to which he had returned to end his life.

Setting his gym bag down a short distance from the stairs, Hugh spread his towel and found four rocks to hold down the edges, though the wind was negligible. He stood up, sucked in a lungful of ocean air and touched the waistband of his bathing suit. He undid the cord's bow, yanked the ends tighter and retied the nylon. Satisfied with the snug waistband, he took a step toward the ocean, and then remembered that Kazuki's new novel was in the gym bag.

In the hours after Hugh had seen Kazuki in the Pasadena bookstore, he read *Enrique the Freak* in one sitting. Having heard Kazuki's words about danger and children had given Hugh hope that this time Kazuki had tossed some crumbs of forgiveness his way. It was that possibility that caused Hugh to retreat from personally delivering the letter. For a few hours, each turned page promised some new perspective on his responsibility for the death of his sons.

Beyond the passage that had raised his hopes at the reading, the book offered Hugh no pardon. No child, no children, appeared. He discerned no parallel to his own life. No hint that Setsuko might have forgiven him. Lacking that reprieve, rehearsals were over.

How would the police, who would undoubtedly find the gym bag, interpret Kazuki's book? Would they draw a motive from the dog-eared pages? He meant to toss it, but there it lay. He picked it up, looked toward the trash can. No.

Hugh returned the book to the bag and faced the sea.

A set of modest waves had drawn the surfers into frenzied paddling. Rising on their boards in one seamless motion, the quickest broke from the pack.

The kayaker, too, turned shoreward and rode the wave.

Hugh walked across the beach, striding a tangle of kelp attracting ten thousand gnats and landing on something that enveloped his foot for an instant, but was not there when he drew his foot away. A red-tipped tentacle gave away the creature: a jellyfish melting under the California sun.

Kurage.

Little more than a month after Hugh and Setsuko returned to Japan from Los Angeles, Setsuko, based solely on her late period, pronounced that she was pregnant, subsequently confirmed by a test. Did he want her to abort? she asked flatly. He recognized that his only answer could be no, and to that response she said, "Good, because I will not, even if we part."

"Part? I want to marry you!"

Though Hugh had dated Setsuko for almost two years, he had not met with nor spoken to Kazuki Ono, who seemed always to be otherwise engaged. Now her father would find the time, Setsuko reported after telling her father of the engagement. For his first meeting with Kazuki, Setsuko, who was not invited to the tête-à-tête, had given Hugh some guidance. Her father would not try to speak much English, but would make use of a translator, though he had little need of one. The translator would allow her father to study Hugh. Her father's purpose wasn't sinister, Setsuko assured Hugh, but simply his way of fixing his encounters in memory. She advised Hugh that everyone her father met was fair game for his craft. It might only be a facial tic, odd mannerism or an unusual pronunciation that Kazuki would absorb for later use, but sometimes it would be the person's character or charm. On occasion, he'd tote the whole person back, though likely that person wouldn't recognize himself—melded, transmogrified—down the road. Numerous times, her father had confessed his practice to Setsuko: a writer had nothing to mine but the world he encountered. *He must always haul around his flashlight and pick.*

Jack the translator, also Kazuki's driver and confidant, was a Brit with a ready smile, a string of jokes and a grip that warned his leaden hand could break every bone in yours. Jack had picked up Hugh from his apartment, a block later saying, "Take his only daughter, will you, mate? Ono's got fans among the Yakuza—*big* fans." Hugh just laughed.

"There's Mr. Ono waiting for us," said Jack, nodding toward a table in the hotel's restaurant, where a tall man with a mane of golden hair had risen, bowing to Hugh when he reached the heat of the candle. Hugh met the bow, and then the flood of brown eyes.

"Good evening. Thank you for coming," said Kazuki in English.

"It's my pleasure to be here," said Hugh in Japanese.

"Please sit down. What do you drink?"

"Biru," said Hugh.

To a server, Kazuki said, "Two beers."

"Scotch and water," said Jack.

After the drinks came, Kazuki spoke in Japanese with Jack, ignoring Hugh. The conversation was too fast-paced for Hugh to understand much, though he mentioned Hugh's name several times. The isolation ended when the server brought sushi. Exotic dishes—blowfish, sea urchin, eel-heart soup—followed by huge bloody steaks and rice and more drinks. It was after they were sated and the desserts lay on the table untouched, that the serious questions began. They were of two general categories: the first, Hugh's biography. Kazuki seemed especially interested in Hugh's father with the unusual given name of Pirie.

An Irish name, explained Hugh, which was one of the few legacies Pirie received from his own father, for Pirie's father and mother had been killed in a car crash when Pirie was six. After their parents' deaths, Pirie and his brother went to different relatives, for one family couldn't care for both. Hugh's father grew up a quiet, studious, shy boy who expected nothing less of the world than chance mayhem and loss. Pirie married a childhood sweetheart, had Hugh and then another boy. Pirie didn't overtly forbid Hugh from doing anything, but whenever Hugh left the house, whether to go to school or play baseball in the park, Hugh was aware of the fear and sadness in his father's face, that certainty that the worst had not yet passed, and he was in for something more. It was with that in mind, that Hugh avoided most of the risks of childhood and adolescence. He had not jumped off roofs. He had left the willing girls alone. He had not gotten drunk or smoked marijuana. The modest risks he took were out of his father's sight. All this changed when he went away to college, beyond his father's melancholy smile. He let loose. He liked it, not being fearful each time he did something new, not afraid of hurting himself or someone else.

"Is that why you traveled to Japan?" asked Kazuki.

Hugh forthrightly confessed that it *was* a bit of a lark. What is life if not an adventure? Kazuki's stony response compelled Hugh to add that he too had writing ambitions— screenwriting. Hugh had a writing partner in Los Angeles . . . looking for ideas . . . Teaching English in Japan was, of course, just temporary.

Kazuki nodded.

To all questions, Hugh told the truth, and then Kazuki moved to the second field of inquiry: Hugh's relationship with his daughter, eventually asking the blunt question that would draw the lie. His daughter had met Hugh while she attended the English school. She was seventeen at the time. Had Hugh been intimate with Setsuko while he was teaching her?

"No," Hugh replied, his heart beating fiercely, for this was the lie that he and Setsuko had agreed upon, though never before had she told her father the smallest lie.

"Good," said Kazuki. "I would find that hard to accept."

It was done. No, not quite.

"Two months ago my daughter went to Los Angeles to attend a cousin's wedding that I could not attend myself."

Hugh nodded.

"Did you meet with her in Los Angeles?"

Yes, for this was defensible, but yes, too, was betraying Setsuko who had not known of Hugh's intentions to fly to Los Angeles until he walked up to her in the airport. In truth, he hadn't known himself until the night before her flight.

"No, I did not," said Hugh.

"Have you ever heard the fable of the Jellyfish and the Monkey?" asked Kazuki, after a few more questions of minor importance.

"I've never heard any stories about jellyfish."

Kazuki sipped his beer, smiled and said, "Long, long ago, in old Japan, the Kingdom of the Sea was governed by a magnificent king called Ryn Jin, or the Dragon King . . ." Kazuki paused and looked away, his gaze fixing on the restaurant's broad window through which poured Tokyo's night light. The glass shuddered as if from a blast of wind, and the lights undulated like lights on an unsettled sea. Turning back to Hugh, Kazuki smiled gently. "Oh, it's a long story. Not worth the effort to get to the end. Another round, hey? Let's talk of your plans . . ."

On another night, Hugh would ask Setsuko about the fable, which involved a hard-backed jellyfish, *kurage*, whose lies to the king resulted in the king's servants slamming *kurage* with their sticks, ". . . so thoroughly was the poor creature beaten," explained Setsuko, "that he turned into a gelatinous, transparent pulp. And that is how the jellyfish we know came into being."

Driving Hugh back to his apartment, Jack played a tape of a British rock group called the Squeeze.

"I hope you were straight with Kazuki," said Jack. "Otherwise you might find yourself waking up as a jellyfish."

Hugh swam for a moment more in that memory and then with his heel covered the dissolving creature under a mound of sand.

An hour from high tide, the rocks were barely visible. He stepped keenly, trying to retain his balance as he made it knee deep. He was about to kneel when a wave rolled through him, bringing a sudden jolt of pain. *Fuck.* He dropped, kneeling on the rocky base as if acclimatizing himself to the water. His hands out of sight, he clawed up two medium-sized rocks with both hands and shoved them into the bathing suit's pockets. Rising with his hands on the waist of his slumping bathing suit, he walked seaward, every step painful and precarious. The water was only two feet deep, but the rocks were too thick for him to pick a path through the sand bottom. It was heaven to reach the deeper water and dive into the shock. He swam underwater, past a few large, mossy boulders that would wreck a surfboard. He labored with the weight of the rocks, glad that if he stopped swimming, he would sink.

The waves that had energized the surfers broke over him. So as not to be thrown back, he dived, feeling the ocean's surge stroke his spine like loving hands. Underwater, the rocks, moved by the crashing waves, crackled like voices in a crowd. He saw the surfers' legs encased in bubble wrap. He surfaced, a surfer rocketing toward him.

Hugh swam with long strokes, keeping his face in the water for three strokes, breathing on the fourth. His lower body sank with the weight of the rocks, so that he had to kick hard throughout the cycle. He did this for one hundred strokes, and then turned over and gently kicked, catching his breath, smelling the salt-drenched air. He swam another hundred yards, floated again, and looked back toward the beach. The shore was a crescent, the surfers distant. Several pelicans glided silently overhead. He gazed at their awkward beauty.

The buoy was another twenty yards away. He would rest there for a moment, before regaining the energy to start the long swim, which would take him beyond the vigilance of the lifeguards, little concerned about strong swimmers, who could take care of themselves. And he would take care of himself.

Hugh took another stroke and reached the buoy. He clung to the cold metal ball and felt his weight disappear. He needed to gather strength for the last stretch, by the end of which his energy would have been drained to zero. He kept his eyes seaward, bobbing rhythmically and trying to remember that black morning's details, which would function as the sedative administered before the general anesthetic.

He pushed off the buoy and swam toward the memory.

Ten minutes later, he dug the rocks out of his pockets, held them to his chest, opened his mouth and gave himself to the sea. As he dropped his arms, glad for the end of his exertion, and sunk one, two, three feet beneath the surface, he heard a soft rhythmic clapping. Someone swimming, swimming effortlessly. He hoped the swimmer would not notice him. He saw through the distorted lens of the deepening water a body pass above, undulating like a sea creature and then melding with the liquid. Elbows locked at his hips, still holding the stones, Hugh lifted his forearms to draw himself ever downward into the dark green depths. He sucked the water into his throat, urging his lungs to take it, inverting the way a woman urged her womb to release a baby. The forms came toward him like the shadow of something below. The forms closed on him. Two swimmers, he thought. *No. Go away. I want no help.* But then he saw that the swimmers were his sons. Takumi was on the right. Hitoshi on the left. Their hair floated above the beautiful expressionless faces. Takumi held something in his hand. Held it out to Hugh. Small, rectangular, ivory-colored: the final letter Hugh had sent Setsuko, the final communication that he expected her to turn back, as she turned back all the others, unopened, unread, unconsidered, deleted.

Hugh took the envelope, which was soft, falling apart. He drew his fingernail along the top and the envelope sprang open. The letter floated out, the ink blurred and streaming.

> *Dear Setsuko,*
>
> *I loved you and our children. Since I lost them—and you—my life hasn't meant much so what I'm doing seems almost easy. Please forgive me, Temperate Child. I think you will . . .*

Chapter 4

Kazuki Ono opened the balcony door of his suite at the Olympic Hotel on Santa Monica's famed beachfront, and scanned the horizon. One hundred miles from shore, the pale blue cloudless sky met the placid sea. To the southwest Santa Catalina rose from a misty shroud. A mile from shore, a low-slung oil tanker slunk north, sounding its horn while a dozen pleasure boats buzzed merrily in its wake. On the beach an umbrella or two rose, a blanket unfolded, a fat man sprinted into the cool green sea. Closer, beneath palm fronds still as stones, a pack of ancient joggers smeared on sunscreen as they broke their sweat.

He considered the day's schedule. Later in the morning, he had an appointment with the studio, where he would listen to preposterous plans for turning his new book into a feature film. He had learned to smile when they suggested this or that director, this or that star. Rarely did anything come of any of it. One book had been turned into a film, and the film had not been very good. In the afternoon, he had an appointment to view some paintings from a Courbet-inspired artist whose subject was cancer victims and schizophrenics. In the evening he had another book signing for *Enrique the Freak*. There was also some research to do for the new book. Jack would drive him.

Kazuki had written much of the novel, *Fingal's Cave*, in Japan, and his intention was to complete it during his time in Los Angeles. There were gaps to be filled, chapters to be rearranged, scenes that required a firsthand look at the settings, a few coincidences for which to arrange plausibility, scenes to add, scenes to cut. The inevitable rewriting. The inevitable rewriting of the rewriting, ad infinitum, ad nauseam . . .

But most daunting was the ending. For Katashi to suffer for his actions, his grandsons must be dead. His actions were surely immoral, though at the time he had spun it as his duty. He simply wanted what was his and there was no getting around it. But if the boys were truly dead, why put their father, Yuudai, through the anguish? Yuudai already had paid the price for his immorality and foolishness. Why should he pay a second time? And what of Sumiko? Usually Kazuki didn't give a shit about happy or tragic endings. The world went on or more to the point didn't go on, for wasn't every individual's death the death of the universe? That was the fine print in the contract. However, *Fingal's Cave* had purpose beyond an evening's entertainment. It wasn't just the fictive dream that Kazuki had to worry about.

Kazuki's stomach growled. He hadn't planned on getting up so early, and room service was late. He sat at the balcony's table, turned on his laptop and opened his journal. The writing was in kanji and hiragana, but as he read from the journal, he translated into English and input English text into the laptop. He usually didn't translate to English until his books were finished, but this time he was translating on the fly. In Recent Documents, he clicked on *Fingal's Cave*.

Page one appeared.

Fingal's Cave/1
HERB

A few distant lights sputtered on as the plane neared its target, which from an altitude of thirty-two thousand feet was clearly visible beyond a few scattered cumulus clouds. Extraordinary only in its untouched landscape—for the city, like four other potential targets, had escaped the nightly bombings so that the damage of the plane's unique weapon could be accurately measured—the town waited like an unsuspecting lab animal about to undergo a deadly experiment, trusting that the benign neglect of previous days would continue into the indefinite future.

At 8:10, the final turn of the screw now in the capable hands of bombardier Major Ferebee, Colonel Tibbets thought briefly and irritatingly if not quite regretfully about the name he'd painted on the aircraft's nose, *Enola Gay*, his mother's Christian name. In minutes, the plane would release a gravity bomb containing 130 pounds of Uranium 235 on the city of 350,000, and the results wouldn't be pretty. He wasn't sure his mother would appreciate the intended honor.

In the rear of the *Enola Gay*, tail gunner Technical Sergeant Herb O'Keefe fought the pounding at his temples, the ache of incomplete knowledge . . .

"Yuudai?"

"Yes, Dad?"

"The mother's hiding these little plastic dinosaurs on the café's patio. The daughter, maybe four years old, puts her head down on the table, covers her eyes. Mama hides the last toy, and yells, 'Iidesuyo.' Right? 'Iidesuyo!' The little girl jumps up, laughs. Runs all over the place looking for those dinosaurs. She finds them—one on a window sill, another under an old newspaper, another stuck in a bush. Every damn time she finds one, she laughs like crazy. Like she's having so much fun that I, that I—"

Yuudai waited several minutes until—

"Yuudai?" said his father.

"Yes, Dad?"

"The mother's hiding these little plastic dinosaurs on the café's patio. The daughter, maybe four years old . . ."

His father had repeated the truncated story six times since Yuudai had entered the hospital room, where Herb had drifted in and out of consciousness for four days. Whether his father's vignette was memory or a dream, Yuudai couldn't say, but he thought his father was somehow comforted by it, for the buckled cheeks and creased forehead seemed to smooth and catch color, though it may have been the glow of the monitor.

Running his finger along the punctured artery of the bone-thin forearm, once as thick as the sweet spot of a Louisville Slugger, Yuudai wondered if Herb himself in some dim neuronal corner knew the story's end. A worn man before his first heart attack (aged fifty), an impaired man before his first stroke (aged fifty-seven), Herb had lumbered on far longer than any of the doctors had predicted. Though repeated like a looped tape, the anecdote was a marvel, thought Yuudai, for Herb's speech and thoughts had become increasingly garbled, and in the last six months impossible to penetrate. It was his third stroke and the scattered family was flying in.

"Yuudai?" the doctor had asked, uncertain that he had this red-headed Caucasian's name correct.

I'm Irish, kiss me.

Yuudai rolled out his own oft-repeated story.

An enlisted man, Herbert O'Keefe had been the assistant tail gunner on the *Enola Gay*, the plane that dropped the first atomic bomb on Japan, though Herb swore that the officers had not told him beforehand the nature and potency of the weapon. When the bomb missed its central target and fell on a hospital, Herb saw in the cataclysm that this bomb was . . . different. Troubled and then profoundly depressed by his part in the mission, Herb left the military and spent his life trying to make amends from his Boston home. He tithed his salary to send money to Japanese charities, studied the country's history and culture, fought the racism, the incessant three-letter slur that flowed through America in the postwar years, and gave his children Japanese names. But he had never gone there, never gone back. To that he left his youngest son, Yuudai, who after his father's first heart attack, was made to vow that when death took Herb, Yuudai would scatter his father's ashes over the site of the hospital that the bomber had inadvertently made ground zero, devote himself to healing the wounds of that tragic day and mix his blood with a Japanese maiden's.

A Japanese maiden that Yuudai would marry, bring back to America—and keep safe.

"Yuudai?"

"Yes, Dad?"

"The mother's hiding these little plastic dinosaurs on the café's patio. The daughter, maybe four years old . . ."

Chapter 5

Hugh staggered from the sea. Bent and shaking like a sick old man, he hid his face in his hands while water streamed from the bulging pockets of his bathing suit. He flopped on the tide line and coughed up the acidic sea-water. Crawling back from the yellow pool, he dropped his head to his forearms, pressing his face to the clammy shivering skin.

The mewing of the gulls and the clap of the waves vanished. Hugh felt far from the sea, and yet he was looking out at the sea, scanning the horizon for the twin swimmers, his sons. The ocean turned grainy and white, and the sounds returned as if from a speaker drawing closer to his ear. He pushed to his knees. His stomach convulsed and vomit filled his throat and mouth. He clamped his lips, but the hot salty mix gushed out, splattering and mingling with the resurfaced jellyfish. Hugh scuttled sideways and collapsed again.

It was another ten minutes before Hugh rose and walked back to his towel.

He was a coward. Neither his boys nor the letter had been there. He did not believe in ghosts. He did not believe in visits from the spirit world. The only things left of his boys were the empty tethers. His sons had been swept out to sea, probably devoured by sharks to become a delicacy for the Japanese.

Digging his fingers into the sand, Hugh glanced away from the surf. Coming up the beach was Aaron, one of his students. Most of the kids he taught chose Santa Monica or Malibu, but occasionally Hugh would meet an outlier at Topanga.

"Hey, Mr. Mac," said Aaron, halting six feet from Hugh's towel, his gaze over Hugh's head.

"Oh, hello . . ."

"This your hangout?" asked Aaron.

"Yes, I guess. Yes." Hugh looked around. "I like this beach."

"Like that commercial, huh? Find your beach," Aaron said with a tight knowing smile.

"You've been swimming?" Hugh asked.

"No, I don't go into the sea. I can't swim or anything. I stay out."

"Makes sense."

"Hey, can I get my story back?" asked Aaron.

"Your story?" asked Hugh.

"Yeah. The one I wrote about my grandpa."

The second story Aaron wrote for the class. Yes, the grandfather's job as hit man for a Mexican drug cartel, until he erred and killed the boss's son, subsequently vanishing and presumed dead.

"I passed all the stories back," said Hugh.

"Maybe I was absent."

"Then I would have put it in the class tray. You know, on the bookshelf."

Aaron shook his head. "I looked."

"I don't know then. You should have asked at the end of the semester."

"Yeah, well I was sick . . . You think maybe it's still there?"

"I don't know—you're sure I didn't—"

"Maybe you could check," suggested Aaron.

"Drop by my class in the fall," said Hugh, tired already of the request.

"I ain't going to be around in the fall."

"Maybe I could mail it to you."

"That wouldn't work. Couldn't you get it?"

"You mean like today?"

"Yeah."

Hugh said, "I don't even know if the school is open."

"Would you try?"

"Look Aaron, I may not have kept it. Maybe in a day or so . . ."

A hand fell on Aaron's shoulder. The nails were bright purple. Anna, Anna of the sleepy brown eyes and *Fuck Like A Porn Star* stenciled on her notebook's spine, Aaron's sometimes girlfriend.

"You were way out," said Anna to Hugh.

"You saw me?"

"Didn't know it was you. Just someone swimming far out. I thought you weren't going to come back."

"Cheaper than flying to Hawaii," said Hugh, forcing a grin.

Anna glanced back over her shoulder. "I don't like to swim."

"You and Aaron both, huh? That's too bad. It's great exercise."

"But you get wet."

"True," said Hugh flatly, not sure that Anna was making a joke.

"So, you going to get me that story?" asked Aaron.

"Why is the story so important?"

Aaron rubbed his knuckles across his chin. "I just don't want anyone to read it."

"I have read it," said Hugh.

"Sure, you. But nobody else. That was the deal."

"I still don't understand—"

"It just is," said Aaron.

"Give me your phone number. I'll call you."

"About what?"

"If I get by the school and can find your story."

"Why couldn't you?"

"If I go by the school, I'll get the story. I'll call you."

"Call Anna, okay?" Aaron made two fists, rapped them together. His face colored as if embarrassed. "I got to take a piss," he said, walking toward the restrooms.

Anna watched Aaron for a few seconds and then shifted back to Hugh. She gave him a tight-lipped smile, shrugged her shoulders and dug her fingers through her hair. She faded into the seascape.

A drop of seawater dripped from Hugh's nostril, and another behind it. He caught the flow with the back of his hand. He should have prepared himself. He should have expected the life force to play a trick or two.

A bullet was not so susceptible.

But a bullet could not be an accident.

In the fall semester, a student wrote a story in which the teenage narrator, bullied by schoolmates, committed suicide. Hugh didn't think that the writer, an easygoing friendly girl, was writing about herself, but her story galvanized the students. Hugh spent the remainder of the class making the case against self-destruction. In subsequent classes, Hugh returned to his admonition whenever he could. If he committed an identifiable suicide, his students would label all his earnest arguments as bullshit. What would stop one— or more—from following his example?

Though today he had missed his mark, it had to be death by misadventure.

"What are those?" asked Anna.

"Pelicans," said Hugh.

A half dozen of the birds flew by. Anna's head swiveled as they skimmed the ocean for a hundred yards, one by one dropping almost violently into the sea. Her eyes drifted away. Aaron was coming back, walking with martial precision, each step the same length and same duration.

"You ready?" asked Aaron upon reaching her.

"Uh huh . . ."

"You give him your number?" Aaron asked.

Anna got out a pen and paper and scribbled her number. Aaron watched as she gave it to Hugh and he tucked it in his gym bag.

"Have a nice day," said Anna.

Hugh smiled good-bye and watched them as they climbed the steps to the exit road. He would not be surprised to see them hitchhiking north on Topanga, Anna with her thumb out, Aaron ten yards away, pretending he wasn't with her and ready to run to the car the moment it stopped, deflating the faux Samaritan.

Hugh dug his fingers into the sand and considered another immediate try at offing himself. But suicide took energy and the ordeal had left him drained.

There was a hurricane off Mexico. A swell was coming. If he were lucky, tomorrow the sea would rage. He wouldn't fuck up his suicide twice.

If Setsuko ever read the letter, she would understand that he kept his implied promise, even if it took two tries . . .

Hugh set his gym bag into the Volvo's open trunk. He lifted the yellow beach towel, backed up a step and snapped it. A volley of sand stung his face. "Shit," said Hugh, releasing the towel and clapping his right eye, as if it were not too late. He waited a moment for the tears to clear the particle of sand, bending his head so that the drops fell to his toes. On his white trunks he saw a blue smear. He scraped it with his fingernail. He lifted his hand. A bit of ivory-colored paper sat under his nail.

He lifted his head to the roar of a truck speeding around the first bend of the canyon. With two quick steps, he could end the stupidity now.

Do it. *Do it*—

"Hey, boss," said a new voice. "How long have you been parked here?"

"What?" asked Hugh, still considering the truck, the road, the distance, the time, barely conscious of another voice that seemed to come out of the past.

A hand tapped his shoulder. Heart beating terrifically, he turned to a bare-chested man, *Kyle.*

"I asked how long have you been here?"

"Couple hours," said Hugh.

Kyle looked away and smirked as if to a companion.

"You see Hanna?"

"Hanna?"

"My old lady. Blue hair. Pretty. Tats. You know her, man. You talk to her all the time."

"I don't think so. Sorry." Hugh stared after the truck, now turning north on PCH. With his thumb, he worked the sliver of paper from under his nail.

"You never saw her here?" asked Kyle.

"We said hello," replied Hugh, looking back toward the sea.

"Where'd she go?"

Hugh shrugged.

"You don't know?"

"We barely spoke."

"She invite you in the trailer?"

"We said . . . *hello.*"

Kyle again gave the self-assured smile to his invisible friend and then drew back his shoulders. He had a boxer's stomach, lean arms and clothesline veins. A motorcycle crackled and roared as it accelerated into the canyon, its chrome shedding sunlight. Hugh felt the engine's throb in his chest. The motorcycle disappeared around the first curve.

Hugh gazed at the sliver of paper, rolled it between his fingers and then flicked it to the dirt. *Stupid. Stupid. Stupid.*

He slammed the trunk, brushed by Kyle and slid into the car. Another breath, another two steps, and he would have been beyond magical thinking and assholes like Kyle.

The interior was a sauna. In the rearview mirror, Kyle walked toward Hugh's open window.

"We weren't finished talking," Kyle snarled.

"Yes, we were." Hugh fished in his pocket for his keys.

Kyle swung the driver's door open. "You ain't going nowhere," said Kyle, bracing the door open with his leg and grinning.

Hugh shoved the key in the ignition. Kyle reached across him for the key. With his left hand, Hugh grabbed the man's wrist. With his right hand, he clasped the elbow, but he hesitated to apply pressure. Kyle's grin faded.

"Hey, Mr. Mac!"

Anna and Aaron sprinted across the boulevard toward him. "Can you give us a ride?" Hugh released Kyle, who drew back from the door, rubbing his forearm and staring hard at Hugh, who had all but forgotten him.

Never let a student get into your car.

"Sure. No problem. Get in," said Hugh.

Chapter 6

The morning fog clearing, Kazuki watched the huge yacht, perhaps two hundred feet in length, inch northward. It dwarfed the nearby sailboats, which followed the vessel like pilot fish follow their shark, white sails billowing against the bright blue sea. Turning away from the festive scene, Kazuki walked back into his suite. He had canceled the appointment at the studio and had spent the morning in his room.

He sat down and tapped the touch pad.

When Yuudai next met Sumiko, at a club in the Shibuya ward of Tokyo, he was singing Elvis Costello's "Alison" through a defective karaoke stage microphone, so that his aim, his voice at least, was never true. Drink in hand, Sumiko approached him and tried heroically to speak English. Yuudai's limited Japanese and Sumiko's severely limited English were not much of a disadvantage in the thunderous club, to which Yuudai had come with a group of associates. Sumiko too had come with friends, but after Yuudai and she met, they were alone most of the night, laughing at each other's language deficiencies and their equally clumsy dancing. They left together shortly before midnight, after which the trains no longer ran. She allowed him to accompany her back on the last train. A quarter hour into their ride, Yuudai pointed questioningly to what seemed to be a castle, strung with dazzling lights.

"It's a Love Hotel," Sumiko said. It was not quite what the phrase seemed to indicate, she explained. It was not for prostitutes but for lovers who could not afford their own apartments.

On the following Saturday night, Sumiko showed up by herself at the club. Though she sat with Yuudai, she seemed solemn, thoughtful, not quite there. Prompted by his friends, Yuudai sang: ". . . isn't you, isn't me, search for things that you can't see, goin' blind, out of reach, somewhere in the vasoline." He sang it well, and for such a sad song, it made Sumiko happy. Once again they took the train home together. He got off at her stop, though he would have to walk a long distance to get to his apartment. They were both still a little high, and in a small park he challenged her to climb a tree with him. He swung into it easily. She refused his helping hand and climbed up herself. They sat in the thick limbs of the core, staring out through the leaves, listening to the wind whistling through the branches. Sumiko's hair hung against the heavy wood like water cascading over black stone, and Yuudai felt the universe turn as if he were at its very center. The moonlight was broken by a cloud of crows falling on the park. The wind of their flapping wings lifted Sumiko's hair, and the branches above shivered as the birds settled into the tree, cawing resolutely. Japanese crows will sometimes attack people, warned Sumiko.

"We can't let them know we're here," she whispered in Yuudai's ear. "We must be quiet and still."

Something flashed by the window. Kazuki looked up to see a huge seagull alighting on the railing. Kazuki's queasiness had passed and he remembered the uneaten pastry on the balcony table. He stood and shouted, but the untroubled bird hopped within inches of the pastry.

Kazuki slid back the screen door to see the bird snatching the pastry in its beak. The bird beat its wings to take off, but the jelly-filled pastry was heavier than the seagull had anticipated. Its take-off was delayed a microsecond, just long enough for Kazuki to grab its tail. The bird cawed and flapped its lustrous wings. Was he only imagining the seagull to be the same color and size as the one in the bookstore? Odd, but no matter. Kazuki tore the pastry from its beak, tossed the bird into the air and chewed slowly on the sweet's perimeter. Returned to his laptop, he typed:

As Yuudai tried not to fidget, he saw out the corner of his eye that Sumiko in her immobility and silence had vanished into the branches and leaves. No crow would see or hear her, nor any other agent of destruction. If she chose to hide from him, he too would never find her. Yuudai dug his nails into the bark. Inches from the gnawing hand, a huge crow studied the worms beneath the white skin. The bird's lust thickened like congealed blood. Not much risk, hop, hop. As Yuudai squirmed indecisively, a three-foot tongue, as if from a Komodo dragon, shot the darkness, coiled the crow's head and retracted swiftly. As the remaining crows, alert to some inchoate danger, took flight, Sumiko found Yuudai's mouth with hers, moved his lips to draw his words.
"Are you sure?" she asked. "Because I am sure."
For an hour they caressed among the branches. When they returned to earth, Yuudai pointed to the fallen crow.
"Would it have attacked?" asked Yuudai.
"Maybe," said Sumiko.
"Keep your distance, vicious birds," said Yuudai, putting his arm around her waist and pressing his lips to her ear. "What else shouldn't get too close? Snakes? Lions?"
"Anyone or anything that tries to take what I love."
"Anyone?"
"Even you," answered Sumiko with a laugh.

"Setsuko . . ." murmured Kazuki, his plea flying like an arrow over ten thousand miles of dark ocean and a

quarter century of turmoil to pierce and tumble a lock in a Urayasu townhome. Setsuko walked into his memory, closed the door behind her. She dropped the key on the crooked brass finger above the entranceway table, beneath which she nudged her shoes. Usually when she entered her home this late, her lips were set in a pensive frown, but tonight, at two A.M., she was smiling. Even when she saw her father standing there, waiting up for her, relieved but disappointed, the smile didn't vanish.

"I was getting worried," Kazuki admitted.

"I should have called."

"Are you all right?" Kazuki asked.

"Oh, I'm very good," said Setsuko.

She moved quickly toward him, kissed him. Her perfume was faint, overwhelmed by another scent: a man's cologne.

"Are you working?" asked Setsuko, sliding away, glancing toward her father's writing desk, the old electric typewriter humming.

"Never past midnight," said Kazuki. "That's when the words fly off the page to do their own mischief."

"They're not too loyal?"

"A dozen I trust."

Setsuko smiled. "So, what's the new one about?" she asked.

"I could ask the same of you," replied Kazuki.

"Do you want to know?"

Kazuki shrugged, took in his daughter's beauty. "It's based on a folktale I once read to you when you were five or six."

"The Jellyfish and the Monkey."

"No."

"The One-Inch Boy."

"Not close."

"Hanasaka Jiisan?"

"Let me reflect," said Kazuki.

~ 46 ~

"The Mirror of Masumi," said Setsuko brightly.

"Right you are."

"How far have you gotten in it?"

"The end . . . of the beginning."

"The hardest part."

"To get right," said Kazuki.

"Have you eaten?" she asked.

"Have I—" Kazuki shook his head. He had not eaten and had forgotten. His stomach was giving him trouble, but he had to eat. He knew that.

"I'll make you something," said Setsuko. As she walked toward the kitchen, she called back, "He's an American."

Chapter 7

Aaron had gotten into the rear seat, but Anna chose to sit up front with Hugh, slinging her oversized handbag into Aaron's hands. They drove silently through the canyon, but on the downgrade into Woodland Hills, Anna unbuckled, twisted backward and fussed with Aaron about extracting some garments from her handbag.

"Please put on your seatbelt," said Hugh.

"One minute, okay?"

A bright ball of fabric flew into Anna's lap. Hugh glanced at his passenger as she pulled a sundress over her bathing suit.

"Seatbelt now."

"Sure, sure."

In the mirror, Hugh saw Aaron slip on an oversized white T-shirt.

"Seatbelts?" asked Hugh.

Groans of compliance. Both students rebuckled noisily.

A block south of Ventura and Topanga, Hugh waited behind a disabled bus with its hazard lights on, discharging passengers into 110-degree heat. Expressionless riders stepped into the hard sun. The older ones held shopping bags from Ralph's and Rite Aid; the young lugged bulging backpacks.

"Can you take us to Reseda?" asked Anna.

"Oh, I don't think, I . . . I don't have much time."

"Ten minutes on the freeway," said Aaron.

Spotting a break in the traffic in the outer lane, Hugh maneuvered around the bus, drove toward the busy intersection.

"Please," said Anna. "can you take us?"

Reseda. *It's a long day living in Reseda* . . . The boys liked the song. He remembered playing it loud as they drove, drove where? . . . *And I'm free, free fallin'* . . .

"Yeah, I'll take you," said Hugh, moving into the intersection, tempting an eastbound SUV that had ignored the light to T-bone him. Hugh accelerated, skimming by the asshole.

"Nice," said Aaron.

"Thanks."

The onramp to the 101 was jammed. They inched forward.

Hugh gazed beyond the line of cars to the San Gabriel Mountains, all but the nearest peaks smeared by the summer haze. Lousy snowboarding, really, but hardly an hour's drive. Surf in the morning, cut the slopes in the afternoon. They had done that a half-dozen times . . . Hugh drove forward twenty feet, braked, remembered patchy snow, complaints—but the morning had been fine . . . in the sea. He drove forward, braked, and envisioned his young sons swimming toward him, holding out the letter. It didn't mean anything. The letter was on his mind, so of course it would flutter into his imagination. He glanced down at his bathing suit. The dark streak remained, but its source could have been one of countless things floating in the sea: oil, tar . . . shit.

As Hugh drove forward another twenty feet, he realized the two passengers entitled him to the ramp's carpool lane. He checked the rearview, cut into the left lane and accelerated. A few cars back, another vehicle followed his example, its engine roaring. As Hugh merged onto the freeway, he glanced again into the mirror; Aaron had twisted in his seat to view something.

"Sick," said Aaron, who appeared to be looking at a primed Camaro not quite tailgating them.

"How long have you had this car?" asked Anna, as Hugh maneuvered into an outer lane.

"Six years."

"It's nice. What kind is it?"

"Volvo," declared Aaron.

"I've never heard of a Vovo."

"Volvo," corrected Aaron. "Swedish. Solid steel frame. Weighs over two tons. It's a little tank."

"How much did it cost?" said Anna, gazing out the window.

Aaron didn't respond, and Hugh didn't feel like discussing the price of cars.

On one of the snowboarding outings to the San Gabriels, Hugh, Hitoshi and Takumi had rolled a giant snowball, put it in the trunk. So fast was the drive back to their Studio City home that the snowball had hardly lost an inch in diameter. In their backyard, they tore the snowball apart and had a snowball fight as the thermometer hit ninety.

After Setsuko left, Hugh had stayed in the leased house for two more years, unable to clear out what remained in the boys' room. Setsuko had taken the skateboards, bicycles, radio-controlled cars, baseball bats, footballs, spinning rods and surfboards to Goodwill, but Hugh was reluctant to part with the less recyclable: the wheel-less trucks and toy soldiers who refused to stand upright, the dim laser swords and the soft, stained pliable playthings of their early childhood. Each night for two years, he settled in the room, choosing a toy to touch and smell, as if he might find his sons' anima within the polymers.

Takumi and Hitoshi were dead, but he could not stop searching for them.

The ritual, which in truth became what he lived for, might have continued indefinitely if it weren't for the new profession. In the Sunday paper, he read a story about a teaching program for professionals who wanted a second, meaningful career. As he contemplated the idea, the word *meaningful* seized him. If he had lost his own children, perhaps he could help others. Yes. Yes. He passed the required tests and applied to a teaching program designed to put him in front of a classroom within six months. At the end of the six months, a school hired him.

The change prompted the move from their home. When he began the teaching program, he called the Salvation Army. It was springtime, and while the workers hauled out the donations, he sat in the backyard watching swallows build their inverted nest in the eve of a neighboring house. When the Salvation Army had finished, Hugh went back into the house, which now seemed vast, infinite. He was afraid if he didn't leave, that one day he would lose himself forever in its depths.

His first short-lived move was to a Warner Center apartment, but the walls closed in on him like a treacherous room in an old science fiction movie. In a long line at the supermarket, he overheard a couple discussing Topanga, where seclusion could be found without forgoing access to the city. Within two weeks, he'd signed a lease on a small house and moved in.

He hoped the new career and home would divert his thoughts, and for some time they did. Controlling classes of thirty-five students, hormones raging, personalities sharpening, ethnicities clashing, guiding them through the thickets of English grammar and idiom, providing solace for the homesick (they were all from other countries, most at war), sympathizing with the lovesick (of course, he likes you. That's *why* he kicked you.), and ministering to the real sick (put your head down for a while. Get an icepack from the nurse. Juan is doing what, Parisa?) left scant time to dwell on guilt or to tour memory. But as the years passed and dealing with chaos became routine, the specter of his sons' deaths entered the classroom, sitting in the back of the room like some cynical observer. *Whom are you trying to fool? Who teaches your children?* When Pouya and Adel, Camille and Natasha spoke, he heard Takumi and Hitoshi, but the observer laughed and asked, "Do you forget your own children's voices? Do you forget your own children's suffocated screams?" His students were not his children. He had not marched these children from life. His sons' deaths were the abyss that he couldn't crawl out of.

He even tried upping the ante: on weekends for the last five years he taught at homeless shelters in downtown Los Angeles. He taught for free and gave the children every blessed ounce of his energy. But even in exhaustion, the memories haunted him.

Good deeds would not buy him salvation.

He had not returned to the Studio City house since the day he moved out. Was there anything left of their life there? Might he find his sons there as he had found them in the ocean? It would be a mere fifteen-minute drive after he dropped his students in Reseda . . .

"Are you married?" asked Anna.

Hugh snapped out of his reverie. "No. Why?"

"You're wearing a wedding band."

Hugh glanced at the tarnished gold band that he had never removed. "I *was* married."

"She die or something?"

"No . . . nothing like that."

"Where'd you meet her?"

Hugh hesitated, but then muttered, "Japan. I was teaching English—to adults. She enrolled in my class."

"Oh. Was she pretty?"

"Very pretty."

"Short?"

Hugh smiled. "Tall, actually."

"What was her name?"

"Setsuko."

"In one word tell me what Setsuko was like," said Anna, echoing the challenge he gave to his creative writing students when asked to describe their stories' characters.

"Indomitable," Hugh decisively responded.

"Umm. What's that mean?"

"Like the bunny that keeps on going."

"A pretty bunny," said Anna with satisfaction.

"She was an artist, a painter. She used these tiny paintbrushes to make lines thinner than a spider's strand." Hugh took his right hand from the steering wheel, held his thumb and forefinger together and pretended to draw. "Seascapes. Most of all, she painted seascapes . . ." He clamped the wheel. "We're divorced."

"Well, that's too bad," said Anna.

Hugh had never mentioned his wife or sons to his students. He wanted to tell Anna more about Setsuko, her dry sense of humor, her tolerance for Hugh's clutter and dreaminess, her love and respect for the natural world—her hand pressed to a slab of granite as if she might draw out its thoughts—her serene, effortless, transfixing beauty, her unflappable poise, her grace under pressure as Hemingway would have put it, but Anna had moved on, no more interested in Hugh's ex-wife than the irrigation methods of the ancient Egyptians. She was digging through her purse. Hugh took his hand from the wheel and gazed at his fingers.

"Where in Reseda are you going?" asked Hugh.

Anna turned to Aaron. In the mirror, Aaron moved his head a centimeter.

"We've changed our plans, Mr. Mcpherson. We're going to Van Nuys. It's not much farther."

"What exit?"

"Van Nuys Boulevard," said Aaron.

"All right."

"We're not putting you out, I hope, Mr. Mcpherson."

"No, it's okay," he said. Reseda, Van Nuys, Sherman Oaks . . . Studio City.

"Mind if I turn on the radio?" asked Anna.

"Go ahead."

She settled on a hip-hop station, but kept the volume low.

"So, when can I get my story?" asked Aaron.

Jesus Christ, *his story.* "I told you, Aaron, I have to find out if the school is even open."

"Why wouldn't it be open?"

"Budget cuts."

"I need that story."

"Yes, you've told me a half-dozen times."

"Two, three maybe," said Aaron.

"Why? Why is the story so important?"

"When can you get it?" asked Aaron.

"That's enough," said Hugh. "Let's drop it for a while."

Aaron beat time on the window, and then said, "My grandfather is pissed that I wrote it. He wants it back. Wants to burn it."

"Your grandfather?"

"Yeah."

"The grandfather in the story was *your* grandfather? You didn't make the story up?" asked Hugh.

"Some," muttered Aaron.

"How much *some?*"

"Fuck, man, you gave me an A."

"The story is about your real grandfather and your real grandfather didn't die?"

Aaron groaned. "If he died, how could he have told me the story?"

"I should have given the A to your grandfather."

Anna laughed.

"Yeah, that's funny."

"As I recall," said Hugh, "his name in the story was Juan Valdez."

"So?"

"That's the coffee bean guy."

"No, it's my grandfather."

"You used his real name?"

"That's what my grandfather said, only he didn't say it that way."

A van pulled alongside Hugh, slid closer. A big blue van with a sign that read GO HOME. Hugh stared in amazement as the truck drifted closer. Hugh hit the horn, accelerated. The truck slipped away, slipped back. GO HOME AND RELAX. LEAVE THE MOVING TO US.

"There are a million stories out there," said Hugh.

"What the fuck does that mean?"

"Your grandfather's safe."

"Fuck you, Mr. Mac," said Aaron, leaning his head on the window.

Juan Valdez . . .

Hugh glanced in the rearview at the truck. He felt a soft flow against his chest, the flutter of the water when his sons swam toward him. *Go home.*

"Teachers aren't supposed to give students rides, are they?" asked Anna.

The twins' presence fled. Hugh's throat tightened. "No, not generally."

"Why not?"

"It's for the students' and the teachers' protection."

"Why would they need protection?"

"The bitch says the teacher molested her," Aaron eagerly speculated. "How can he prove he didn't?"

"But how can she prove he did?" asked Anna.

"Why did he give her the ride?" asked Aaron.

"But why would she lie?"

"Maybe she asked him for money and he refused."

Anna leaned toward Hugh. "Mr. Mac, would you loan me twenty dollars? Pretty please?"

Hugh ignored her.

A weight light as a leaf slid down his thigh.

"Anna!" said Hugh, swiping away her hand. The car veered into the right lane. "Why the hell did you do that? That's terrible!"

"I was joking," said Anna, giggling.

"That's a joke? You think that's a joke? Goddamn. Goddamn." Despite the air-conditioning, sweat slicked his forehead.

"Yeah, Anna," said Aaron.

"I touched his leg. Big deal." Anna turned up the radio.

"He rejected you. *Reject*," taunted Aaron.

"Please, down the music," said Hugh, breathing hard as if he'd just sprinted.

"Down the music? That don't sound right," said Aaron with a laugh.

Hugh jabbed the radio's off button.

"Leave my radio alone, all right? Leave everything alone," said Hugh, wiping the sweat from his forehead.

Anna huffed and crossed her arms. "God. Now everything's all tense. You never yelled in class, Mr. Mac." She reached over the seat and took Aaron's hand.

Mr. Easygoing. Yeah, Mr. Fucking Easygoing.

At the White Oak exit, Hugh changed lanes. The traffic was thickening and approaching the 405, the 101's lanes reduced to two. He pulled in front of a tricked-out BMW. In the rearview mirror he saw Aaron's head turn. The boy liked cars and guns. In the computer lab, if he left Aaron alone for a moment, he'd be researching assault weapons. The district's computer system filtered out sex but not .45 Magnums. When Hugh monitored his viewing, Aaron's face colored a little, but he didn't close the page. Most kids would be slamming the X.

Hugh glanced at the cloudless sky. Satellite surveillance captured such detailed images of earth that individuals could be seen slipping into porn shops, buying drugs in alleys, cheating on their spouses. At this moment, an employee of some bleak agency could be considering a digital image of Anna getting into his car.

You're going to kill yourself, man, what the fuck's the difference?

Passing the 405, Hugh maneuvered into the far right lane to take the Van Nuys Boulevard exit. Aaron whispered something, and Anna twisted in her seat.

"Sorry, Mr. Mcpherson, we've changed our plans again. We want to go to North Hollywood. Sorry to put you out."

"You said 'Van Nuys Boulevard.' This is it." Hugh slowed as he took his place at the end of the line of exiting cars.

"It's only another ten minutes. Please?"

"Is this a game? Are you playing another game with me?" asked Hugh.

Anna giggled nervously.

"My grandfather lives in North Hollywood," said Aaron.

"Sure," said Hugh, "your grandfather. Your *story*. I'm sorry, but I've got something to do. I can't be chauffeuring you around all day."

"Hey, this ain't no limo. Where's your cap?"

Hugh swung out of the exit lane, floored the accelerator and zipped across several lanes, horns sounding angrily.

"Get off at Cahuenga," said Aaron.

They approached an overpass. If Hugh took his hands from the steering wheel, just let the car drift with the road's camber . . . flipping, flipping, flipping. But his passengers were innocent, weren't they? He clasped the wheel at ten and two, and glanced in the rearview at Aaron, eyes cold, mouth turned down.

Go home.

As they approached the 101 split, where to the left the 134 would continue on to North Hollywood and Burbank, Hugh crossed lanes to the right.

"Hey, wrong way," said Aaron.

Hugh accelerated into the far right lane, the Tujunga Avenue exit.

"Maybe he's taking a shortcut," suggested Anna.

The exit wrapped around so that if they turned right he'd be heading north, not south as the off-ramp led one to expect. When the family lived in the area, Hugh frequently took this exit, and he never rid himself of the feeling that when he turned left, he was turning the wrong way. He turned left.

"This ain't the way to North Hollywood," said Aaron.

"It is to Studio City."

"Don't make any sense."

"I'll let you out at the light," said Hugh.

"But this isn't where we're going."

"It's where I'm going," said Hugh.

He stopped at the light on Moorpark. "Should I let you out here?" There were plenty of people around to watch them depart.

"What the fuck, man?" said Aaron.

Hugh pointed back over his shoulder. "North Hollywood's that way."

"Come on, Mr. Mcpherson. You're not like that," pleaded Anna.

"So long, guys."

The light turned green. Hugh crossed through the intersection and pulled to the curb.

"It's because I touched your leg, isn't it?" asked Anna.

"I've got something to do," answered Hugh.

"Don't be mad at me," said Anna.

"I'm not."

Anna got out and walked to the driver's side. She tapped on Hugh's window. He rolled it down. "Does my lipstick look okay?" she asked, licking her vermilion lips. The wattage jumped.

"Yes. Fine."

"Do you like this color?"

"Sure."

The back door slammed. Aaron stood in back of Anna. Leaning against her, his chin on her shoulder.

"How about loaning us fifty?" asked Aaron.

"Fifty cents?"

Aaron guffawed. "Fifty dollars, maestro."

"Why would I do that?"

"You're leaving us in the middle of nowhere. We need bus fare."

Hugh took his wallet from the console and slipped out a five dollar bill. "Here's your bus fare. Smile."

"Come on, you can spare more than that."

"Tell Aaron to take the money and back off before I fucking, fucking—ah, shit."

Anna's eyebrows jumped. "Mr. Mcpherson!"

"Hey, teach, you let a student rub your leg," said Aaron.

Hugh sat back in the seat, turned his eyes away. "This is bullshit, total bullshit." Hugh crunched the five-dollar bill and threw it out the window.

"Just joking," said Aaron as Hugh pulled away.

"Sorry about touching your leg," Anna said, the thin eyebrows disappearing into her bangs like the steps of an escalator.

"Remember my story!" shouted Aaron.

In the rearview, he caught them staring thoughtfully after him, like parents watching the morning school bus leave.

Hugh drove through Tujunga Village. Outside the Aroma Café, a star of a TV forensics team twice removed from the original series inspected his lunch. Hugh passed the Italian restaurant where Robert Blake had dinner with his wife before she was murdered. The jury found him innocent, and the tour buses came by twice a day.

When he reached Ventura Boulevard, he turned east. He hadn't driven a hundred yards, when a car swerved within a foot of the Volvo. Hugh punched his horn. The car slipped back into its lane only to meander closer a moment later, sliding by Hugh. An old primed Camaro with tinted windows. Was it the car that had been behind them on the on-ramp? It drifted closer again. "Get the fuck away," shouted Hugh, honking repeatedly. The car returned to its lane, slowed and vanished into the traffic behind.

"Asshole," muttered Hugh, but by the third stoplight, he had all but forgotten the encounter.

The next turn took him back a decade. As he gazed at the familiar houses, Hugh eased up on the accelerator.

Turning onto Rosegate Street, Hugh gripped the steering wheel tighter, for his body felt weightless, as on the first plunge of a roller coaster. Here a tree had been climbed, a curb jumped, a driveway chipped by the edge of their skateboards.

At the end of the street, a cul-de-sac, two children were forming figure eights on silver scooters. For an instant—but, no . . . always skateboards.

Hugh stopped in the middle of the street, leaving the car in neutral. He didn't yet look at the house, but stared at the freeway noise barrier that twenty years ago served as a backstop for his pitches to Takumi and Hitoshi.

The two children on scooters, noticing his gaze, scooted off.

Executing a U-turn, Hugh pulled up in front of his former house and turned to face memory's indictment.

Chapter 8

From the pier restaurant's second-deck dining area, Kazuki watched the fat fisherman break the bonito's jaw. The blood leaked to the wooden slats, pooled in a perfect circle, bulged as if in mitosis and formed a rivulet that trickled down the inch-wide space between the slats and emptied into the sea twenty feet below, drops striking the water like little red bombs. The angler tossed the improved fish into a bulging gunnysack.

At the end of the pier, the breeze was strong and cool. Kazuki hoped it might tamp his fever while he worked. But his stomach was in turmoil, and he would soon have to use the bathroom. He bent over the keyboard, gazed somberly at his words.

Katashi Ito twisted the ring on his left index finger.

"This isn't right," said the slight man with the crescent scar below his right eye. "The mistake was made in Seoul."

There was no air-conditioning in the dockside warehouse, and summer Tokyo's nightly steam bath did not relent. The man's white shirt was dark and clingy with sweat as were those of the two broad-shouldered men who flanked him. Katashi's shirt was as if freshly pressed. Three years ago, a surgeon had removed Katashi's apocrine glands as a precaution against the spread of a malignant melanoma. Katashi did not perspire. He turned his ear to the ratcheting of a saltwater reel and smiled. Someone fishing on the dock. So late!

"Relax," said Katashi.

Kazuki tapped Pg Dn several times, then slipped the curser to the vertical scroll bar, pulling the manuscript a few hours forward.

Deep in the ship's belly, Katashi led his associates down the intricate path of ladders and narrow passageways. As a young man he'd worked in the merchant marine, and as they descended, the thickening smell of oil and brine comforted him, took him back. At the base of the final ladder was the bilge, where a tall, thin, bare-chested figure kneeled on a catwalk above the black pools streaked with rainbows . . .

"Are the fish jumping tonight?" asked Katashi.

Slipping his fingers from the keyboard, Kazuki stood up and placed his palm to his midsection. Below, a small girl in red dashed about, checking the big plastic paint buckets that most of the anglers used to hold their catch. On newspapers spread beside their husbands' tackle, wives prepared lunch, bright bowls of salsa, pork, onions, and chicken to be scooped into corn tortillas. In the midday sun, the meats swam in their juices. Without warning, the pier shivered as a docking boat slammed against the pilings, engines then roaring and flooding the patio with diesel fumes.

Holding his stomach, Kazuki staggered toward the restroom.

On his knees, Kazuki vomited into a shit-flecked toilet bowl. He gazed at his deposit, trying to remember the English words for its consistency and color, but Katashi and his men intruded.

The dark figure stood, arms raised, stretching taut a piece of rope. Behind Katashi, the slight man made his pitiful case. Even if he were not completely innocent, what of his family? How would they get along in this hard world?

The restroom door squealed and banged. Kazuki listened to the creak of a zipper and the hesitant stream of piss, and—after long delay—the rapid flapping of penis. The door squealed and banged again. Without washing his hands! Kazuki peered into the bowl. On the white slope, a cockroach struggled to find traction. Teeth chattering with a sudden fever, the author yanked off a piece of toilet paper, rolled it in his fingers and pointed the tube at the insect. Should he nudge the creature to safety or push it back into the fetid pool?

Katashi met the man's pale and tear-stained face. "I'd forgotten your family, Makoto."
"Yes?" asked the man, face brightening.
Katashi shielded his eyes with his hand. "Will you forgive my thoughtlessness?"
"Of course," said Makoto.
"Thank you."
Katashi nodded to the dark figure, turned and began his ascent even as the two large men carried Makoto, screaming and kicking like a baby fresh out of the womb, to the dark waiting figure.

"Forgive me," said Kazuki, poking the tube at the archaic shell of the struggling insect. It toppled down the white slope into the last of Kazuki's breakfast. Teary-eyed, the author fumbled for the toilet's handle. His deposit swirled. The cascade of fresh water swept the roach into the rich whirlpool, whose consistency was that of coffee grounds, and whose color was that of tangerines.
Liver cancer.

Chapter 9

Gathering himself, Hugh got out of the car. He walked up the cracked asphalt driveway to the garage. Above the garage door, a rusted basketball hoop framed a well-trafficked cobweb. A dozen insects slept in the fine mesh.

Hugh lifted his hands to shape a basketball. He shot.

"Air ball," shouted Takumi.

"Extend your wrist, Dad," advised Hitoshi.

Here they had lived. Rushed out that green door into a thousand fiery mornings. Hammered that Spalding into their dark court. Sprang on impossibly smooth strong legs to shoot and block and pass. Never pass in the air. Protect the ball. Head fake.

Their first home. Their only home.

Setsuko and Hugh had moved into the house when the boys were still infants. It was not an easy time. The boys were colicky and refused to sleep on the same schedule, leaving one always awake. One time this went on for four days. Setsuko did not sleep, not any sleep that Hugh had seen. She spurned Hugh's offers of help. He couldn't feed them anyway, and they cried in his arms. Setsuko never complained. Not once had she even sighed at these impossible responsibilities. After four days, the babies settled back into their normal sleeping patterns, which was for both to sleep for two to three hours. Now Setsuko slept, Takumi nestled on one side of her, Hitoshi on the other. How still and silent all three were, like moonlit winter snow. When the babies woke to be fed, it took nothing else than their stirring to wake her from her first sleep in one hundred hours. She sat up and fed Hitoshi first, singing to Takumi to conciliate him.

She had a beautiful singing voice, but Setsuko only sang for their sons.

Hugh peered over the side gate. The valley oak had grown enormous, its branches formed an umbrella over the entire yard. Deep into the north end of the property remained the stump of the mulberry tree, which Hugh had cut down, holding his boys' shoulders as they took turns using the chain saw to reduce the fallen limbs to firewood.

"I do not want to pick up their fingers," Setsuko had said as she watched in stony dismay.

"They're fine," said Hugh, who in actuality controlled their every movement. But they had to be taught, and this is what Setsuko could not quite grasp. To teach them about the world required going out into the world, chasing its mysteries, following the stream to its source, the owl into its cave, that will-o'-the-wisp into its swampy domain.

Hugh leaned over the gate, tempted to lift the latch, four inches beneath his fingers. He wondered if the old hay bales remained. Perhaps a weathered arrow sticking out of the painted target. He craned his neck.

Weeds grew tall. Junk and plastic storage boxes of various sizes, the largest the length and shape of a coffin, were visible like islands among the sea of weeds.

From the backyard, his sons called out to him.

"Hold on, guys," whispered Hugh, tapping his hand on the rusted metal gate and feeling for the latch. So simple, but . . .

Sighing, Hugh stepped away from the gate and walked to the front steps. Planters on either side once held stunning arrangements of flowers, but now housed only weeds and a few gladioli. In the dirt by one of the sad plants, a small American flag, discolored and tattered, no doubt left by a real estate agent on some distant Fourth of July, fluttered. Hugh looked for the doorbell but it had been torn out. The blinds were drawn. It was possible that the house was unoccupied, but equally possible that some frightened elderly person was peering out through a crack in the blinds.

As he stood on the step, the house seemed to recede.

He understood clearly why he had not previously returned to the neighborhood and home. There was nothing here for him, nothing to be derived, no sons to be found. He turned to walk away, but glanced once more at the little American flag. Hugh bent down and plucked up the flag by its stem. Beneath the faded red, white and blue, he read:

Nakamura Realty. Beneath the name was a phone number.

Hugh turned his head toward the loud rumble of a muffler. The old primed Camaro was stopped halfway down the block. The car did a slow K turn and drove away. Even through the tinted rear windshield, the driver's long black hair shone.

Was he being followed? It seemed like it, felt like it. He remembered other times, distant times, when he thought someone was tracking him. A stranger seen at too many places during the course of a day. A woman at a bar smiling too generously. Intense eyes in the rearview mirror, eyes looking for his eyes.

Hunted like game. But no one ever took him down.

Well, who doesn't have their run-in now and then with paranoia?

Chapter 10

Fingal's Cave /16
AN ODD ENCOUNTER

Yuudai guided Sumiko from the Marina del Rey restaurant, where they had dined and danced, to the nearby cove.

"Mother's Beach," said Yuudai, gesturing at the pale, narrow crescent of sand bordering the dark glassy bay. "Water's shallow. No waves. No riptides. Safe as a bathtub. Also cruelly known as Stretch Mark Beach."

"I don't understand," said Sumiko.

Sumiko's English was more advanced than Yuudai's Japanese, but she was challenged by idioms and wordplay. Yuudai took her hand and puffed out his belly. He held her hand to his skin and separated her fingers. "Marks left when the woman's skin stretches during pregnancy. Stretch marks."

"Ah, sutoretchimāku."

They wrapped their arms around each other, shrugged off their shoes and stepped into the still-warm sand. It was July and in Los Angeles it had been in the nineties during the day for the last two weeks. It was mild compared to a Tokyo summer, and perfect beach weather, but Sumiko, wary of the sun, would only go to the beach in late afternoon, and even then hide beneath an umbrella. How relaxed she seemed now, sunbathing at midnight. Not once had she mentioned her guilt.

When Katashi asked if she would be alone in Los Angeles for the art exhibition that featured one of her photos, she had lied to her father. Too many times had she voiced her regret to Yuudai, dulling the brightest moments of their stay.

At those moments, too, Sumiko would survey their surroundings and hint at something more. Her father may have been ailing, but "he took care of business . . ."

At the water's edge they stopped, swaying to the music that slipped from an open door of the restaurant like a bird escaping from a cage. On the bay, the night-lights of a hundred boats danced like fluorescent sea creatures. Yuudai dug his toes into the moist sand, took Sumiko's arm and guided her out into the shallow water. Holding hands, they walked in the warm bay toward a shadowy bulkhead that ran down the beach and into the water. Beyond the bulkhead was a lit dock, on which a dozen shiny sea kayaks stretched out in all directions like seals on a jetty. The bulkhead throwing a convenient shadow on the sand, Yuudai and Sumiko lay down beneath the dark pilings. Yuudai offered his chest as a pillow.

"I would like to capture this," said Sumiko, gesturing at the shimmering lights on the gentle water. She framed the scene with her arms.

"Night or day?" asked Yuudai.

"Night. Yes, night."

"We'll come back."

"No, I don't think so."

"Pessimist," he whispered, kissing Sumiko's nose and then her lips, shaping them to his. But realist was more accurate. Sumiko knew there wouldn't be time. She'd need tomorrow night for packing. She had no instinct for pretending.

He took off his shirt, laid it on the sand and unpeeled Sumiko's jeans. She trusted him wholly, had from that night in Tokyo when they danced, and he fell in love with her grace, soft laughter, slender beauty—and self-possession. There was no other word for it.

Yuudai held his hand against Sumiko and stared back across the beach at the restaurant's picture windows where the dancers were so densely packed and their movements so similar that they appeared as one organism. At one of the docks, a boat was tying up, its hull tapping rhythmically against the wood.

Yuudai rapped his hand on the sand in time with the tapping boat.

He knew that if not for her father, Sumiko would leave Japan to be with Yuudai in America, but how to break her father's spell?

"Let's go for a swim," said Yuudai to Sumiko.

"All right."

Yuudai took off his jeans. Sumiko slipped off her T-shirt. They crept across the sand, staying in the bulkhead's shadow. They slipped into the water like amphibious creatures tired of the obstinacy of land. At first, the water was too shallow for them to swim, so they crawled, digging their fingers into the mud and sand, their bodies floating on the water's surface. Every few yards, the bottom pulsed as the stingrays and flatfish darted from cover. Eventually the water became waist deep, and they let loose the seabed. Sumiko had swum on her high school team. Yuudai had to labor to keep up with her, but it was not long before they reached the rope and buoys that signaled the limits of the bathing area. They clung to the rope. Yuudai held his hands up and dropped to the bottom. His feet touched in an instant. The water reached his forehead, just deep enough to drown. Bending his knees, and then straightening, he resurfaced. With arms resting on the rope, they clung to each other, kissing hungrily, faces sinking into the sea until they remembered their breaths. The water had the faint smell of oil, and he tasted it on Sumiko's lips. A pelican swooped down out of nowhere, skimming the surface, its huge whiteness unexpected. Sumiko stared into Yuudai's eyes as he slipped off her panties. She wrapped her legs around him. His hand barely clasped the rope.

Yuudai's toes brushed the sea bottom as he stretched to hold Sumiko's weight and still breathe. He thrust into her, lost himself in the firm silky body until unable to hold back his ejaculation, he stepped forward to keep his balance and felt a prick to the arch of his foot. "Fuck," he said, slowly releasing her.

"What is it?"

"I stepped on something."

"Are you cut?"

"Damn, I think so."

"Glass?"

"Not glass. A ray, I think."

Sumiko's eyes went big. "A ray bit you?"

"No, no. A stingray They don't bite, but their tails have stingers." Yuudai held to the rope, lifted and bent his leg. He drew his fingers across the spot that burned. "My foot will swell up. I might get sick. We better go in."

Sumiko nodded. She turned over and swam on her back, watching Yuudai as he thrashed angrily at the sea that had ruined the moment.

As they dressed, Sumiko said, "I want to kill it and eat it."

"What do you mean?"

"The stingray that bit you."

"It didn't—I don't—"

Sumiko tossed down her clothes and walked back toward the bay.

"Don't be crazy."

But she was already in the water, diving, disappearing.

He dropped down on the sand, inspecting his foot.

Fifty yards from the beach, near the rope where their lovemaking had been thwarted, Sumiko disappeared.

"Come on. It's funny, okay. But enough's enough."

She appeared on the surface, swimming toward the shore. Nearing the shore, she stood up, the boat's lights sparking off her wet black hair.

To her chest, she held something gray and the length of a man's shoe. It was only when she was upon him that he realized it was alive and vibrating. She gazed at Yuudai, lifted the stingray to her mouth and bit. Blood flicked across her cheeks.

"Sumiko!"

She dropped the wriggling wounded stingray to the sand, where it was quickly coated like a fillet in batter.

In Sumiko's womb, the little fish swam toward its intended.

Kazuki leaned back, cradled his head in his interlocking fingers. Setsuko gave birth to Sumiko but Sumiko in turn gave birth to Setsuko's truest self.

Chapter 11

Stretched out on the lounge chair, Hugh listened to the songs that seeped out of his home's screen door. To the beat, he twirled the little flag, his *souvenir from a dream*.

An hour passed. The sun dipped beneath the western ridges. The insects set to with their call and response. His little chipped statue of Buddha, which sat upon the stump of a scrub oak, found the evening's last direct light.

A glint of sunlight blinded him. To block the ray, Hugh held up the flag and it was then he noticed the typo: *Nakamura Reality*. Reality?

Hugh leaned from the lounge chair and jammed the flag into the dirt. A few minutes later, he picked up the flag and took out his cell phone. It was past six, but real estate firms kept late hours.

"Good evening," answered a honey-voiced woman.

"Is this Nakamura Realty?" asked Hugh.

"No, you've reached Nakamura *Reality*."

"Not real estate?"

"We are a fabrication company. The film industry mostly."

"Props and stuff."

"Yes, props and stuff."

"Sorry."

"Are you looking for a realty company?"

"Not—well, yes."

"I highly recommend PB Realty. I don't have their number but they're listed and you can find them online."

"PB Realty. Great. Thanks."

"You're welcome."

The phone went dead.

Hugh twirled the oddball promotional item for a few seconds, stuck it back in the dirt, but then retrieved it.

Later, he sat up in bed, holding a Lunesta between his thumb and index finger. The little gray tablets were almost invisible at night. He would use them for a month at a time and then stop cold turkey so as to meet the requirement of his health insurance, which would only allow renewal of the thirty-pill prescription every sixty days.

Before the Lunesta was Fuguelle, which promised restful sleep but delivered mostly comforting delirium. After taking the drug, he would bring the Buddha inside, set it on the floor before the couch and stare at the figure until it danced and multiplied into dozens of damaged Buddhas, each whispering a wonderful story, offering him access to the secrets of the universe. Though far from meditation, the state was comforting and freed him for a while from thoughts of his sons and Setsuko.

He took the sleeping pills and loathed them, for the price of his broken sleep was the nightmare, whose mutable terrain changed not at all its draining frustration. In the dream he could not find his way to the place of his appointment, where the consequences of his absence would be disastrous. Each logical step toward his destination—seen in the distance—led absurdly away from that destination. Each street, each corridor, each path, though as familiar as the length of his arm, tricked and betrayed him. Every turn was wrong, every door was the wrong door, every certainty was uncertainty. He ran in bewilderment through these implacable settings, pulverized into helplessness—a helplessness and uncertainty that would come upon him in waking hours like a flash of gout.

But this was not the dream's ultimate horror—

. . . Apparently extracted from the dream, sitting on a luxurious sofa, Hugh gazed at a television on which Takumi and Hitoshi, perhaps three years old, clawed from inside the screen in a paroxysm of pain and terror, mirrored in their faces. "No, Daddy," they begged, tears streaming. "Come get us!"

"Mr. Mcpherson? Mr. Mcpherson, are you awake?"

A woman's voice, vaguely familiar. The smell of bleach and urine. His right thumb nagging his fingers, one by one . . . *This little piggy goes to market. This little piggy stays home. This—*

Hugh opened his eyes. The woman attached to the voice smiled down at him, brown eyes in a round brown face.

"There you are," she said. "Remember me?"

He spotted the silver name tag on her white jacket: "Yes," he whispered. "You've been very kind."

"I try," said Miranda.

The black letters on the silver nametag smeared as she leaned into him. "Here, just a little water." She lifted his head and pressed the plastic cup to his lips. The cool water trickled down his throat.

"Groggy?" she asked.

He remembered that he'd awakened before. Several times. He'd awakened and then—blank. He nodded.

"Well, you should be. Would you like some breakfast?"

"Breakfast?"

Hugh glanced at the IV in his left forearm. He pressed his right hand against the mattress. He rose a few inches.

Miranda eased him back. "If you stood up, you'd fall down."

"My sons . . ." said Hugh.

Miranda's lips tightened and her forehead lined with concern. She knew the truth, and she knew that Hugh did also.

Later, the young man with the gleaming shaved head came in. He looked like his sons might look when they reached their twenties. He stood at the foot of the bed; above his head, on the television, stock market quotes zipping across the base of the television screen. Securely on the far right the date. *July 22.* Hugh had been in the hospital for five days.

"It's not just found in soldiers returning from combat," the young man had explained in an earlier consultation. How earlier? A day? Hugh could not remember. *Repressed memories. Glucocorticoids. Neuronal damage. Depression.*

Hugh recalled swimming furiously, shouting his sons' names with liquid breath. The sea was everywhere; his sons were nowhere, the realization piercing his brain like a bullet.

"Did you bring the paper?" Hugh asked.

"Yes, but—"

Hugh held out his hand. From his briefcase the young man withdrew a newspaper and handed it to Hugh, who merely lay it on his chest.

"Nothing?" asked Hugh.

"I'm sorry, Hugh."

Hugh tapped the paper as if keying in a password. He opened it, turned a page, saw the photo. Again he recalled the numbing vastness of the ocean as he searched for their forms, black as night in their wet suits.

"Nothing," said Hugh, as he looked up from the paper to the dark eyes of the expressionless woman who stood in the doorway behind the young man. Hugh tried to hold her gaze.

"Setsuko," Hugh called out, but his voice did not appear to reach his wife's ears, for she turned away.

He popped in the pill, took a sip of tea and lifted the book he would read until sleep.

Before he opened to the dog-eared page, he thought of the letter, the real letter. He wondered if it had made its way across that vast ocean. Was Setsuko at this moment breaking the seal or had Kazuki tossed it into the sea?

Hugh slept until dawn, awakening to a pain on his side. He yanked out the book, which had lodged between his arm and chest. His sleep had bent the hardback's cover and wrinkled its pages beyond redemption. He tossed the disaster to the floor.

In the kitchen, he quartered two oranges and ate them from the peel, spitting the seeds in a plastic grocery bag. He boiled the water again and had high-fiber maple and honey oatmeal. After eating, he was alert enough to realize that he stank. The accumulation of the ocean and the exertion. He took a shower, put on fresh jeans, made another coffee and went out bare-chested into the backyard. The sun was breaking over the eastern ridge. He watched the hills light up.

A couple of rabbits nibbled at the weeds. Sometimes deer would be there, walking from the higher elevations to the creek. Hugh glanced along the path that paralleled the stream, which fed into a deep wide rock pool. Something moved in the water, maybe one of the brown trout that were illegal to fish. The fish, no, a *hand* broke the surface. A body unfolded. The morning light struck a slender tapered back, raven hair spreading across the smooth white shoulders. Hugh rose, dropping the coffee cup.

A woman swam face down, her butterfly strokes taking her to the far end of the pool.

"Setsuko—" cried Hugh.

The pool was no more than twenty feet across and ten wide. The body turned underwater like a screw, quickly reaching the far bank.

"Setsuko!"

The swimmer's arm came out of the water. The long, elegant fingers dug into the moist soil. She pulled herself onto the bank, and then scampered into the brush, almost on all fours, the way an animal would escape.

Hugh ran down the path along the creek, halting at the rock pool. He looked for movement within the brush. It was insane to think the swimmer had been Setsuko. He hadn't even seen her face. Some back-to-nature hippie chick taking a cool morning bath. Hugh strode along the bank to where the water resumed its slow flow in a shallower area, the creek clogged with deadwood and rocks. He picked his way across the debris, realizing he was barefoot. He walked toward the spot where the woman had disappeared. Something stirred in the brush.

He looked back at the pool, where several small brown trout glided a foot beneath the surface, passing over a motionless crayfish and disappearing into clouds of sediment stirred up by the swimmer. Hugh climbed the slope, scanning the ground for broken twigs, footprints, signs. Through the trees, a house was visible, one of those dark stone houses that from the road might be taken for a rock formation. Solid as a fort and uninviting, along the sides, a wall of bamboo. A path appeared.

He felt a prick of pain. A trickle of blood appeared beside his right toe. He thought about returning to the house for his shoes, but the woman would be long gone by then. On either side of the path, the brush was thick. Despite the open wound, he sprinted along the path.

As he ran barefoot, his heartbeat rising to the effort, the adrenaline flowing, he felt the urge to remove the rest of his clothes, to run naked on the hard dirt in pursuit of the woman who would not be Setsuko. He ran several hundred yards and stopped, panting and dripping sweat, his ears abuzz, his skin tingling. Flat initially, the path now sloped upward, vanishing into a thicket of briars. He must have kicked something as he ran, for his left toenail bent up at a right angle like an empty clam shell. He pinched it in his fingers and tore, flicked it into the brush as he walked forward into the thorns. They had not grown there naturally. They were not rooted. Someone had cut them up and stuffed them in the path as a barrier. He looked around for a stick, found a divining rod and stuck it into the clump of briars. As he worked it out, a radio played, and the odor rose of roasting fish. He dislodged the barrier. One hundred feet down the path, under a scrub oak, several men sat around a small fire. The men looked like the day workers who waited outside the post office. Not old, but aged, not worn, but weary. As he walked closer, they turned to him, their eyes sharp and defensive. He expected to see the woman hidden among them. But there was no woman, just the old homeless man whom Hugh had seen along the highway, now huddled in a blanket and roasting two small fish, identical even to their split bellies, on a spit.

Chapter 12

Kazuki glided past the slender thighs of a pubescent girl, swaying like a reed in the shallow end of the pool. He slid his hands across the second step and pushed, so that he rose with an explosion of water. Grabbing the silver rail, he yanked himself to the deck. He walked on the warm stone, halting a few feet from the lounge chair to tilt back his head, grab his hair and twist. He faced the sun for a few seconds, grateful for its cancerous rays, then strode to the shade of his umbrella. He toweled off, waved away a beautiful hostess and dropped to the chair. He felt feverish. The swim hadn't helped. He lifted his glasses from the laptop, asleep on the hardwood table, checked the thick lenses for smudges and jerked them on. He swiveled sideways on the chair, poked the touchpad. The screen lit up. Kazuki read through the scene of Yuudai's first meeting with Katashi. Satisfied, he scrolled ahead seven years.

Bone dry, the rock pool. Ducks, frogs and crayfish disappeared. Along the cracked brown track, James and Brent silent, Yuudai divining. Fifty yards, not a drop, not a river, not an ocean. Did you? . . . Feel it, boys? Feel it soften? Vegetation thicken. Prehistoric. Cautious. Snake rattle. Fan palms.

Before a bundle of broken branches, Yuudai hunched down, pressed his hand to the earth and felt moisture.

Glancing beyond the interlaced branches, he saw a glistening. He pointed and urged the boys to move closer. Though it was a hardly a yard in diameter, the little pool seemed miraculous. As they moved toward it, their feet sank into soft earth. When they were two yards away, a second pool revealed itself, something moving at the bottom. Flashing claws threw off a brilliant orange light. Two crayfish, either mating or consuming one another. For a closer look, Yuudai had his sons gather dead branches and lay them down over the first pool. Crossing on the dead branches, they hunched down before the second pool to see the crayfish. The creatures were a good four inches long. Yuudai snapped off a twig and touched a claw. The creature scuttled back under cover of a fallen tree. In the silence insects buzzed and birds chirped. From deeper in the woods, came a shout: "Iidesuyo!"

Yuudai jumped to his feet.

"What's the matter, Dad?" asked Brent.

"Did you hear it?"

"Hear what?" asked James.

Yuudai pivoted, listened for the voice. "There," he said, pointing in the direction of a fan palm.

"Look," said Brent, gesturing at the pool where the larger of the crayfish had reappeared.

Still listening for the voice, Yuudai slowly turned to Brent. Merely the echo of a memory, thought Yuudai, turning his attention to the crayfish. Dropping to his haunches, he instructed James to keep the crustacean occupied with the twig while Brent grabbed its tail. Is there a claw on his tail? No. No claw. No stinger. The boys were thinking of scorpions or stingrays . . . James stuck the stick in front of the crayfish, its protruding eyes darting about, and it pinched the stick. Brent dipped in his hand and pinched the crayfish by its tail. The boys laughed. The crayfish flashed its claws. It wasn't brilliant orange out of the water, and was not the monster crayfish that had first appeared to them. Brent set it on the mud.

"Iidesuyo!"

Yuudai jumped up.

"Dad, it went back in the water."

"Look, it's digging a hole."

But Yuudai could not take his eyes from the quivering fan palm, stabbed, uprooted and flung aside by the horns of a triceratops.

Kazuki pushed back his chair and rose. He walked over to the far side of the pool with its view of the Pacific. A mile from shore, the enormous yacht motored north. Had the story reached the point where Brent and James would be taken from Yuudai? The crayfish had disappeared in the little pool, perhaps dug in under a rock or broken branch. The boys would plead to be allowed to catch it one more time, and though it was getting dark in the noxious dry swamp, where radioactive isotopes had seeped into the soil, Yuudai, ignoring his hallucination, would urge them to recapture the crayfish. They dug their smooth slender hands into the muddy bottom of the pool. Laughing in the warm dusk, they reached deeper until the mud was up to their elbows. How deep could the crayfish bury itself? Could it rip through the underlying bedrock? Was it a real crayfish at all? Titanium claws, digital brain . . . Wincing, Kazuki remembered that he'd used a mechanical crayfish in *Enrique The Freak*, though the crayfish, central to one of the twins' stories, should have been saved for—was promised to—*Fingal's Cave*. He steadied himself against the rail, closed his eyes and drew a long breath. For most things his memory was no better than average, but he could summon up his own words as if they were projected before him on a teleprompter. He scrolled the pages of the books he had written during the last ten years for other errors of inclusion. For everything his grandsons had told him, he had one intention, which was to supply the raw material for *Fingal's Cave*. But he had drawn in the detail accidentally, as one practicing casting from the shore might snag a fish by its tail or fin. Without intention, an echo of his error, he pinched a strand of his still damp hair and drew it to his lips, nibbling and tasting chlorine. On the periphery of his vision, through the crawl space of his not completely closed eyes, the strands were like steel cable. Whether he stood there a minute, an hour or one hundred years, he was uncertain, but when he stepped back, his hands shaking like those of an alcoholic deprived of his next drink, he watched the last page of *Enrique the Freak* crawl into the rafters like the final credits of a movie. He had found no other betrayals in the thousands of words, yet something gnawed at him. Had he transformed an artifact of his grandsons' experience into a shape that he no longer recognized? Had a memory stored in the *Fingal's Cave* neural network seeped into a nearby other and donned a disguise? Had he given away his secrets in potentially decipherable code?

What a drag it is getting old.

How did you know it so young, Mick?

Kazuki glanced at his fingers, which held something that he did not recognize. A spider's web? No, a dozen strands of his hair ripped from his scalp. Although it may have been the sun reflecting off the bougainvillea, the tips appeared red. He drew the strands apart. Closer to white than silver, but for the odd still-blond thread. Many thought it dyed, but he was born with a Viking's hair, his brows and beard yellow, too. A freak, he kept it close-cropped as a youth, and it drew little attention. In the 1960s he let it grow like everyone else, and as his reputation as a writer grew so did his hair, longer and wilder, going years without an inch trimmed. It was the mane of a lion, or the costume of a Kabuki actor. When Setsuko was a toddler, Kazuki would get down on all fours and flop his hair forward to the floor. Setsuko would crawl under it as if behind a waterfall. She would laugh as she poked and peeked through the strands. He watched her enchanting face as if a god who had parted the clouds to look down from heaven.

Gimme a head with hair / Long beautiful hair / Shining, gleaming, / Streaming . . .

But though inseparable from his image, there were times it seemed a burden. He wore it with the feeling he was carrying someone on his shoulders.

He tied a knot in the strands and snapped the wen against the rail. How old would Setsuko be? Forty-four? Yes, forty-four on November 17. His daughter was no fan of birthdays. She wanted no part of them or any other anniversary. He never forced them on her. There were no special days, each day the same in its emptiness. Her aversion began with her mother's death. She was eight, and would be ten before she ventured out from under the black umbrella of shock and despair. Ten before she truly looked again at the world. He tried to make her life joyous, but she smiled rarely, laughed never. She asked for nothing, he gave her everything.

But not enough. Huck Finn paddled all the way from Los Angeles to Tokyo.

The big yacht was gone.

Kazuki swung the knotted strands like a weapon. Released. It whirled like a bolo, stretching and thickening as it flew above the walkway and beach, a monstrous propeller, whipping and blowing the sand into a yellow tidal wave that fell upon and covered the sea.

Kazuki returned to his laptop. The muddy pool would not open up like the earth under the singing Persephone, and Hades's golden chariot would not take the boys away.

Not yet.

Chapter 13

Hugh parked the Volvo, crossed PCH and climbed half-way down the stairs to the beach when a voice called him from the memory he had packed like a box lunch for the journey.

"Hey, Buddha."

Standing at the top of the steps, Hanna grabbed the rails and swung up one leg. Lines of text ran across the ball of her foot.

"I'm sorry about the other day. About Kyle, I mean." She fingered her black lip stud. Her hair was now red with a blue streak.

"Don't worry about it," said Hugh.

"I didn't know he was home. The sneak was hiding under the newspapers. Scared the shit out of me."

"Newspapers?"

"Kyle has been collecting newspapers to sell to the Chinese. He heard they're paying big money for cardboard boxes. He figures newspapers will be next. Anyway, he's got them stacked up five feet high all around the trailer. He's got little tunnels in there. He's like a gopher."

Hanna dismounted from the rail and scampered down the steps, stopping two steps above Hugh. She stuck out her hand. "Hanna."

"Hugh," he said, taking the soft weightless fingers.

"We've met before." She giggled. "I mean before before. The Peace & Love, right?"

"We did, briefly."

"Did anyone ever tell you that you look like Eric Clapton?"

"It's the haircut," said Hugh.

"Do me a favor?" She glanced at her shoulder, where a beige bra strap ran across the pink skin. She stuck a finger under the strap and sniffed.

"Smells funny. Does it smell funny to you?"

"No," he said, taking a perfunctory sniff. "It smells laundry fresh."

At the top of the stairs appeared a family composed of two heavyset women and a half-dozen children. They were loaded like pack mules and catching their breath. The oldest child, a boy of nine or ten, carried a watermelon and was doubled over with the weight. As the boy climbed down, the melon slipped from his grasp, falling toward the hard steps.

Hugh flung himself forward and grabbed the watermelon, his knuckles brushing the concrete.

"*Gracias!*" said one of the women.

"Do you want me to carry it for you?" asked Hugh.

"No, I got it," said the grinning boy, taking the melon. "My hands were just slippery. Thanks, mister."

Hugh stepped aside as the family descended the steps and tramped across the beach, the boy twice turning back to nod and smile at Hugh.

"Pretty good goalie," said Hanna. "Down for another swim?"

"Mostly."

"Mind if I tag along?"

She jutted out her hip and nibbled her lip. "I don't want to be rude," said Hugh, "but I'd rather you didn't."

"Kyle's not around, if that's what you're worried about."

Hugh looked toward the point. The ocean was flat. Twenty surfers floated motionless, dead in the water. The storm had not yet generated the promised swell.

"I have some reading I want to get done."

"That's all right."

"I don't want to talk."

"That's cool by me. You never talk anyway. Well, I knew you were silent, and now—" She pointed toward the boy with the watermelon. "—I know you are strong and flexible."

"I'm really—"

"Please?"

"I only have one towel."

"Oh, that's a real dilemma," she said, tugging at her ragged red bangs and then tapping her lip ring.

She followed him as he trod down the beach, halting near the lifeguard stand.

He set his bag down, removed his towel and spread it on the sand, anchoring it with two nearby rocks. He took off his sandals, putting them beside the towel, and then removed his T-shirt, conscious of Hanna staring at his chest and back, not quite as hairy as an ape. For some women it was a turn-on, for others it was repulsive. Except for the bouquets of hair at his nipples, her boyfriend, Kyle, was sleek as a porpoise. Hugh folded his T-shirt and tucked it in the bag. He took out his sunscreen, rubbed a layer on his face and offered it to Hanna.

"No thank you. I've sworn off that stuff," said Hanna smartly.

Hugh powered the cell phone, floating for a few seconds on Radiohead's oceanic melody. There were no messages. Setsuko had not called. His sons had not texted from heaven . . .

"Man, that's an old phone," commented Hanna.

"I get the same calls," said Hugh.

"Maybe you wouldn't if you had a new one."

Hugh flipped the phone shut, dropped it in the gym bag and took out Kazuki's book. As he was driving to the beach, thinking about the woman in the rock pool—his morning mirage—he remembered the brown trout and the crayfish. It occurred to him that there was something about crayfish in *Enrique*. *Mechanical crayfish*. The narrator was describing a dinner at a bizarre restaurant and *mechanical crayfish* was one of the items on the menu. With his sons he had hunted crayfish, and there was that one day . . .

He planned to skim for twenty minutes before dog-earing the page, returning the book to the gym bag and then going for the long swim. He opened to Chapter Seventeen. He read a page and then thumbed backward.

Hanna cleared her throat, her eyes begging attention. So ignored, a puppy would yelp.

"I told you . . ."

"I know, I know. Can I read one of your books?"

Hugh thumbed the pages of *Enrique*. So there was a crayfish—so what? He handed her Kazuki's book.

Opening to the first page, Hanna read aloud, looking into his eyes every few sentences to gauge his interest, just as he had done when he read to Takumi and Hitoshi as they settled into their bunk beds. In the morning, Setsuko read to them in Japanese, but at night it was Hugh reciting English. He read from Brothers Grimm and Hans Christian Andersen. The Grimm stories were dark, violent and erotic. The Andersen tales were romantic, filled with lost love and small heroisms. When he read the stories to the twins, he felt he was weather-coating their emotions for storms to come. Their favorite was "The Steadfast Tin Soldier," which told the story of the one-legged toy infantryman who fell in love with the beautiful paper ballerina doll who sat on a nearby mantle, both residents of a child's bedroom. Pushed from the room's windowsill, the soldier fell into a toy boat floating in the gutter and traveled miles and miles to sea. But eventually, he found his way back to the bedroom and his beloved ballerina. Yet he had only a moment of fulfillment before the willful child tossed him into the room's fireplace. As the soldier melted, a breeze from an open window blew the ballerina too into the fire. The toy soldier melted into a heart. The ballerina consumed but for a single spangle.

More than once as he closed the book, his sons in their steady sleep, he thought of how happy he would be to die like that with Setsuko. Immolated, reduced to symbols. He never told her. She would have laughed.

Hugh would swim farther than he ever had. He would swim until he couldn't swim anymore and then he'd swim some more just to be safe. In his imagination, he projected the effort, felt the sea in his eyes, mouth and throat.

Hanna read aloud, "Any attempt to hide or cover the body, for example when guests came over, would break the lease. The landlord advised against inviting children into the apartment, not that the children would be disturbed by the sight, but because even the best-behaved sometimes get into mischief, occasionally putting their own lives in danger. Any damage to the chamber would be his responsibility. He agreed, knowing he constructed this arrangement or had he was the question . . ."

Hugh pressed the back of his hand across one eye and then the other.

"Are you crying?" asked Hanna.

"For Christ's sake, no," he said sharply, but his body trembled. As if he might fall, he leaned into her. His tears pooled in the hollow of her shoulder, transformed for an instant into Setsuko's hollow, Setsuko's breast. When the boys sucked from her, the clear milk was indistinguishable from her skin, leaving her ruby red nipples like islands.

"I fucked up."

"It's okay," she whispered. "We all fuck up."

He wanted to spill it all out to her. How he had left his sons alone in a dangerous sea, and upon returning found them gone. How he had swum a mile from shore searching for his sons among the dark, tangled kelp. How he had begged God to perform one more trick. How he had lost his fucking mind.

But he only repeated Hanna's words. "Yes. We all fuck up." *But some more than others.*

His chest heaved as if to throw off a weight, and he realized his arms were around Hanna, his lips pressed to her neck as if there he might find a nipple and a drop of mother's milk. He whimpered and then it was done. Drawing away from Hanna, who grimaced with disappointment, he met a nearby older woman's disapproving stare. Hanna more than the tears, he supposed. Hugh drew up a laugh like phlegm, bellowing as if the funniest joke in the world had just been told.

The older woman, who nibbled a sandwich, a bright red slice of tomato hanging out like a second tongue, eyed him now with pure hostility. Her tomato slid out from the sandwich and dropped to the sand. She looked at the tomato and then back at Hugh as if it were his fault. *Old men with young girls, enough to make a sandwich explode.* But Hanna's presence made suicide an even less likely interpretation, Hugh thought, and to confirm his old goat status, he patted Hanna's thigh, remembering wondrously how muscle felt beneath smooth cool skin.

"You okay?" she asked.

Hugh nodded, drawing back from the girl, gathering himself.

"I broke up with Kyle," said Hanna.

"Congratulations."

"It was time for a change."

"New horizons."

"I knew it was a mistake. From the beginning, I felt like I was giving up something to be with him. My independence, I guess. Kyle spouts all this hippie stuff, but he's the jealous sort. Well, you know that. But I got something too, and not just drugs—I'll bet that's what you were thinking."

Hugh shrugged. She wanted him to consider her, to open up a Hanna file in which the pages of her life would accumulate. Despite their age difference, it was not such an odd choice. At the café, she had seen him numerous times silent and composed, but hardly unapproachable, for he would answer any question put to him. But he neither started nor entered conversations. He would be a good listener, she must have thought. He might have secrets. He wore a wedding band, but he was not married, common knowledge at the café, for he had mentioned it once (perhaps to the plumber), and in the P&L such things echo forever. As all could see, he had no girlfriend. He was likely kind, and not bad looking. He had a trouble-free car and a kept-up house. Oh, what a prize!

Hugh didn't ask about and Hanna didn't disclose the additional benefits Kyle offered beyond the implied drugs.

Last night, she explained, she slept over at a friend's. In the morning, she hitchhiked back to the trailer. She came back to tell Kyle that she was moving out, but he wasn't there. She didn't have anywhere to move out to anyway, though.

She was fishing for shelter. Hugh would be dead before the afternoon was over, so what difference would it make if she squatted at his place for a couple of days? When the rent became due it would become her problem. But how would it strike the cops? How would it look in the newspapers to his students? To their parents? It was one thing to sit on a blanket at the beach, but it would be spun as a middle-aged teacher shacked up with a girl barely out of her teens.

"If it was night, I could show you something," said Hanna.

"Oh, Hanna, don't—"

She pointed at the sky. "Right straight over there is Hercules." She swept her arm to the right. "Over there is Ophiuchus. That means the 'serpent bearer.'" She dropped her arm. "That's Scorpius." She laughed. "Of course, you can't see them now. But tonight that's where they'll be."

"How many are there?" asked Hugh.

"Eighty-eight, just like the keys on a piano," said Hanna. She gazed across the sky as if she were seeing all of them. A cool breeze touched the back of his neck, and it was seconds before he realized it was Hanna's hand. "How's that feel?"

"Nice, but—"

"Do you live in a house, Hugh?"

"I can't give you shelter."

She asked more leading questions, but Hugh turned to the sea's unfolding. Offshore, a pelican glided one hundred yards, sharply plummeted and smashed into a boil. Greeted by a couple of foraging gulls, the bird reemerged with a plump fish thrashing in its reddening bill. The surfers carved their trails. Hanna picked up the book and read, her voice competing with the crashing waves and crying birds.

". . . Enrique descended the dimly lit flight of stairs whose tubular enclosure narrowed with each step at a rate that soon he would have to be a mouse to continue. Not being a mouse, he stopped, turned around, and preparing to retreat drew an astonished breath, for he saw that the tube diminished equally in the direction from which he had come. Easier to be a descending than an ascending mouse, he pivoted, hunched his shoulders and dropped another step. The cohort of odd sounds that had drawn him to the passage rose again and was quickly gone. Tucking into himself, Enrique went down a dozen more steps until the passage ended in a small door offering three doorknobs of different shapes: round, square, triangular (Enrique wasn't sure that a doorknob could be anything other than round, but he couldn't think of alternative descriptors). He chose the doorknob shaped like his face, grasped the knob tightly and turned. The knob resisted. For his second try, he chose the knob with the shape opposite his face. The knob turned like a pinwheel, but was clearly unattached to a lock. But the third knob did the trick. The door swung open. Enrique shielded his eyes from the dazzling golden light of a huge heap of gilded bones. Peeking through his fingers, fearing he'd stumbled on the lair of a carnivorous monster, he laughed with relief. Not bones but brass instruments: trombones, trumpets and tubas, piled disreputably atop one another, like the discarded shells of crustaceans after a summer feast. Curtains covered each side of the enclosure for the instruments, but above them only sky. One of the curtains stirred and the odd sounds that had drawn Enrique to the passage swelled again. Ah. The brass were being played by the lips and tongues of innocent winds. Enrique dislodged a trombone from the pile. He put it to his mouth to blow, and something sweet dripped from the mouthpiece. He let it drizzle on his tongue but then sucked vigorously. He drained the trombone of its nectar, cast it aside and picked up a tuba. It too was filled with the sweet liquid, which flowed into his mouth in a succulent stream. Emptying the tuba, he blew a triumphant note, and then grabbed a trombone—"

"This is pretty freaky stuff," said Hanna.

"Keep going," said Hugh, who could not remember reading the passage, but now found the words utterly compelling.

"All right, let's see . . .

". . . Enrique sorted through the instruments, drinking from each one's lips as a hummingbird might gather its nectar from a thousand flowers . . ."

"Try it, guys. It's really good." Hugh held the tubular stem of the plucked honeysuckle flower to Takumi's lips. Takumi sucked lightly and then forcefully, his cheeks drawing in. The flower emptied, Hugh pulled it from his son's mouth. "More!" said Takumi. "Try it, Hitoshi. Better than candy!"

For an hour Takumi and Hitoshi drank from the wild honeysuckle. He had told the boys not to mention sucking the juice to their mother. The story was nowhere in the world, yet it had found its way into Kazuki's novel, transmuted, but recognizable. Or had Kazuki himself drunk from the honeysuckle as a child? It was foolish to think one had a monopoly on experience. There were no two things without correspondence if you were intent on finding it. Or perhaps the boys had told their mother, and Setsuko told her father. That was the most likely explanation, and yet— not as if they had eaten wild mushrooms—but still, they would not tell their mother that. What had been Kazuki's source?

Hanna set down the book. "You know, I'm easy to live with." She slid her hand across his. He pulled away, his train of thought broken.

"As I said, I'm a teacher."

"Well, I'm hardly your student."

"There's a principle involved," said Hugh with sad slyness. "I'll loan you some money."

Hanna licked her black stud. "I don't want money."

Hugh took the cool Gatorade out of the gym bag and offered it to her. She shook her head languorously, while laying her hand on Hugh's shoulder.

"I'm going to go for a swim," he said, sliding from under her hand.

"I've made you uncomfortable," sighed Hanna.

"I came down for a swim."

"You want me to leave?"

"If you like . . ."

"I can take a hint," said Hanna. She walked a few feet away, turned and smiled at him and then continued toward the stairs, off to solve her own problems. Maybe to start a new life, but most likely to move back in with Kyle and keep the old one going.

Good-bye, Hanna.

Good luck with your astronomy career. See you in the heavens.

There, too, he would see his sons, *if he didn't see them now*.

For that was the long-shot hope. The last chip on the wheel's green slot.

One more chance to believe.

Hugh waded out and dived, skimming the bottom. He pulled himself through the silence. An arm's length ahead, sand spurted as a stingray abandoned its disguise. Hugh swam without rising to breathe. Sixty seconds. Seventy seconds. His blood pulsed. The biggest sound in the big sea. He swallowed the swell of his tongue, a trick he'd learned as a boy in the creek behind their home. *If it be now, 'tis not to come. If it be not to come, it will be now. If it be not now, yet it will come—the readiness* . . .

I'm ready, sons.

His lungs burned as he drew a few oxygen molecules from the stale air. A strand of kelp whipped by his face. A second strand struck Hugh's chest, like a man making a point. And then he was in it, a tangle of slick smooth snarled tubes, which should have embraced him, but instead provoked a drunken brawl. As he struggled in the kelp like a fish in a collapsing net, his movements drove the mass to the surface, where it popped up like a space capsule, his inhalation a cheer from ground control. He kicked to stay on the surface, working to extract his upper body from the kelp until he realized he was battling the water like someone learning to swim. The kelp was gone. He turned 360 degrees, scanning the rising swell. He turned on his back and stared at the sky until his breathing became regular. Someone blew a whistle. Someone called. He looked toward the shore, saw no one that saw him.

One hundred yards away, a boat motored parallel to shore. It moved slowly, visible one moment, hidden by a swell the next. Behind him, the whistle blew.

Ignoring the whistle, Hugh swam west toward the slow-moving craft, which seemed oddly familiar to him. He had seen the boat somewhere, sometime. He was tugged now by a current that took him toward the surfers. One hundred yards away, the first wave of the set rose. The pack maneuvered in anticipation. Pressed to their boards like lovers, they paddled tenderly, waiting for the sign to attack. The wave rose higher and drew into itself, moving faster now, casting off light and signaling to the experienced where it would crest. Hugh swam hard to keep his distance, but the current pushed him closer. With certainty, the pack broke. A dozen of the strongest arms broke free of the others and paddled furiously to reach the wave at its height. Unable to turn away, Hugh watched the sea hollow out before the wave's base as the water was sucked into the form. Twenty surfers met the wave and turned, now soaring down its face.

A surfer rocketed toward him. If Hugh could leap like a dolphin, he could catch the surfboard's tip in his chest, if lucky, piercing his heart like a spear. He would rise to his sons. But he could only watch as the surfboard passed overhead and he fell beneath the wave. Below the surface, the sea turned in on itself, unleashing gravities that pulled him in a dozen directions. He was helpless but couldn't open his mouth to let it fill him, to let the sea fill him. When he came to the surface he was encased in a cloud of bubbles, in the midst of the surfers who, having missed the first wave, were preparing for the next. No one saw him or no one cared. The second wave was not far off.

In a moment, the lifeguards would spot him among the surfers. He dived, trying to get beneath the boards. If he could just swim until the wave passed overhead, he could lose the surfers and could continue out to sea. He pulled himself ten feet down, kicking hard and pulling forward. A boat's motor whined. If he could reach the boat, swim into the propeller.

Where are you, sons? Take my hands. Take me.

Just as his breath was exhausted, the wave passed, its force shaking him. He waited five seconds and rose to the surface. As he broke, a light flashed. He turned to its source and saw the boat coming toward him at an oblique angle. On the bow, two boys kneeled, clutching the gleaming safety rail. "Hitoshi! Takumi!" Hugh cried as the boat closed on him. Treading water to suspend himself, he waved his arms frantically. "Sons!" he cried again. The boys, releasing the safety rail, pointed downward at the hull. Hugh gazed in bewilderment as something solid struck him.

Chapter 14

For three hours straight, Kazuki wrote, unaware of the sun's passage or the transformation of his hotel's pool. Yuudai and his eight-year-old sons ascending Yosemite's Half Dome during autumn's first and unexpected snowfall:

For two hours the flakes melted on the stone, but by the time they reached the rope ladder to draw themselves up the final hundred yards, the snow stuck to the granite. Yuudai looked up to see Brent's foot come out from under him—

Yuudai and his nine-year-old sons shooting guns in the Mojave:

Brent rocked back on his heels from the force of the .38's explosion, but the rusted can remained unmoved. "One more shot, Dad, please?" pleaded Brent. James stood nearby with Sumiko, steely eyed. "It's James's turn," said Yuudai. "It's okay, Dad," responded James. "Let Brent try again." Brent grinned and raised the gun . . .

Kazuki stopped, aware of an atmospheric shift. When he looked up from his laptop, there were hundreds of beautiful young men and women dancing and preening to thunderous music. A banner had been strung across the pool proclaiming Mid-Week Pool Party. Behind an elevated table, a DJ sat at the controls of a massive sound system.

Returning to his room, Kazuki ordered a beer and a shrimp cocktail from room service. His work was done for the day, but his thoughts remained with the story, especially its unresolved ending. *Fingal's Cave* was divided into three books: The first chronicled Yuudai's relationship with his father. The second book followed Yuudai's journey to Japan, his surreal attempts to obey his father's guilt-ridden schematic for reparation and his meeting and love affair with Sumiko. The remainder of the second book told the story of the marriage, the birth of the twin sons, Yuudai's relationship with Sumiko's family, the Itos, the argument with Katashi Ito—whose ties to the Yakuza, the American had slowly discerned—and the subsequent return of Yuudai and family to America. Many pages of the second book were devoted to Yuudai's exhilarating but dangerous adventures with his sons, Brent and James, and the growing estrangement between Yuudai—an evolving adulterer—and Sumiko. It was toward the end of the second book that Yuudai would lose his sons and begin his difficult and painful journey to untangle the great mystery of their disappearance.

The third book.

With the completed manuscript, he could approach Hugh in good conscience. The novel would not only explain the inexplicable, but provide solace to the inconsolable, for it would give Hugh back what had been taken from him, if not in flesh, at least in words indestructible. But it would do all that only if Kazuki could solve the problem of the ending . . . But if Kazuki didn't or couldn't finish . . .

He started writing *Fingal's Cave* almost ten years ago, but abruptly stopped, and locked away the first rough chapters. He thought about those scenes many times, but he evaded responsibility by launching into one new book after the other. True escapist fiction.

Kazuki finished off his beer, though he had not touched the shrimp. What the hell, he would order another beer. But as he picked up the phone to call room service, Mendelssohn interrupted. Kazuki looked down at his cell phone's caller ID:

Nakamura Reality.

Chapter 15

One more time. Hugh's stomach heaved. He spewed into the frothy yellow puddle. On the far shore, a small brown foot shoveled sand over the mess.

"Oh, God," rasped Hugh.

"You're going to be all right, sir."

Hugh licked his tongue across the roof of his mouth, gathered the residue of the vomit and coughed it onto the sand. A young man with bright blue eyes and several days' growth of blond beard straddled Hugh's torso. On the service road that led to the beach, flashing red lights penetrated the bougainvillea and cactus.

"Best you get checked out," said the young man. "The paramedics will take you to emergency. Better to be safe than sorry, boss."

Hugh touched the throbbing lump on his forehead. "Please let me get up," he said to the young man with *lifeguard* stenciled on his orange trunks. The young man stepped away as Hugh got to his feet. A dozen beachgoers surrounded him. He pushed through the stubborn spectators.

"Where did the boat go?" asked Hugh, walking to the water's edge and scanning the horizon. He touched his hand to his chest and winced. A streak the texture and color of ground beef ran diagonally across his left breast. Blood welled at his touch. Two paramedics jogged up and scuffled with him as they attempted to get a blood-pressure cuff around his arm. One shone a penlight into Hugh's eyes.

Later, Hugh would wonder if he responded at all, for separating him from his inquisitors was that seascape of the Oceanside Beach where his sons had died. Beyond the frozen cresting waves glided a boat. The same boat he had seen moments ago carrying the apparitions of his sons.

Hugh pulled away from the paramedics.

"Did you bring me in?" he asked the blue-eyed lifeguard.

"Only the last ten yards. A swimmer grabbed you."

"Did you ask—the swimmer?"

The lifeguard's attention had been drawn elsewhere. Hugh tapped his arm. The lifeguard met his gaze.

"Ask what?"

"About the boat?"

The lifeguard glanced at the paramedic and rolled his eyes. "No, I haven't had time. I'll make sure I do that."

"Which one was it?" Hugh gestured toward the pack.

"I told you he wasn't a surfer. And he didn't stick around."

"Someone had to have seen the boat."

"You just got slammed by a surfboard. What's with you and this boat?" asked the lifeguard.

The paramedics spent another ten minutes trying to persuade Hugh to visit emergency, but Hugh refused. Shrugging, the paramedics gave him a sheet listing the warning signs of a concussion and then marched off. The crowd had long dispersed, except the watermelon boy who stood beside him gazing toward the unseen boat.

"What's your name?" asked Hugh.

"Apollonius," said the boy.

"Did you see it?"

"The boat, you mean?"

"Yes, the boat that was out there."

"There were a couple of boats," said the boy.

"This one was big, really aero—fast-looking."

"Maybe I saw it." He shrugged. "I think I did." The boy's shy eyes and drawn lip said uncertainty. He had not seen it. Only Hugh had seen it.

"Apollonius," shouted the boy's mother, "*vete aquí.*"

The boy looked toward his blanket, "It's okay, Mom. He's my friend."

The mother frowned and said something to the other woman, who stared at Hugh.

"My mom's afraid of kidnappers. She thinks they're everywhere."

Hugh shivered. He pulled his forearm to his mouth and blew on the goose bumps. "She's right. A parent can't be too careful."

"Do you have children?" asked Apollonius.

"I—I have two boys."

"How old are they?"

"They're . . . they would be . . ." He veered from the calculation. "They're gone."

"Where did they go?"

Hugh shook his head hopelessly.

"Were they kidnapped?" asked the boy.

He thought the parents paranoid who drilled fear into their children, making them run from every stranger's smile. How many kidnappers were out there? Plenty, maybe. Children snatched up and hidden in nondescript houses, high-fenced backyards. To satisfy some freak's pleasure. There were other motives, too, so common as to be considered the price of living in some places. Not pedophiles so much as thugs terrorizing families for ransoms. He had several Mexican children in his classes, sons and daughters of the upper class, who were in the United States because of that real threat.

"Did the boat take them?" asked Apollonius.

Hugh glanced down at the boy. "The boat?"

"I guess," said Apollonius.

"No, the boat didn't take them."

"Who did?' asked the boy, bristling with concern.

Hugh gestured toward the sea.

Apollonius frowned. "A different boat?"

"No. My sons drowned."

"Both of them?"

"Yes, both."

Apollonius dug his foot into the sand. "That's bad. Do you go see them sometimes?"

"See them?"

"At the cemetery."

Hugh shook his head. "I—we didn't get to bury them. Their bodies were never found."

"So maybe they're not really dead."

Hugh couldn't respond.

"Maybe the boat did take them," said the boy.

"Maybe," said Hugh softly. He gazed at the ocean, searched for the boat that was merely a memory. One hundred yards out, a horizontal black bar unfolded across a length of sea; a parallel rule appeared along the water's edge. *Page three.* In the hospital room, someone had handed him the newspaper with the story. The roiling sea, the fragile surfers, the sleek yacht. "Page three," the gift-giver had said.

Page three . . .

Who had been that messenger? The nurse Miranda? No, not her.

"Appolonius, ven a comer su bocadillo."

"Well, see you later. Sorry about your sons."

"Apollonius—the man who pulled me out of the ocean . . ."

"You mean the lifeguard?"

"No. There was another man. Surfer—no, swimmer."

"Oh, yeah. I saw him."

"What did he look like?"

"Pretty tall, like you. Skinny. Tattooed like crazy."

"What kind of tattoos?"

"He had this cool tiger on his back."

The boy's mother called out again.

"Later," said Apollonius.

Hugh returned to his towel. A half mile away a party boat crawled north, a huge catamaran swiftly gliding across its wake. The boat at Oceanside wasn't a sailboat, but a cabin cruiser or a speedboat. There was something futuristic about it, almost fantastic. Of course, the boat he had seen today could simply be the same model as the one he had seen at Oceanside. There were probably hundreds of them. Or was it just a memory? A memory on which he had imposed his lost sons. Hugh scooped up a handful of sand. The sand rippled as a buried bee broke the surface.

A young woman walked by, glancing at the stunned bee and then at Hugh's forehead. He had forgotten about the wound. His forehead throbbed, wanted ice.

Perhaps his sons had gotten dragged into the boat's propeller. He had read how large objects could become lodged against a hull, stay there for hundreds of miles. Or perhaps tangled in kelp, and the kelp caught on the propeller. There were nets, too. It would explain why the bodies were never found. But in his vision today, his sons were pointing at the hull—to tell him what? That their deaths were a measure more complicated than he supposed?

At the crossing, where he stopped to wipe off his feet and put on his sandals, an old primed Camaro was parked on the roadside with its hood up. A man was leaning over the engine and smoking a cigarette. He wore baggy, low-slung jeans, aviator sunglasses and a wrinkled dress shirt, sleeves stained with grease marks. He glanced at Hugh, who nodded to him as he sat on the guardrail. As Hugh wiped the sand from between his toes, he looked at the man's profile. He had a firm jaw, broad, protruding cheekbones and long straight black hair. His lips were fine, but his nose bent and blunt as if it had been broken a few times. He turned and smiled at Hugh. He could have been of South Korean descent or Japanese. He looked something like his sons would have looked if they had reached their midthirties. Something else though. Not just a resemblance to his sons in an imagined future, but also a resemblance to someone in the past.

"How you feeling?" asked the man.

"Yeah, better. You saw what happened?"

"You almost bought it."

"Were you the one who pulled me out?"

"I look like someone who goes in for that hero shit?"
Hugh slipped on his sandals and stood up. The man set
a chrome cover over the air filter. He held up a chrome nut
and said, "Call this a wing nut. You know why? Because
it has little wings on it." He drew the nut in an arc above
his head. "Butterfly, same kind of word. Like butter flying."
He grinned. "Back to your nest, little bird." He screwed it
down and turned back to Hugh, wiping his hands on a rag,
though his fingers appeared spotless. The Camaro's engine
compartment was in cherry condition.

"Hey, you got your light," the man said, pointing to the
highway.

Hugh glanced back at the blinking walk sign. "Thanks—
what's your name?"

The man seemed to give it a moment's thought. He
smiled. "Jason."

"Hugh."

"Cool."

"You happen to live in Studio City?" asked Hugh.

"You're going to miss that light, boss."

As Hugh reached the north side of the intersection he
looked back to see the young man getting into his car. He'd
taken off the shirt. His back and arms were covered with
the full-body tattoos that the Japanese call irldenzi. In the
center of his back was a tiger.

"Hey, Jason," shouted Hugh, but the Camaro's owner
had started his engine and gone like Speed Racer.

Hugh stared after the vanished car. Hugh was sure that
he had encountered him before. If he could remember the
context, he would remember the young man, but the context eluded him.

Chapter 16

When he returned home from the hospital twelve years ago, Setsuko had asked him where he wanted to put the newspaper, which he would just as well have left on that unmade bed if Setsuko hadn't taken it. He told her to put it into the black sea chest he'd had since college.

As Hugh slid the trunk from his bedroom closet, he tried to recall when he'd last opened it and for what reason. Perhaps to deposit the pink slip for the Volvo or a copy of an income tax form. He'd taken nothing out in years, certainly not that paper. There was no solace in that angry sea or the misnamed inset photos of his sons. But returning from Topanga Beach, he again considered that strange boat. It had remained offshore all the time that he and the boys had waited. It was there when the boys entered the water. But when Hugh returned to find his sons, the boat was speeding off. He would not allow himself hope, but he wanted to know more about that boat. If he had its name . . . He set the trunk beside his bed and snapped back the latches.

He remembered the trunk overflowing with a lifetime's paperwork, but it was less than half full. He sorted through the envelopes, canceled checks and faded memorabilia. CDs and ancient tapes. High school and college degrees. Warranties, loan papers and instruction manuals. Setsuko had taken the boys' documents: the report cards and birth certificates, the sports plaques and medals. She'd taken the photographs too, all of them. He suspected she'd burned them—for what was the point of these two-dimensional memories, false positives of life.

He envisioned the San Diego paper as if it lay before him. The headline: Brothers Missing in Surfing Tragedy. The large photo of the angry sea at Oceanside, the insets of Takumi and Hitoshi, their names reversed, and in the upper left of the photo, the boat. He dug deeper into the trunk's contents. In ten minutes he'd dug through to the bottom, scratching the ribbed silky fabric. He leafed through everything again, turning each item upside down, snapping and shaking. For a moment, one item held his attention: a glossy brochure for a cemetery, High Meadow.

For years the salesperson had called him to make her low-key pitch: "We have the most beautiful sites and very affordable." Hugh remembered playing with her, asking inane but not unbelievable questions. What was the history of the land? Were there any Indian burial grounds nearby? Was the ground hard or soft? Clay or loam? What sorts of insects were there? What kinds of birds? (He didn't like crows or vultures.) How often was the grass cut? Did they employ a night watchman? Was a gravesite ever marred by graffiti? Did they bury atheists at the same depth as Christians or did they give them short shovel? He had thought that the salesperson, Gina, would sooner or later catch on to his whimsical game and stop calling, but Gina had stamina. No matter how outrageous his questions, she would try to answer or say she would research it and get back to him. He did not think she ever got the joke, but if so she hid it well. Eventually he gave up jokes, but after all his joking, he didn't have the heart to tell her he wasn't interested. In that lush season of young manhood and success, who can take the grave seriously? And so he put her off with innumerable excuses. He could not remember when Gina stopped calling. He could not remember when the Thursday ritual ended. He wondered if she were still out there, pitching her plots. He would be surprised. Her voice was meek and frail and he imagined her then as a woman in her late sixties, perhaps earning a deserved discount on her own grave.

He tossed the brochure in the trunk, closed the lid and shoved the chest back into the closet.

In the kitchen, he waited for the teapot to whistle.

Perhaps Setsuko had not followed his instruction or perhaps she had taken the newspaper with her when she left.

How difficult would it be to get another copy of the newspaper? He could go to the university library. Perhaps it was available online. Again, he imagined the picture of the surf, the boat. There was a name. There might be a serial number, some sort of registration.

The newspaper was called the *San Diego Sol*. A bright-yellow smiling sun above the title.

Hugh slipped his cell phone from his pocket and dialed information. The operator informed him that there was no listing. She suggested the *San Diego Union*.

"No, I'm sure it was the *San Diego Sol*. Do you have a phone number for a San Diego newsstand?"

"Do you have a name, sir?"

"I don't know. San Diego News?"

"I'll try."

She came back with, "Here is your number."

"*What* paper?" asked the gravel-voiced man who answered the phone at the newsstand.

The tea kettle pealed. "Hold on," said Hugh.

"Hey, I've got customers."

Hugh stretched to turn off the flame. He repeated the name.

"Christ, that paper's been out of business for years."

"I'd pay $100 for a copy of the July 16, 2000, edition."

"You kidding me?"

"If you can find one, any condition, call me. Here's my number."

Hugh hung up, and not bothering with the tea, walked into his living room and flopped on the couch, feeling tired and heavy, weighted by the awareness of how quixotic were his thoughts. *Taken*, which opened the possibility that—
Impossible.
Never once in the years since their disappearance—death—had such a thought occurred to him. But now a vision in the sea, a memory . . .
What could he really see of the boat in the photo?
Quixotic.
But clearly his sons were pointing at the boat's name. A delusion, meaning nothing or meaning everything.

He gazed across the room at the bookshelf built when he moved into the house. It held perhaps five hundred books, mostly paperbacks. The exception was the row of Kazuki Ono's novels, the dust jackets still shiny and bright on the hardcovers. When Hugh and Setsuko, three months pregnant, had left Kazuki's Tokyo home for America, the author had ceremoniously presented Hugh with his first five novels, each dutifully inscribed to his son-in-law. In turn, Hugh had purchased each new novel as it appeared. *Deadpan All The Way*, Kazuki's first book, was on the far right; six novels to the left was *Living in Camus*, which Hugh read shortly after the birth of the twins; two books farther left was Hugh's favorite, *Riding, Riding, Riding*, an eight-hundred-page labyrinth attacked by as many American critics as it was lauded by European critics for its strings of coincidence. The Euros maintained that the novel was structured to evoke seriality, a theory that all events are connected, and that coincidences are the visible signs of the interconnection. In the year the twins entered kindergarten, *Riding* was a best seller for six months. *Enrique the Freak*, at the moment in the bottom of his gym bag, would complete the collection. Hugh thought of the book, Hanna's recitation. The passage that had so much brought to mind the memory of his sons' sipping honeysuckle returned to him with inexplicable urgency—*Enrique sorted through the instruments, drinking from each one's lips as a hummingbird might gather its nectar from a thousand flowers . . .*"

He envisioned Takumi's pretty lips on the honeysuckle stems.

"Try it, Hitoshi. Better than candy!"

Displacing the honeysuckle, the scent of marijuana, an odor that after the sun went down wafted through the canyon like mist, seeped through his open screened window. Pushing off the couch, Hugh peered through the window into his backyard.

Hanna sat on the patch of crabgrass beside his vegetable garden and fed apple slices to a rooster standing between her legs. In her other hand, she held a lit joint. She wore cutoff jeans and a wrinkled green blouse, the tails knotted at her little belly, the canvas for a plump tattooed infant, likely Jesus. Her tan skin glowed, but couldn't hide the pitted hollows of her cheeks. She opened her mouth wide to pick something resistant from the gap between her two top front teeth. She weighed maybe ninety pounds, not much more than his sons. Her eyes were pale blue, pretty. She wanted to be an astronomer.

As Hugh approached, she rid herself of the bird, wiped her fingers on her jeans and turned. "Why that bruise looks awful. Are you all right?"

"Yes. I was swimming . . . a surfboard." He tried to smile, but her presence unsettled him. He didn't have visitors.

"Put raw meat on it. That helps," she said.

The rooster struck out for the garden, attacking the mesh that kept the birds and rabbits out of the blueberries and tomatoes. The sun hung above the crest of the farthest hill, still spreading its warmth down the canyon. High above, a hawk circled.

"How did you find my place?" Hugh asked.

She stuck out her tongue and moistened the black lip ring, as if it were a plant that needed watering. "I followed your trail." She laughed. "Asked around the café. Alphonse the plumber told me he did some work for you. I walked up here." She offered the joint to him.

He waved the offer away.

She took a long drag, looked around. "This is like paradise. Adam and Eve, you know?" She picked up the open penknife lying beside her foot and closed the blade. She offered the joint again. He shook his head. Hanna grinned. "You going to expel me and my rooster from the garden?"

"I've got my routine, you know . . ."

"Oh, I know," Hanna said, grinning.

Ten minutes later, Hugh flopped down in his lounge chair, pressing an ice-filled sock to his forehead. He took the sock away to adjust the ice.

"Looks like a kiss," said Hanna. She sat on the second chair, lay back, closed her eyes and beamed. The two of them were stretched out like his own parents in their backyard lounge chairs, drinking iced tea and nibbling from a shared bowl of snacks.

Hanna hiccuped, laughed and opened her eyes. She leaned to one side, smiled and tapped Hugh's shoulder.

"This is nice, you know?"

"I have work to do, Hanna."

"You always say that. You a workaholic?"

She pulled at her blouse, letting the air in, and then rolled over on her stomach and nestled her head against her arms. He hadn't noticed her perfume before, a flower child fragrance that smelled like raspberries cooked for a pie. Hanna laughed to herself and then raised her head. "You think they make you work in hell?"

"Why would you ask that?"

"In case I go there."

"You won't."

"How do you know that?"

"I just know it."

"Well, do they?"

"Some circles."

"What's that mean?"

"Hell has circles. A circle for gluttons. A circle for the carnal. A circle for suicides."

"That's it?"

"No. There are many circles. And in some, the sinners work."

"Well, I've never worked. Never had a job."

"Princess Hanna."

"Hardly. If I needed something, I'd steal it. When I was fourteen, sixteen, I'd steal things all the time, and never get in trouble. They'd always let me go, like I couldn't have done whatever it was I did. Even if someone saw me, they didn't see me. I was young, blonde and pretty."

"A get-out-of-jail-free card."

"That's it." She laughed. "You ever steal anything?"

Dogs bark, boys steal. But in his father's domain, theft was not a prank. His father had never stolen anything in his life, not an apple off a tree, a fallen apple even. Once, he and his father had been walking and came upon a five-dollar bill lying on the sidewalk. As Hugh stopped to pick it up, his father said leave it, that the person who lost the bill might come back to look for it, and that person surely needed it more than Hugh needed it. Hugh argued that it would be a person other than the owner who found the money and took it. Pirie didn't bend. We can't be responsible for that person's actions, his father said, only for our own. His father was balsa wood in the face of the physical world but his morality was granite. He would no more pick up a stranger's coin than a strange woman at a bar.

Hanna slipped off her lounge chair and sat at the bottom of Hugh's. They watched the hawk circle.

"Did you?"

"I suppose . . ."

"So what happened?" she asked, leaning back and resting her head against his thigh.

He nudged her away. "No."

"It feels so nice."

"I mean it, Hanna. I don't want you to." But his leg felt carved away where her head had lain. One stupid thing jostling another stupid thing for attention. He was afraid that if she touched him again, he'd have her on the ground.

"You don't like me?" she whined.

"I'd rather you sat in the other chair."

Hanna pushed against Hugh to get up. The heat of her hand sunk into his leg, radiated to his groin. His throat constricted.

"It wouldn't hurt you to get a job," he said, hoping to divert his own thoughts. "You wouldn't need Kyle then. You could take night courses at the community college. If you want to be an astronomer, do something about it." *Be all you can be.* Could he be any more banal?

"Who's gonna give me a job? Work experience: zero, zilch."

"Make something up. Say you worked at one of those chain stores that went out of business. They won't check."

"I guess . . ."

"It slips away."

"What does?"

"Everything. You go for a cup of coffee and it's gone. The whole world vanishes in an instant."

"Then why bother?"

"Don't be lazy."

"Okay, I'll look for a job, maybe. Happy?"

Hugh nodded, thinking again of the boat. That was his job now.

She brightened. "You read a lot, huh? I see you reading at the P&L. What books should I read?"

"I don't know. *Frankenstein*, maybe."

"Frankenstein? I don't want to read *that*."

"You might be surprised."

"What's that story about the guy who goes down to hell to get his girlfriend?"

"Why all this interest in hell?"

Hanna waved her arm. "The flip side of paradise, isn't it?"

"Orpheus," said Hugh.

"I like that story. I'm glad he did that. I mean, get her back."

"He didn't get her back. Orpheus's wife, Eurydice, was to follow him out of the underworld, but Hades ordered Orpheus not to look back at her until they both reached the upper world. Just as they were almost there, just as they had it made, Orpheus fucked up. He looked back. Eurydice disappeared then, never to be seen again."

"Why did that guy who ran hell—what's his name?"

"Hades."

"Why did *Hades* not want him to look back? Why did Hades have that rule?"

"You have to follow the rules, in this world or the next."

"Maybe he's like Kyle. Kyle tells me to do things all the time. He doesn't care about them being done. He just wants to see I follow his orders."

A fly landed on Hugh's arm, jumped to his neck, then his cheek. He swatted, missed and imagined that he'd squashed it. The fly relocated to the back of his hand, then his arm again, where he could feel each leg snagging the hairs. Why had he left the beach that day—even for a minute? What the fuck was he thinking? If he had stayed. If he had stayed . . . He touched his forehead. He recalled the boat's looming hull, the letters that would not emerge from the jumble and blur.

He breathed in the urine-scented air of his hospital room. His head floated above the pillow. He stretched the rattling paper to quiet it, but it would not be still.

A soft pelt and then another. Hugh glanced at the bright green leaves of the dollar tree, then at the fallen ones on the ground. The fallen were pale brown and pale red. One turned redder.

"What the hell?"

"Accident," Hanna said, setting aside the knife, as she too watched the drop on her wrist form and fall.

"I don't want you doing crazy things like that. You can't be here if you're going to do things like that." *Be here?* Why did he say that?

"Jesus, it was a mistake. You never cut yourself?" She licked her finger, drew it over her wrist's red smear and lay her arm on her leg. Cross-hatching spanned her wrist . . . Beneath the cutting, Hanna's veins looked as narrow as kite string.

She offered him a shy grin. "I won't do it again. Promise."

Hugh sliced the clove of garlic and tossed it into the pan with the tomatoes, mushrooms and oil. The P&L closed at two P.M. He'd have to drive to the café on Ventura to get on the Internet. He would feed her before he embarked on his research.

"Nice table," said Hanna, fingering the wood.

Hugh nodded. The table was a bamboo and glass construction that Setsuko had chosen and Hugh had inherited after the break-up. The table and chairs had to be twenty years old but showed no sign of weakening except for a few broken strips of raffia. He remembered Setsuko sitting across from him, knife held in her long uncolored fingers, cutting up the boys' steaks into perfect half-inch squares. She obsessed about what they ate and how they ate it. No canned anything, everything fresh with strict ratios of vegetables to grains, fruits to meat. Meat separated into safe symmetrical pieces. If Hugh slipped in a treat, something sweet, something processed, it would be the cold shoulder for days.

"That smells good."

"We'll eat and then I'll drive you back down."

"I love Italian food," she said, pretending not to have heard. "Mexican, of course. Thai, too. You know those flat noodles with lobster sauce? Yum. The only thing Kyle and I eat is Top Ramen and those plastic cans of soup, which is all right. My mother was a good cook. Roast beef and potatoes. She tried to teach me to cook, but I never listened. I didn't want to know, just seemed like something else I'd have to do if I ever learned it."

"That's very . . . practical."

Hanna yawned and stretched her arms. Her shirt rose on her belly. Hugh glanced away and lit the gas under the pot of water. In the days following his return from the hospital, when Setsuko still seemed capable of forgiveness, there were several nights when the passion was as strong as during courtship. It started with Hugh talking about the boys, and Setsuko coming on to him as if out of a dream. She would go to sleep afterward, though Hugh would lie awake, touching her hair, breathing in her delicious scent, pressing his lips to her cool arms.

One night Hugh dragged her to a support group, composed of people who had lost sons and daughters. They listened to other people's stories and they were all painful, but had no bearing on their own loss. They were just stories and Hugh knew that this was true for all the others. But the others had at least buried their children. Even the ones that had been in horrible automobile accidents like the couple who were driving home from buying Christmas presents when a tractor-trailer plowed into them, compressing the rear half of the car to three feet and the two children to shadows. They buried shadows. But better shadows or skeletons than . . . nothing.

But on that night, too, Setsuko and he had made fierce love. Hugh pushed away from the memories.

He opened a bottle of white and set it on the table with two glasses. He asked Hanna if she liked wine and she nodded. He filled the glasses and then set down the plates.

"You're not going to lay a napkin on my lap?"

She seemed transparent, not hiding anything, and yet he wondered if it was a clever mask. Perhaps she and Kyle plotted to rob him in the night. She'd leave the door open, and in the morning his money and valuables and Hanna would be gone. Hugh twirled the linguine onto his spoon.

"Why do you do that?"

He put the linguine in his mouth and chewed, enjoying the texture of the tomatoes and the earthy taste of the mushrooms.

"The pasta doesn't trail over your chin," replied Hugh.

"I always thought it was just showing off. You know, the way people do these little things so others will notice them. The way they always want the pepper ground over their food, or their martinis dry."

She drew up a forkful of the pasta and shoved it in her mouth. "Wow, this is good," she said, her mouth open, the pasta gushing out, childlike. He didn't watch her eat after that, staring at the reddening sky. She cleaned her plate, leaned back and burped. Hugh expected her to draw out a toothpick and pat her stomach. No, he didn't desire her.

"Shit," said Hanna, jumping up.

"What? What?"

"Pecky. I forgot about my rooster."

He followed her outside.

"Here, Pecky! Here, Pecky!"

Hanna dashed about the yard, looking under bushes, behind trees. Ten yards down the path, a small coyote emerged from the underbrush, its head turned away. It didn't move, perhaps assuming it couldn't be seen in the shadows. Hugh walked to the path, held his finger to his lips. The coyote remained frozen. As Hugh drew closer, the coyote turned, its mouth filled with rooster.

The coyote made eye contact, and keeping Hugh in view, started walking away. It didn't seem in a hurry, as if it knew that Hugh had no chance of catching it. Hugh walked slowly and tried not to panic the animal, which kept its distance. The animal stopped again and Hugh charged forward. The coyote didn't move. Would it turn into Setsuko as in some magic-realist tale? But the coyote remained a coyote as Hugh slammed into it. The animal took three quick strides and vaulted into the shadows.

"Dad, let's chase it!" shouted the twins.

"Go, right, Takumi! Left, Hitoshi!"

"What's happening?"

Hugh picked up the bedraggled but live rooster and carried it back to its mistress.

Holding her rooster in her lap, Hanna sat on the couch and watched television as Hugh cleaned the dishes. By the time he was finished Hanna was asleep. The rooster watched Hugh with interest and admiration.

Hugh turned on the local news. Budget cuts. A brush fire near the Getty. A picture of the surf at Trestles. The reporter announced that for the next few days the surf would be enormous. Seven- and eight-foot swells were coming. The video showed surfers and Boogie Boarders. There would be a riptide.

He watched Hanna and the rooster, wondering if the rooster might shit on her. It would get cold later. He put a blanket over Hanna and the rooster, who winked at Hugh.

He would let her sleep and wait until morning to search the cloud.

In the dream, Hugh was teaching. The class was unruly and he was being observed, officially observed, though the observer was not to be seen. He had nothing to teach. No lesson plans. The observer who could not be observed was

~ 118 ~

taking notes. If he could get the children in their chairs. He yelled a few words in Farsi.

"*Gooshkan! Book Sha!*"

A young Israeli girl, perhaps eleven but younger looking, raised her blouse, revealing her belly. It was covered in intersecting lines. Another girl, Indian, blushed and cried out, "Mr. Mac! Mr. Mac! Look what she's doing!" "Please put that down," said Hugh. "You can't do that. Cover yourself."

The students were marching in single file. There had been a fire alarm. But they weren't marching toward the physical education field, but toward the library. From which flames were shooting.

Hugh coughed up blood. The observer was angry. "Where are your lesson plans?"

A hand moved across his thigh, the touch hard, insistent. It wasn't a dream touch. He recognized the thing beside him as a body, its contours firm, but giving. The calf bone against his.

His penis hardened and she moved to it. He remained still as she wrapped her hand around him—lips at his ear.

"Let me, huh?"

"No," he said turning away. "Go to sleep, Hanna. Just go to sleep."

But Hugh did not sleep.

Chapter 17

Kazuki did not sleep. He tore the sheet away to see his erection leaning leeward from the slit in his boxer shorts. He had neglected to draw the curtains and a light from that enormous yacht, which seemed to ply the Santa Monica Bay like a watchman, found the tip, so that it glowed like some exotic sea plant, undulating in the currents. The ship passed, the room darkened, his penis shriveled. For three hours, he had been trying to sleep, but the story's gaps poked at his consciousness, like the miniature devil children who poked poor Mr. Hood.

The tendrils of story found nothing on which to cling. He needed a listener to frown at his errors, smile at his felicities, but he had no ear, no living ear.

Another stray beam swept the room. Kazuki's penis rose again, as if it had been waiting for the spotlight.

In the old days, he would have turned to his wife and fit himself against her like two pieces of a puzzle. She would have wriggled closer, reached back to take his hand and whispered, "Now you will sleep," and he would have slept.

But Manami was gone, only returning in dreams, which were never nourishing, and most times depleting. Manami had been four years old at the time of the Hiroshima blast, miraculously escaping external injuries though her family lived within four kilometers of the hypocenter. But the radiation had damaged enough cells that she died of leukemia at age thirty-four, leaving Kazuki with their young daughter.

Kazuki rolled out of bed, took three long breaths and walked to the balcony. Tolstoy would not mourn even for the death of his youngest son. It was God's will and plan. What was there to mourn?

Staring at the heavens, he caught his breath at the tender touch of the stars, as if each was a woman's loving finger.

Chapter 18

At the Peace & Love Café, the patio was empty except for the poet, an older denim-clad man who sat on his bench, rocked and muttered a mantra as he awaited customers. He sold his poems ten-for-a-dollar, but Hugh, like most of the regulars, refused to purchase, fearing it would become the expected gesture, so most of the poet's customers were strangers, visitors. Occasionally, Hugh would place a dollar on the deck where the poet could find it, not suspecting that it came from Hugh, perhaps thinking God was a fan of his poems—and that was their amiable relationship. Hugh nodded to the ever-nodding poet, took the table under the dollar tree and plugged his laptop into the extension cord that ran out of the café. The blue power light didn't come on. He checked all the connections, but the light remained off. The battery wouldn't last more than an hour. He followed the extension cord into the café where it led to an outlet beneath the table of a customer whose back was to Hugh. He peered under the customer's legs. The plug had fallen from the outlet.

"Excuse me," said Hugh, tapping the man's shoulder.

Twisting in his chair, Kyle glared back.

"I need to plug in," said Hugh.

As he had done at the beach, Kyle smirked and looked past Hugh as if to share some comedy with a friend.

"I'm using this outlet," said Kyle.

"No, it's empty."

Kyle pushed aside his chair and rose, backing Hugh to the window. Kyle stayed with him like a dance partner. The man's hot skin radiated through his tattered T-shirt, which smelled of dried perspiration and tobacco. Hugh went soft under the man's weight, like a dog that bellies up to avoid a fight, but Kyle wasn't letting him off that easy. Hugh prepared for a head butt.

"What's she see in an old man like you?" asked Kyle.

"Nothing. And there is nothing."

"I smell her on you."

"Do you mind if I plug in?"

"What is it, old man?"

The café had grown quiet.

"What the fuck you got on her?" asked Kyle.

"Just let me plug—"

"I thought we were beyond this stuff," said Melinda, the tarot card reader.

"Hey, you guys, take it outside," said Rick.

"You paying her?" asked Kyle.

"No, son."

"Not your son, asshole."

"Right you are."

Simone, the café's owner, walked up. "This will stop."

Kyle grinned at Simone. "Just messing around."

Hugh nodded. "It was nothing, Simone."

"I hope so," said Simone, shaking her head and walking back to the counter where a customer waited. "C'est toujours le même refrain," she sniffed.

Kyle stepped aside, allowing Hugh to bend down and insert the plug. Kyle wouldn't jeopardize his day job.

"See you later," said Kyle, as Hugh pushed through the screen door.

It was a mistake to feed her, to let her stay, to leave her sleeping in his bed.

But those regrets shriveled as the desktop icons appeared. Keywords: *2000, Oceanside, boat.* He thought the craft to be the size of a sport fishing boat, which was how large? Several times, he'd taken the boys on a party boat out of San Pedro. He typed in "sport fishing, San Pedro." The fleet of sport fishing boats came up, one of which was named the *Sea Mist.* Beneath photographs of the boat was a box of information. Length: fifty feet. So the length of the boat was about fifty feet, maybe a few feet more, or less.

His search produced fourteen million responses.

Christ. He would not find the boat, he thought dismally, and even if he found it, what then? What would he do?

Hugh slumped, weighted by the awareness of how ridiculous the search was. Next he would be attending séances. He would be like the woman he encountered at the Coffee Bean who had lost her dog. She searched her neighborhood and the surrounding neighborhoods for weeks, hired people off Craigslist to put up reward posters. In local papers and online, she devoured the descriptions of found pets. She haunted the pounds and animal shelters. At the café, she asked everyone she met, strangers even, for ideas on how to find her dog. Some buoyed her with suggestions, some just shook their heads. One day he heard her talking about a psychic and on a subsequent day she described the method the psychic suggested to get her pet to return home. Turn a spotlight on your house at night. Show your pet that you still love it. More than one person told her that certainly a coyote had gotten little Jack, but she rented a spotlight to illuminate her house and beckon home her pet.

A boat?

But Jaycee Dugard disappeared from the world at age eleven, the age of his sons, and was found eighteen years later. She could not have been alive and yet she was. How many thousands having lost someone took hope from this story? That the desert was not gnawing away at the bones of their children? This was what he hoped. This was the stupid thing. That somehow his sons had not died. That it had all been a big mistake. That he would wake up from the nightmare to find that he was not irrevocably separated from his sons as he knew he was, and knowing felt his heart plunge as if to the first harrowing drop on a roller coaster.

Hugh pushed back his chair. That he could find his answer through this plastic screen, that he could dig through the digital world and bring his sons back from the dead, that they were sitting on the bow of a boat waiting for him to find them—this was the idea that had stolen upon him. Wasn't that the promise of this depthless vault of information? That everything could be retrieved—even the dead.

He needed more parameters. He needed to know more about the boat. He clicked on a link that took him to yacht sales. One could choose to search for boats by length, age, price, category and manufacturer.

A loose slat groaned. Hugh looked up. "Peace and love, brother," said Kyle, snapping off a branch from the olive tree and scratching his neck with it. "Just want to give you some news. Your friend was looking for you."

"A friend? Driving a Camaro?"

"El Camino, candy-color. But he wasn't driving. Shotgun."

"Long hair, Asian?"

"*His-pan-ic.* You know, the banger. Kid you gave a ride to down the beach."

"Aaron," muttered Hugh. "He's not a—"

"Came into the café and asked for Mr. Mcpherson."

"When?"

"Yesterday."

"Did he say why?"

"Just wanted to know if you came here."

"What did you tell him."

"Said you were here just about every day."

"Was there anyone with him?"

"Yeah, the one driving. Another banger. Big tattoo around his neck."

"A girl?"

"Yeah, she was squeezed in there."

"Thanks for letting me know."

"No *prob-lem*." Kyle licked his finger and spit. "When you see Hanna, tell her I want to talk to her, huh? Tell her I'm sorry. Will you do that?"

"Yeah. *If* I see her."

"That's what I meant," said Kyle, smiling.

Hugh dropped his eyes to the screen, yet he could not avoid watching the hovering Kyle, who obtained a pack of cigarettes, noisily sucked one out and let it dangle from his mouth. With a grunt, he dug a neon-colored lighter from his pocket, lit up and puffed vigorously. Blowing out a delicate smoke ring, he nodded, turned and walked toward the parking lot, where he stopped, glanced back at Hugh and then smirked at his invisible friend. Waiting until Kyle got into his old Sentra and chugged onto the boulevard, Hugh returned to Google.

Ten thousand images of yachts awaited his perusal.

Chapter 19

Under a brisk wind, a plume of smoke danced above the ravine where he lived, but the smoke quickly dissipated and Hugh was not concerned.

But as the paved road turned to dirt and potholes, the flames became visible. Hugh floored the gas pedal, racing up the last one hundred yards and tumbled out of the car leaving the door open. A line of flames danced along one eave of the house, and gray smoke seeped from the front door and windows. He ran to the spigot, unhooked the coiled hose and turned on the water. The hose thickened and squirmed. Opening the brass nozzle, he played the jet stream over the roof. He blasted the flames along the eave, which erupted in a white cloud. There was a loud crack like a splintered bat.

Hanna's rooster, wings afire, sat embedded in a wreath of glass shards. It's dreadful black eyes settled on Hugh's as the flames spread around its neck, flashing on the glass shard penetrating its throat.

"Hanna!"

Hugh drew out his keychain, found the house key. Stepping forward, he sprayed the front door. The water sizzled on the hot wood and spattered his face. He aimed at the doorknob for a few seconds and then inserted the key. He grabbed the doorknob, twisted and kicked the door. Dense white smoke hung slovenly in the doorway.

"Hanna!"

He shuffled blindly across the room until he collided with the ottoman. He fell forward, fingers groping the couch. His hand slipped beneath a warm wet cushion.

Flames sprung from the bookcase like headlights in the fog. He dropped to his haunches, spraying upward and burying his face in the stink of burned hair as he duck-walked toward the bedroom. He got two yards before the hose tightened. He yanked once, twice. He retreated and snapped, hoping it had just snagged a chair leg. He heard the fowl's skin pop and smelled the obscene mouthwatering odor. He snapped the hose again and felt it loosen but remain weighted. Dragging the reluctant hose, he crawled down the hall.

"Hanna!"

In the bedroom, the smoke was thin, there were no flames and the bed was empty.

A deep low sound rose to a wail

By the time, he'd backed out of the house, a half-dozen fire trucks had roared up and numerous firemen in bunker gear were rolling out their hoses. A half-dozen silver streams slapped down the flames. Water poured off the roof. Hugh soon stood in a puddle, muddy water slopping at his ankles.

As the firefighters doused the blaze, others had gone inside and were throwing out smoldering furnishings. The fringed tasseled ottoman tumbled into the now muddy backyard, plastic fringes curled up into themselves like tiny fists. Books and magazines, smoky tendrils rising from blackened pages, lay in a heap. Hugh bent down before the pile, sorted through the damage. He pulled *Deadpan All The Way* from the bottom. The glossy dust jacket was a breath away from turning into ash, the back and spine were scorched, interior threads showing through, but the front cover was intact. Hugh peeled away the jacket and ran his thumb across the burned spots.

Not more than a quarter hour had passed when a voice summoned Hugh into the house.

Hugh was surprised to see that aside from the bookcase and furnishings not much had been consumed by the flames. Some of the wooden floor was scorched and the ceiling blackened, but the structure looked intact.

Two firefighters were examining the north window in the living room. "Do you normally keep this window open?" asked one of the men.

"Yes. A couple of inches."

"You see the screen."

"Yeah."

"Was it ripped like that?"

The firefighter pointed to the floor where a dark streak ran across the hardwood, ending at a stack of half-burned newspapers. "Looks like somebody ripped the screen, played a little lighter fluid over your hardwood and tossed in a match."

Hugh recalled Kyle's neon-colored lighter.

"You had any problems with neighbors lately?" asked the cop. Hugh noted the policeman's nametag: Escher. He had a wad of cotton on his freshly shaven throat. Hugh thought of Kyle's smirk. "No . . ."

"Does anyone else live with you?"

"I live alone."

"No guests?"

"There was a woman here the day before, but she . . . left."

"Did you have an argument with her?" asked Escher, pressing the cotton ball, which exuded a red spot.

"No. She wouldn't have done this."

"Not on purpose?"

"No."

"By accident?"

Hugh glanced at the broken screen. "She was here when I left. She wouldn't have to—"

"No, that's right," said Escher. "What's her name?"

"Hanna."

"Last name?"

Hugh shook his head.

"But you know her?"

"I don't know her last name."

"Local . . . ?" he asked insinuatingly.

"Yes, if you mean from the canyon."

"What's her address?"

"I . . . I don't know. I met her down at the beach."

"So you just invited her for the night."

Another cop entered. He was carrying something. He took Escher outside. The two came back a moment later.

Escher asked, "How old was Hanna?"

"What's going on?"

"Take it easy. How old?"

"Twenty-five, twenty-six . . . I don't know."

"How old are you?"

"What does that matter?"

"Fifty?"

"Forty-nine."

"Is this Hanna?"

Escher held out a clear plastic bag that held a photo of a young woman. It sucked the air from Hugh's lungs. It was Anna.

"Where did that come from?" Hugh finally managed to ask.

"Found it in your car. Your door was open, windows rolled down. Maybe it blew in from Chatsworth."

"Like hell," said Hugh. "That was not in my car."

"This isn't the girl that stayed with you."

He dredged up a monosyllable. "No."

"You're certain?"

"Ab—absolutely."

"Absolutely. Okay. Sounds firm. Hanna was twenty—"

"Twenty-five or twenty-six, maybe a year or two older."

"So, older than this girl."

"Considerably."

"This girl looks fourteen or fifteen."

"Yes."

"Have you seen this photo before."

Hugh glanced at the slim, provocatively posed, naked body. "No."

"But you know this girl?"

"She's . . . a student," said Hugh, his heart in his throat.

"Your student?"

"She was in one of my classes in the spring semester. She graduated."

"Was this the girl that was here?"

"No."

"That was Anna?"

"Hanna."

"The thirty-year-old."

"I think I need a lawyer."

"We just want to get things straight. Anna, Hanna. It's confusing. This is a photo of—"

"Anna."

"Anna? Got a last name?"

"I don't . . ." but he did. "Mendez. Anna Mendez. She was a student in one of my classes."

"Did you know her outside of school?"

"No."

"No?"

"I'd seen her at the beach. I was swimming at Topanga. She was there the other day with another student."

"Another young woman?"

"No. A boy. Aaron."

"How long ago was that?"

Hugh thought. "Three days ago. Look. They were hitch-hiking. I gave them a ride home. She had a purse. It must have fallen out of her purse."

"The photo?"

"Yes."

"You didn't take it? She didn't pose for you."

"Of course not. What the fuck do you think—"

"Take it easy," said the cop.

"I gave them a ride and it must have fallen out of her bag. She was putting on her dress . . ."

One of the firefighters laughed.

Hugh glared at the man. "She was coming back from the beach," he said in a rush. "She was putting the dress over her bathing suit."

Escher snatched off the cotton ball and tossed it. "Where did you take them?"

"Van Nuys." No. Studio City. But he did not correct himself.

"So the picture may have been left in your car accidentally?"

"That must be how it happened."

"When did your relationship with her begin?" The fire trucks cut their engines. The rearrangement of his furniture ceased. The voices quieted. They had been transported into outer space. Vast and still and silent.

"I was her teacher."

The firemen had disappeared. It was just Hugh and the cops.

Oh, Jesus. From a quarter mile distant, a blue grass band that practiced twice a week tuned up their banjos. He had tried to kill himself, he thought, which should take the edge off anything anyone else would want to do to him, but he felt weak anticipating the whirlwind of accusations.

"I'm not speaking without a lawyer."

"We haven't charged you with anything," the second cop said.

"It must have been the boy who took the photograph."

"Hanna's friend?" asked Escher.

"Yes, no. Anna's friend. *Aaron.*"

"Have you ever been charged with anything of a sexual nature?"

"No, no fucking way."

"Anything with children?"

"Absolutely not."

"Child endangerment perhaps?" asked the second cop, smiling slyly.

Hugh looked away, shook his head.

"Do you have a family?"

"I—no, I don't." Would it have been better to say, "I did, but *now* I don't"?

"You shouldn't go too far until we clear this up. We'll need to do a formal inspection of your house, but other than the living room, there doesn't appear to be much damage. You can probably get back in a day or two. Will you be staying with anyone, a friend?"

"I have—no. I'll get a room." They stared as if waiting for him to make the reservation in front of them.

Hugh watched Escher walk to the Volvo and open the door. The interior light revealed a woman's face. The uniformed officer glanced at Hugh through the rear windshield. Her eyes were as yellow as a cat's.

In the house, under the watchful eyes of a CSI team, he gathered his clothes and shaving kit.

Hugh drove slowly through Topanga. At Abuelita's Restaurant, the parking attendant scrambled to deal with a rush of cars. The attendant appeared hemmed in by the vehicles. At the restaurant's door, a brightly garbed waitress served margaritas to the blossoming line of waiting patrons. Hugh considered stopping at the bar. His blood pressure felt astronomical, and his head ready to crack. He had twice cheated death to go through all this shit? Death had cheated him. The radio played a song about the body as a cage. He smelled the tequila, but didn't stop, turning left on Old Topanga.

On the old road, Hugh accelerated, his tires squealing on the turns, the headlights glancing off the granite walls and the occasional fugitive house behind the trees. The road straightened and the houses grew more substantial. He drove past the school with the paddock, where globular brown eyes looked up under the curious headlights. He remembered walking down the aisle and seeing Anna's notebook. The hard, drear words. Older than his boys, but a child still. He wondered if the photo had just slipped out of Anna's purse. Surely they hadn't planted it? Hugh had refused to take them to their destination, but they wouldn't be that vindictive—would they? The road ascended then, climbing at every turn. There were several hairpins where it would have been easy enough to twist the wheel, left or right and go sailing into the night. At the peak of the road, he pulled into the turnoff, rolling until the bumper tapped the chain like a key turning in a lock. There was no possibility now of staging an accidental death. He remained in the car a moment, remembering a summer night when the universe seemed to radiate from his fingertips, as if he had thought it all up himself.

Not bothering to lock the car, he scuffed along the shadowy horse trail that wound between the hilltops. The air was sweet with jasmine. Where the trail split, the valley spread out in a sheet of innumerable lights until it collided with the San Gabriel Mountains, icy black against the inky sky. An animal scurried past. Hugh walked to the edge of the cliff. Not quite ninety degrees but close enough to do the job. He would just run for the lights. Would the pole-vaulting coyote eat his corpse? Would he be the one that landed with a puff?

Gazing out at the sea of lights, he saw something huge floating east across the valley. He thought it a cloud, but then its lights became clear. The Goodyear blimp, or was it now named for a foreign corporation?

He followed the blimp's slow smooth flight above the earth; he had seen it a hundred times, yet it seemed impossible floating there, something out of H. G. Wells, something out of a future that was always a fiction.

As he walked back to the Volvo, he looked west and saw a car parked tight against the roadside. The Camaro? The lights of an oncoming car lit the driver's head in outline. The long hair gave no clue as to whether it was a man or woman.

Hugh walked toward the parked car and then sprinted as the engine started, the whine rising to a roar. It's headlights shone, flicking to high beam and blinding Hugh as he got within fifty feet of the vehicle.

"Hey!" shouted Hugh. "Hold on!"

Its tires burning, roadside dust swirling in the headlights, the car sped toward Hugh, veering into the center of the boulevard and quickly disappearing around the bend. Hugh caught a glimpse of the taillights.

He bent down, picked up a stone and hurled it after the vanished car.

"Fuck. Who are you?"

It was ten P.M. by the time Hugh had checked in to the motel across the street from the café. After dropping his gym bag in the room, he crossed the raging boulevard with his laptop, dodging twenty-something Persians in sports cars, windows down, hip-hop blasting from their speakers. He walked toward the café entrance accompanied by the random notes of the trumpet player serenading a man in a parked van, in the back of which a goat chewed straw and stared contentedly at a group of helmeted motorcycle riders standing beside their *pocket rockets*. The bikes could go two hundred mph. While standing still, the bikes appeared in motion, appeared like the blimp from the future.

"Can I help you?" one of the group asked as Hugh approached.

"Your motorcycle," said Hugh, smiling. "I was admiring the design. What do they call the design?"

"Twenty thousand dollars," responded the man.

The others laughed.

"Thanks. Real helpful," snapped Hugh, gazing once more at the bike.

Nodding to the Israeli bunch, smoking cigars and talking boisterously, Hugh entered the café, ordered his coffee and sat down at the handicapped table with its view of the parking lot. On a brown napkin he sketched the handlebar cowling of a bright yellow-and-blue Kawasaki. He erased and redrew until the napkin fell apart. He went through four napkins before he was satisfied with the drawing. With the adjustments, the Kawasaki's cowling mirrored the boat's pilothouse. The part determining the whole, he then drew the deck and hull.

He set the napkin beside the keyboard. He brought up yachtworld.com. On the search form, he typed in the length as forty feet minimum and seventy feet maximum. He checked powerboat and the year of manufacture as between 1960 and 2000. He hit search. There were nine thousand results. He scanned the first page, which took perhaps thirty seconds. Finding nothing close to the boat in the picture, he clicked next. The page took maybe five seconds to appear. He scanned the second. Each page had ten photos. He could browse twenty photos in a minute. That made twelve hundred in an hour. He could see every photo in the course of a night. Two hours later, there had been a half-dozen times when he thought he had found the boat, but bringing up a larger picture, he could see that each was different from the boat that had motored off the beach that day. It was already midnight, the café closing down, but he didn't want to stop. He checked the available Wi-Fi sites and saw that the motel was equipped.

Returning to his motel room, he made a pot of coffee on the courtesy coffee maker and powered up his computer. As he watched the coffee drip into the pot, he started at a tap on the window. Bending back the Venetian blind, he scanned the parking lot, but for a cat padding across a car's hood, it was still and silent. With a sigh, he let the blind drop and returned to work. An hour later, he found a boat so similar to his drawing that he might have traced it. He brought up a larger photo whose caption read:

GOTO, 50', Twin 3208 turbocharged Caterpillar diesel with 575 hours. Tempter Pilothouse Boat. Very Fast, 1989.

He continued to read the sales pitch until he came to a line in capitals: RARE BOAT. ONLY 100 MANUFACTURED.

"Fuck yes," Hugh said.

This particular boat was being sold in Bradenton, Florida. He clicked through a dozen pictures showing the boat from various angles. One showed the name *Magnolia* on the stern.

He returned to the search form and typed in the new information. There was one response: The Bradenton boat. He Googled "yacht sales" and found a dozen sites. He searched on all twelve and found sixteen of the Tempter Pilothouses for sale. Four were in Europe, five in Asia, two in South America, one in Mexico and four in the United States. Of the US boats, the first was the one in Bradenton, the second was in San Francisco, the third in Redondo Beach and the fourth in Marina del Rey. Was it common for these boats to move halfway around the world? What could he ask? He brought up the page for the boat in Mexico. There was one picture of the boat and it didn't show its name. Hugh thought that even the colors were the same. But if this many were for sale, how many existed that were not. Why should one of them be the boat?

He composed a generic e-mail and sent it out to all sixteen sellers.

At three A.M., he took two Lunestas, drank a beer and fell asleep.

When he awoke, he was staring at the computer screen-saver. He reached across the bed to jiggle the mouse. The screen took its familiar form. The AOL mail page showed twenty new messages. He rolled out of bed and climbed into the chair, clicking on the link. The messages appeared on the screen. The first was from Zazzle. The second was from Barnes & Noble, the third was from papandokolis.J@gmail.com. The subject line was Re: Tempter Pilothouse. He clicked on the message.

> *Dear Mr. Mullen,*
> *I regret to inform you that my boat has been purchased. The advertisement should have been removed. Thank you for your interest.*
>
> > *J. Papandokolis*
> > *Athens, Greece*

Hugh clicked reply.

> *Mr. Papandokolis,*
> *Thanks for the quick response. I've been interested in acquiring a Tempter for about fifteen years now, since I viewed one in Southern California. Just curious if that could have been your boat. Have you ever sailed your boat in Southern California?*
>
> > *Sincerely,*
> > *Pirie Mullen*

Sent.

Without showering, he dressed and dodged the early morning traffic on the boulevard for a coffee and bagel. When he returned to his room, there were two new messages. One was from the Greek: *No.*

The second message was from honestabe78@hotmail.com. Subject, re: Tempter Pilothouse.

Hi Pirie,

   I was pleased to hear you were interested in the Tempter Pilothouse. She's an amazing boat, and there are very few on the market. The boat is now docked in Marina del Rey. I live aboard so it's possible for you to view the boat anytime. Just give me an hour's notice to tidy up. Looking forward to meeting you.

Albert

Hugh clicked reply.

Chapter 20

Kazuki placed the CD in the player. Finding the volume low, he turned the knob another quarter turn and restarted the disk: Mendelssohn's *Symphony Number Three*, the *Scottish* symphony.

A visit to Scotland had inspired Mendelssohn to compose the symphony; the overture was the composer's musical response to the eerie magnificence of the grotto known as Fingal's Cave in the Hebrides, a rocky, windswept archipelago off the west coast of Scotland. Mendelssohn called the sea cave a natural cathedral. In the music, Kazuki heard the sounds of the North Atlantic waves breaking and reconstituting—dying and aborning—at its entrance, repeating themselves in stirring, weirdly unsettling variations against the basalt walls and columns. Some believed it a sacred portal: an earth womb. Others, a sepulcher.

Kazuki sat down before the laptop.

Fingal's Cave / 27
THE DISAPPEARANCE

On Yuudai's left the forest drew back, revealing a low, dark green meadow divided by a silver stream, the mirror only broken where it ran over boulder and bough. Above the lush field a hawk flew in a lazy circle, and above the hawk interminable blue, flawed only by a silver jet crawling west.

Through the car's open windows, mingled with the scent of pine and juniper, the breeze carried the meadow's sweet breath, like a waiting girl's. Yuudai adjusted the rearview mirror, which had loosened and would not remain steady. He centered Brent and James. An hour ago, they stopped along a stretch of redwoods, wandering for an hour in the cool dusky air under the umbrella of the enormous trees. Spotting a blackberry bush, Yuudai popped one of the riper ones in his mouth and urged his sons to fill themselves on the plump fruit.

"Some of these trees are a thousand years old," said Yuudai, as they chewed the berries, bending back his head to stare at the nearly invisible treetops. "Imagine. Centuries before Columbus discovered America."

"He didn't," said Brent. "It was Leif Erikson."

"The Indians were already here," added James.

Father and sons joined hands to see if they could encircle one of the trees, but no matter how close they hugged the wood, their outer fingertips would not touch.

The family had planned the camping trip months ago, but at the last moment, Sumiko developed a painful stomach flu. She had found the open campsite, not easy at the height of the season, made the reservations, packed the clothing, but she was too sick to go. She urged Yuudai to take the boys. They looked forward to doing so much: fishing, mountain biking, swimming under waterfalls, finding Indian arrowheads. How could he disappoint them? Yuudai agreed, and he didn't slough off a pledge when Sumiko made him promise not to take chances.

As they drove deeper into the mountains, Yuudai's pulse quickened. As a boy, Yuudai had not once gone on a real outdoors vacation. His father, Herb, was too entangled in his cause to bother with family outings. In fact, Herb had taken the family on only one trip. It was to California. The family flew and then rented a car. Yuudai remembered driving across a vast valley of apple orchards, not knowing clearly where his father was taking them. In the distance were snow-peaked mountains, but they were not going to the mountains. At some point they got behind a caravan of cars, all apparently going to the same destination. When the other cars pulled to the roadside, Herb parked behind them. Yuudai was surprised to see that most of the people getting out of their cars looked like the people in the picture books his father collected: Japanese. Herb led his family to the site where the people were gathering. There wasn't much to see. Some big posts, some tombstones.

"Where are we, Dad?" asked Yuudai.

"Manzanar," said his father, his sleeve to his eyes.

The boys' bikes were mounted on the car's roof. As a strong oblique wind struck the car, the wheels whirred.

"How much longer, Dad?" asked James.

"Just around the bend," said Yuudai.

"Think there's fish in that water?" asked Brent, pointing to the winding stream, which threw off rainbows.

"I can see the trout jumping," said Yuudai.

"Let's go for it," said Brent.

"Oh, we'll have plenty of time."

Yuudai glanced again in the mirror. He loved the intensity in his sons' eyes when they anticipated their next adventure. Concentrated light, like laser beams. But in the rearview, he saw nothing, as if they had jumped out of the car. It took him only an instant to realize that the mirror was totally out of whack. He adjusted it, found his sons.

They reached the promised bend in the road. The meadow disappeared behind them and the forest closed in. A sign told them that Hawk's Flight Camp was two miles distant. Yuudai accelerated past the speed limit, squealing around a tight curve. James and Brent discussed motocross techniques. The sun touched the treetops.

Hawk's Flight Camp One Mile.

In the cooler were hotdogs and beef patties. He would have to start a fire. He tried to remember if he had brought the propane stove. There was so much camping stuff to remember.

Hawk's Flight Camp Five Hundred Yards.

Yuudai glanced to a clearing on the left-hand side of the road. There was a tavern: *Boom Boom's for Beer and Pizza.* There were a couple of cars in the parking lot, one a vintage red Mustang. Red interior, too. Pretty.

"Look, Dad, pizza."

"Yeah, I see that . . ."

As the bar slid by, a woman got out of the Mustang. Yuudai caught her shapely profile.

It was a big, well-situated campsite and the ground was level where they pitched the tent. In an hour, they had the tent up, the sleeping bags arranged inside. They had every-thing they needed but the propane stove.

The boys were already riding their bikes on the trails around the campsite. Nearby were numerous families set-ting up camp or cooking. The smell of the grilled meat made Yuudai's mouth water. He remembered the woman who had gotten out of the Mustang. She wore a red and white checkered shirt. On a nearby path, Brent raced his bike toward a mound, pulling back on the handlebars but then leaning forward as he hit the little hill. The bike flew above the ground, landing with a satisfying thump. James followed, not quite as fast.

They took the jump again.

"Boys, how does pizza sound?" called out Yuudai.

The nearby families, the smoke drifting lazily into the treetops, a doe and fawn foraging at the edge of camp.

"Come on," said Yuudai. "Lock up the bikes."

"Can't we stay?" asked Brent.

"Better come."

"We'll be fine," said James.

Yuudai again considered the surroundings. How could such peace not be trusted?

When Yuudai pulled into the parking lot of Boom Boom's, the Mustang was still there.

Like most roadside bars in the mountains, the tavern was an accumulation of discards and therefore familiar and comforting; its walls were covered with license plates from every state, no doubt removed from wrecks and cars that had given up the ghost on the long ascent, and its log tables etched with countless visitors' names, many long out of fashion: Jeds and Mabels. A nice place to have a beer, but Yuudai would order his food and go.

Extra large. Half mushroom, half pepperoni.

Adjacent to the take-out counter, a worn hardwood bar supported the arms of a few rustic patrons. The woman from the Mustang occupied the nearest stool. Maybe a year or two older than Yuudai from the lines around her mouth when she smiled at him, she was very pretty with a petite figure, the slope of her breasts visible within the unbuttoned collar of her worn flannel shirt. When Yuudai glanced at her, she took off her glasses and set them on the bar, pushing back her straight auburn hair. Her soft green eyes stayed on his and her full lips broke into an amused smile. Why not have a beer while he waited? From the rough-hewn bartender he ordered a tall beer and slipped onto the chair beside her. She was pretty and laughed at his remarks, but he wasn't looking to cheat on Sumiko—even if he had a second beer, bought the pretty woman another Jack and Coke and held his breath when she pressed her leg against his. He felt the firmness and heat through the denim.

"I'm Demi. What's your name?" the woman asked.

"Yuudai O'Keefe."

"Yuudai? What kind of name is that?"

"Japanese."

She pulled back her head. "No offense, but you don't look Japanese."

"It's a long story."

She lifted her drink. "I'm in no rush."

Yuudai began, "My father, Herb O'Keefe, was assistant tail gunner on the Enola Gay . . ."

"Wow, that's one hellacious tale," said Demi, as Yuudai drummed his fingers on the pizza box that had cooled during the length of his family chronicle. Demi stilled his hand with hers, pressed against him and whispered in his ear, "You smoke?"

The old Mustang smelled of marijuana, and its red leather upholstery was soon absorbing another sweet cloud. She unbuttoned easily.

He didn't think of the camp at Manzanar. He didn't think of the boys getting hungry. He didn't think of Sumiko's illness. He didn't think of Sumiko. He thought of this pretty body that he'd never seen or touched.

By the time Yuudai got back to camp, it was eight P.M., an hour later than when he'd told the boys he'd return with dinner. He wasn't surprised when they weren't at the campsite. They'd gotten bored and were no doubt riding their bicycles on one of the nearby paths. He waited for ten minutes, as the forest squeezed out the remaining sunlight and an owl hooted. By flashlight he walked the paths, calling out their names. He went to each of the nearby campsites—marshmallows and s'mores—a staticky baseball game on a boom box. No one had seen them. He returned to the paths. Each breath growing shorter, he drove back to the bar, thinking that his restless sons might have taken their bikes to find him. Another woman had replaced Demi, nudging up to another man, downing another Jack and Coke, her flannel shirt opened another button. Yuudai leaned across the bar, calling to the bartender. "My sons . . . I can't—"

"It happens all the time. They wandered away. They'll be fine. Probably found their own way back by now."

But the bartender said he would call a ranger just to be safe.

Like the bartender, the ranger who showed up an hour later assured him that they would find his children. A mile deep in the woods, hungry and crying, but okay.

The ranger took a description of the two boys and told Yuudai to remain at the bar. He would look for them on horseback. *Have a beer, relax.*

Yuudai had a beer, ignored the woman speaking with him, stared at the collection of abandoned children's playthings on a shelf below the beer bottles. A toy soldier, a ballerina, a Rubik's Cube, a fire engine, a tiny watch, a set of dinosaurs—a fierce charging triceratops. Yuudai heard his father's voice.

"The mother's hiding these little plastic dinosaurs on the café's patio . . ."

When the ranger hadn't returned in an hour, Yuudai told the bartender he was going back to his campsite. The bartender urged him to stay, but Yuudai couldn't breathe. With each attempted inhalation he drew in Demi's checkered shirt, as if someone had stuck the fabric in his mouth and he was sucking it in, choking himself, drowning in flannel.

He forgot to turn on his headlights, and one hundred yards beyond the bar, he couldn't understand the black stretch of road, so he accelerated to get beyond the dark. *Get back to camp, get out on those paths.* He would hear their cries in the night.

He had the momentary sensation of flying, as if he had hit a little hill and had pulled back on the steering wheel, and then a boom and cartoon lights and then blackness.

The instant later was three days later when he awoke.

"Where—"

"I'm sorry, Mr. O'Keefe. We've searched . . ."

Brent and James had vanished into the forest.

His children were gone.

Chapter 21

Twenty years had not altered the fissured and weedy parking lot at Mother's Beach in Marina del Rey, where Setsuko and Hugh had regularly taken the twins as toddlers. So unchanged was the flat gray slab that Hugh turned to reassure himself that his sons were there, but they were not there, just the bare backseat awaiting the infant car seats.

As Hugh got out, he turned at the throaty growl of a car engine and saw the primed Camaro. He turned, walked a few steps toward the beach, stopped and looked back. The car was gone.

A couple of teenage girls scampered by him.

Hugh stopped, opened his wallet and took out the scrap of paper on which Anna had written her name and phone number. He tore the paper into a dozen little pieces. He let the scraps sink into the garbage like hot pistols into the sea.

Under the covered patio bordering the beach, smoke rose from barbecues tended by seniors in sunhats, *Venice, California,* silk-screened on their baggy T-shirts, from whose sleeves hung frail arms bright with sunspots. As breakfast patties sizzled and cranberry juice flowed, a wilted flower child bopped to "Whole Lot of Love" while her man smoked his doobie, thrusting his hips. Leaning against the wall of an outdoor shower, a homeless man with a face like dying embers clawed at his despairing yellow dog.

"You need coolin', baby, I'm not foolin' . . ."

Across the dull brown sand, mothers spread their blankets, distributed juice packs, mini-donuts and bagged cereal. A sailfish tacked the inlet, and one hundred yards away, a cabin cruiser pulled out of its marina, gray exhaust bubbling up from the water. Hugh took off his sandals, cuffed his jeans and walked down the beach.

Half a life ago, Setsuko and Hugh had eaten dinner and danced at Sol Luna, a restaurant that overlooked the marina and the little public beach.

Later they left the restaurant to sit on the dark sand, watching the night-lights of the docked boats and passing crafts sparkle on the water. Hugh challenged Setsuko to strip down to her panties and bra and go for a swim with him. For most of the two weeks they had spent together in the states, Setsuko had been on edge. She hadn't called her father to tell him that Hugh had gone to Los Angeles with her, and it troubled her to think that she would not be able to tell Kazuki, for then she would have to tell him all of it. Under Hugh's tutelage, Setsuko had agreed to lie to her father—each lie, even if only one of omission, would widen her orbit, so that one day she might be pulled from his gravity—but that didn't free her from the guilt. Tonight, though, a day before they were to return to Japan, she seemed utterly relaxed and didn't hesitate to unclothe and dash into the water.

They swam out to the rope that signaled the limits of the bathing area. Clinging to the rope, they made love.

It was perfect, but—

Hugh never mentioned the odd pulse of the water as they joined, and he could not have then guessed that its source was a hundred circling sharks. Nor did he mention the vague, solitary creature hunched down on the shadowy sand, perhaps watching them, perhaps admiring the lights on the water, perhaps eyeing their heaped garments; for when Hugh and Setsuko returned to the beach, Hugh found nothing missing, and he didn't want to frighten her.

Hugh looked back toward the road where a moment ago he saw the Camaro. That night on the beach with Setsuko, Hugh assumed that the person hunting through their clothes was a denizen of the beach. A vagrant looking for a few dollars or something to sell. But nothing had been taken . . .

Likely Hugh's glance had frightened him off. He had never considered another explanation . . . Hugh turned his gaze back to the placid bay.

The calculations that Setsuko would later make put the conception of the twins at Mother's Beach, and it was to Mother's Beach that they would bring the boys as toddlers one hundred times.

One hundred times . . .

It was low tide. Rippled sand and mud—smelling of oil—stretched in a broad crescent like a black quarter moon. As he walked along the tide line toward the docks, he stopped to watch two boys dig a moat for their castle. A woman, hugely pregnant, rushed to their side, eyeing Hugh. He smiled at her and moved on. The cool wet sand sunk beneath his feet, exuding another memory, a memory of mud.

Takumi and Hitoshi, a year old, sat at the bay's edge, water lapping their toes. They dug into the mud, ripping out handfuls to toss aside or to taste, provoking their mother's quick catch and release.

"It won't hurt them," said Hugh, lazing on the blanket, digging a beer from the ice chest, and wondering if the mud would truly not hurt them.

Their chubby white backs glistened with sunscreen. Setsuko coated them before they left the apartment, leaving not a sliver of skin unprotected. Their diapers protruded over their bathing suits like the petals of flowers. Their hair was not so dark as their mother's, but still black and dense. Hugh drank his beer, walked to the water's edge and dropped to his knees before them. He held out his hands palms up. Both boys got it right away, dropping the mud into his hands until it overflowed.

"We should go," said Setsuko.

"We just got here an hour ago," said Hugh, dipping his hands and shaking them clean. He hoisted both boys under his arms like sacks of flour and strode out knee deep. He dropped to his haunches, balancing each boy on a knee. They slapped at the water.

"Too much sun is not good," said Setsuko.

"Ten minutes," he lied.

She turned and walked back to the blanket, where she would refuse the beach chair to sit cross-legged beneath the umbrella and sketch seascapes, later to turn some of the sketches into delicate, iridescent watercolors. He followed her prideful walk up the beach. As with everything she wore, her bathing suit was modest, hiding her shape. Though he detected little change, she insisted that the pregnancy had deformed—Henkei shi ta—her body. She didn't dwell on it, and if it weren't for the loose clothes that she preferred to wear, in contrast to the revealing dress of their dating days, Hugh would have thought that she wasn't aware of it at all, though he suspected, considering the sharpness of her occasional self-criticism, that she wanted him to be aware. She wanted him conscious of her flaw. But it was only at the beach, where her pronounced concealment betrayed her self-consciousness, that Hugh took notice. Hugh scuttled backward like a crab, carrying his sons deeper into the water, so that the yellowish suds came up to their chests. He shook and bounced them until they were near hysterical.

Jesus, he loved their warm little bodies.

"This is where it all began, guys," he whispered, gazing at the safety rope that Setsuko had held as she floated upward to catch him in her legs. "Conceived among sharks, my little boys. Well, your mama says it began so."

The Tempter was docked in Holiday Marina, a small anchorage less than two hundred yards from the beach. A concrete walkway and chain-link fence ran perpendicular to the quays. Hugh reached the gate to the first dock and paused to watch an elegant sailboat pull out of its slip, the water rushing across its hull. He placed his hands on the gate and let the metal's heat burn his skin. Failure rose in his gut like bile. An ultimately fruitless quest, like those that drove on the steadfast but hapless detectives who trudged through the noir screenplays he once wrote. His sons were gone and beyond recall. It was irrational to believe that he'd find even a trace of Takumi and Hitoshi after all this time. He stopped, a gloom settling on his intentions. He had no chance. He was like—it came to him, the boys' favorite cartoon. He was like Road Runner's Wile E. Coyote. Having vaulted off a cliff in pursuit of the bird, he was trying to find purchase in the thin air but succeeded only in climbing to the top of his vaulting stick, which upon pivoting left him at pole's bottom again, plummeting ever downward to the dusty canyon floor where Coyote's previous falls had etched the sand.

There must have been dozens of Tempters not for sale. The odds were low that the boat he was about to view was the Oceanside vessel. Better that he go home and turn spotlights on his house.

To forget time, to forgive life, to be at peace.

For an instant he took solace in that promised death, that green current passing over him, or the earth packed around him, the bugs tunneling through his moldering corpse, a city's cold dark thoroughfares. But at the periphery of his vision, Hitoshi and Takumi swam toward him, Setsuko's letter fixed to his fingers, crayfish roamed beyond their domain, the honeysuckle, Nakamura Reality, the boys on the boat, Jason.

Hints, surely, but hints of what?

No, he knew. Be honest, Hugh.

He had no choice. He had to believe in the absurd quest. Click my heels three times and believe.

Two minutes later, he was at the gate of Dock Three Thousand. He dialed Albert's number.

The phone rang a half-dozen times.

"Hello?"

"This is Mullen. I've come to see the boat."

"You make an appointment?" asked a rough, sleep-drenched voice.

"Last night."

"What's the name?"

"Mullen. Pirie Mullen."

"Oh, yeah, yeah. Where are you?"

"Outside the gate to your dock."

"Um. Give me a minute and I'll buzz you through. Last slip on the right."

It was several minutes before the gate buzzed and unlocked, the click like an errant heartbeat. Until now, his thoughts had been tangled, snagged on their own implications. He could not avoid the idea that his sons had been taken. An opportunist. A barren couple or lonely man who wanted a child to nourish. The news frequently reported childless women snatching infants from hospital incubators. One could almost sympathize. But there were others whose carnal and sadistic desires recognized no boundaries. That was the black sickening thought he couldn't accept. If you believed the radio talk shows, the predators were behind every tree, at the wheel of every dark van, at the helms of yachts trolling the beaches. Drugged and bound. Hidden in a shed in the high-hedged backyard. Forced to—his thought shriveled up. He couldn't bring his imagination to that foul place. But why hadn't he considered it then, in the days after? No, it was no mystery. He had accepted their deaths because he was responsible for their deaths.

He had accepted and he had lost his mind. Not with baby steps like Alzheimer's, but all at once as the abortionist's machine sucks out a fetus. Behind his back they whispered *zombie*.

Hugh walked down the quay, taking in the vessels. On half of the boats there was activity, middle-aged men in polo shirts and shorts inspecting winches and inboard motors. Pretty young women applying sunscreen and brushing their hair. Day laborers lugging supplies aboard for voyages to faraway, exotic places. An old man with rheumy eyes and gray beard looped a line around his hand and elbow, smiling at Hugh as if he knew a secret.

The boat sat between the fingers of the outermost slip, bow abutting the dock. Hugh glanced from the pilothouse to the forward hull, reading the boat's name: *Pearl*, in arced black letters against the ivory hull. Showing through the white paint at each end of the arc were faint traces of additional letters. Or was he imagining the pale letters? He walked to the end of the dock where the transom was visible. *Pearl* again with the faint trace of other letters. He looked up at the eye-catching pilothouse. Even among the larger and no doubt more expensive crafts, the boat stood out. It evoked speed, breaking limits. The *Pearl* rose and fell in the backwash of a monstrous motor yacht.

"Impressive, huh?"

A shirtless man stood at the *Pearl's* transom, pointing to the yacht motoring by. Hugh's lips felt dried and cracked.

"How—big was that?" Hugh managed to ask.

"Ninety feet. That's as big as this marina can handle. That what you're looking for?" asked the man.

Hugh turned his gaze from the oversized yacht and pointed to the Tempter.

"I like this," said Hugh,

"You ever been on one?"

Hugh hesitated. "No."

"I'm Albert Abe."

"Pirie Mullen."

Hugh took Abe's hand, big and soft as an oven mitt.

"Come onboard," said Albert. "I'll give you the twenty-dollar tour."

Albert could have been Hugh's age or ten years younger, his age deferred by a deep tan and gravity-defying pompadour. Amerasian for sure, but finer than that Hugh couldn't guess. Albert smelled of alcohol and a swampy cologne.

"You own a boat now?" asked Albert.

"No."

"You have, though?"

"No. Never."

"Like making your first car a Shelby Cobra," said Albert, picking at his pomp. He examined something between his fingertips and then flicked it over the side.

"I've read about the Tempter Pilothouse," offered Hugh.

"Reading's not racing—or motoring. Excuse me." He retrieved a Bloody Mary from a cup holder. He stirred the drink with his celery, sucking the red from the stalk before taking a gulp.

"Make you one?"

"Thanks. I'll pass."

"Coffee?"

"I'm okay."

"Good. I ain't got any. Let's make you salivate," said Albert, gesturing for Hugh to follow him.

"Now here," said Albert, as they entered the pilothouse, "is what makes this baby special." Albert spun. "Three-hundred-and-sixty-degree visibility. Air-conditioned, two Cat Vision monitors . . ." Albert recited a dozen features. "Beauty, huh?"

Hugh nodded and asked polite questions as Albert touted his merchandise.

"How long have you owned the boat?" asked Hugh.

"Eight years for me, twenty years in the family."

"Long time."

"My father bought it new."

"It looks new now."

"Takes a shitload of work. My old man drummed that into me. Last thing he said was to make me promise to take care of the boat. Loved it, he did. She was his mistress. He couldn't part with it. I can. How serious are you?"

"Pretty damn serious," said Hugh.

"You want to go for a ride?"

"Sure."

"Give me five minutes," said Albert, exiting the pilothouse.

When he returned, Albert took a helm seat and ordered Hugh to sit in its companion. Albert started the engines. As the owner maneuvered his boat from the dock, Hugh studied Albert's hair, which looked like nothing so much as a gathering wave, blacked with crude oil. Hugh wondered if it was fake.

"Elvis," said Albert, catching Hugh's gaze.

"Oh?"

"Vegas."

"You're an impersonator?"

"It's just a goof. Bunch of us go out there a couple of times a year." Albert's head swayed and he bellowed, "Well, since my baby left me. Well, I found a new place to dwell. Well, it's down at the end of Lonely Street at Heartbreak Hotel . . ."

In a quarter hour, they were motoring past the breakwater. On the rocks, fishermen held their casts to follow the boat's progress.

"Hold on now," said Albert as they reached the open sea. The engine went from a throb to a roar as the bow rose. The acceleration pushed Hugh deep into his seat. The hull slapped the water, flinging up great white bells of ocean.

For a moment Hugh was caught in the exhilaration of speed. The shore receded. They were on the open sea. They continued at that speed for another five minutes. Albert pulled back on the throttle.

"Here, take over. I'm going below to mix up another drink."

In Albert's absence, Hugh steered due west. When after five minutes Albert didn't return, Hugh moved the wheel a degree to the right. The boat responded. The speedometer read fifteen knots per hour. Albert had had it up to sixty. Hugh increased the speed. He drew in a lungful of the moist, salt-drenched air. The sky was the faintest blue and went on forever. Over the rushing air, he heard his sons' voices.

"This is a cool boat," said Hitoshi.

"Let me drive," said Takumi.

Were you here, boys? Was this the boat that took you?

"Get the fuck away," said a muffled voice.

Hugh backed off on the throttle. He looked around for Albert, though it wasn't a man's voice Hugh had heard. He *had* heard a voice. It wasn't in his head. Someone had shouted. He looked at the deck.

Albert came back carrying two Bloody Marys. He handed one to Hugh, who took it without protest. Hugh sipped the drink as he piloted.

"Three hundred thousand is a deal for this," said Albert.

"Like buying a home," said Hugh.

"Better than a home. You can't buy a shitbox in LA for $300,000. The slip is no more than homeowner's fees: three hundred a month. No property taxes."

A quarter mile away a pelican glided across the ocean's surface.

"How does it handle in rough water. I mean storms."

"Like a bullet through plasterboard."

"Have you always kept the boat at the marina?"

"Most of the time. Redondo now and then. San Diego once."

Hugh swallowed. "In 2000?"

"It was in the late nineties. Could have been 2000, I guess. Why?"

"I thought I saw it there. *Oceanside.*" He wondered if Albert would see his heart ramming through his breastplate.

"This boat sticks in the memory, but still that's a long time."

"Yeah . . . a long time."

Albert took a step back, looking over Hugh as if he were about to take him on in a fight. "What do you do for a living?" asked Albert.

"I'm—I'm a teacher."

"Professor?"

"Middle school."

"And they pay you that kind of money?"

"I've got the money."

"Independently wealthy?"

"Yes, in a way."

"Give her the gas then."

"That's all right."

"Give her the gas."

Hugh eased back the throttle. The engine roared. The bow leaped, obscuring the sea.

"If you turned the wheel fifteen degrees now, what do you think would happen?"

"Don't know."

"You'd flip us. We'd both be dead men."

The hull beat on the sea, sending up white flames. Hugh pulled the throttle. The boat left the water altogether, gliding above like a seabird.

"Easy now," said Albert, putting his hand over Hugh's and pushing back the throttle. The bow dropped. Hugh was breathing hard. He steadied himself.

"Was *Pearl* its original name?"

"That was mine. Before that she was the—Jesus, what the hell was that name?"

Pearl . . . earl . . . real. The name floated into Hugh's consciousness as if from the bottom of the sea. "*Reality,*" said Hugh.

"*Reality*! That's right. *Reality.* How the hell did you know?"

"I told you. I've seen this boat before."

"When?"

"Summer of 2000."

Albert squinted, shifted in his seat, glanced sharply at Hugh, and then shrugged, his face drained of interest.

"Funny name for a boat," said Hugh. "Why did your father choose it?"

"No idea," snapped Albert.

"Would it be possible to see below decks?" asked Hugh, as Albert finished tying the boat to the dock.

Albert glanced at his watch. "Love to show you, but I'm running late. Got to meet my lawyer in Century City."

"Just a quick look?"

Albert shook his head.

"I'll give you an answer within twenty-four hours," said Hugh.

"Five minutes. In and out," said Albert, leading Hugh below.

"Galley and eating bar," said Albert with a sweep of his arm. "Pardon the—*untidiness.*" He pointed forward to a small closed door. "In the forepeak you've got the guest berth. Queen-size bed and shower."

Hugh grinned. "May I see it?"

"Not today," said Albert. "Let's take a look at the salon and then I'll show you the master stateroom."

Hugh gazed at the forward door, which seemed to expand as if about to explode in the way they depicted such a thing in cartoons. Albert called for him to follow, but Hugh froze as from behind the door came a distinct cry.

"Guest," explained Albert with a wink.

"Ah," said Hugh. Of course. Why not?

"Impressive," said Hugh, as he followed Albert into the salon.

"Custom-made for the boat." Albert flopped down on the salon's leather couch and slapped the fabric. Hugh walked to a bulletin board covered with photos which depicted the Abe family on the boat in different marine settings. There were many children, who grew older or younger with each photo, but his sons were not among them. Perhaps Abe had been following his boys for some time. Perhaps it was because they were beautiful half-Japanese boys, his predilection. From the photos, Hugh picked out Albert's father. White-haired and trim, the older man was deferred to by the others whom the camera captured. Albert was in several photographs: a slimmer, healthier Albert, whose Asian features were more discernible. Had Hugh seen either of them twelve years ago? He closed his eyes and let the projector display a hundred scenes from those days, but there was no Abe, no Albert. At the top right corner of the bulletin board were several photos that contrasted with the other happy scenes: a funeral. A large headstone, the family gathered around a gravesite, a procession of cars driving through the gates of the cemetery: Ornate letters spelled out *High Meadow*. Hugh stepped closer to the photographs.

"My old man's funeral," said Albert over Hugh's shoulder.

"Where?"

"Where what?"

"The cemetery. Where is it?"

"Simi Valley. Why?"

"Nothing."

But it was not nothing. He remembered the brochure in the trunk. He remembered Gina's voice, the regular Thursday evening phone calls. But hell, how many people were buried at Forest Lawn? Perhaps High Meadow could rest as many thousands.

Albert clapped Hugh's back. "Sorry, but I've got to throw you out." He directed Hugh back toward the galley. Hugh stopped to gaze at the forward door.

"Here you go," said Albert, stretching over the rail to hand Hugh a manila envelope. "It's got all the information you'll ever want on the boat. Copies of maintenance, repairs. Everything."

A boy of fourteen skateboarded down the dock. Hugh followed his progress, glancing at Albert, who was also looking at the boy.

"Good-looking kid," said Hugh.

"Hey, Satch, come here," Albert called to the kid.

The boy leaned back on his skateboard, skidding to a stop. He kick-turned and faced Albert. "Yeah?"

"I'm missing an iPod."

"Don't look at me."

"You or one of your buddies."

"Ain't me."

"Come here."

The boy picked up his skateboard and strutted over.

"Here's the deal. You get me my iPod back or you find yourself another boat to crash in when your father is looking to kick your ass."

"Dude, I wouldn't rip you off."

"Find it."

"I'll ask around."

"Yeah, you ask around."

The boy shrugged, dropped his skateboard and zipped away.

"Sorry, man. What were you saying?"

"Nothing," said Hugh, his insides in knots.

Albert tapped the envelope in Hugh's hand. "So, you're interested?"

"It's a hell of a boat."

"Good. By the way, what happened to your face?"

"Surfboard."

"Be careful, man."

Hugh set his foot on the ladder. "I'll be in touch."

"Good." Albert checked his watch. "Gotta run."

Hugh walked down the dock, glancing back to see Albert descending into the boat's interior.

On Mother's Beach, Hugh sat on the sand near the children's play area, from where he could see the *Pearl*'s transom and some of the dock. But he had a clear view of the walkway and the entrance to the tenants' parking lot.

No more than ten minutes had gone by when Albert strode down the walkway and entered the parking lot. Hugh waited another ten minutes.

At the gate to the dock, Hugh didn't hesitate, vaulting the gate like a yachtsman who didn't have time for such bullshit. Smiling at all those he passed, Hugh boarded the *Pearl* without incident or question.

Clasping the door handle, Hugh turned. "Bless you, Albert," he whispered as he drew back the door. The light was on in the galley. The guest berth door was still shut.

Hugh took out his cell phone and set it near the sink.

He knocked on the forward door. Nothing. He knocked again.

"Go away, Albert," said a voice from the interior.

"I'm not Albert. It's all right."

Something clattered in the room, followed by a thump.

"Do you need help?" asked Hugh.

"Who the—"

The door swung open. A woman of about forty, her body wrapped in a red sheet, stared in bewilderment at Hugh.

"Who the fuck are you?" she asked.

Hugh stepped back, unsettled by the sheet as much as by the woman. Blood red. Lurid. "I'm sorry. I came to see the boat. I think I left my cell phone here. I just came back to—"

Hugh smiled with embarrassment and looked around. "Jesus, I see it. There it is." He scrambled over to the sink.

When he turned back, cell phone in hand, the woman had stepped out of the room and the sheet had fallen a couple of inches, partially exposing her breasts, across which a violet rash spread. Her perfume made Hugh's head throb.

"Want a drink?" asked the woman, tightening the sheet but not pulling it up.

"All right, sure," said Hugh.

"Let me change."

Leaving the door open, she dropped the sheet on a chair. Her body appeared and disappeared as she gathered some clothes. She came out a minute later in an oversized T-shirt, no less revealing than the sheet. The rash seemed to spill over the T's neck, but it may have been just a stain. When she closed the bedroom door with her hip, he was glad.

"I'm Janet," she said, moving to the bar. "What you in the mood for?"

"A beer is fine."

"I've told you my name, what's yours?" she asked as she scanned the refrigerator's shelves.

"Hugh," he replied, forgetting he was Pirie.

"*Hugh*. Hugh Grant. Hugh Hefner. Hugh Laurie. Do you watch that show?"

"*House*? I've seen episodes."

She popped a beer and handed it to him. He watched her pour a vodka and tonic. Drink in hand she moved close to Hugh.

"Skol."

"Skol," Hugh repeated.

She sipped her drink, looking at Hugh over the rim of her glass. "I love that show," she said.

"It's very funny."

"Yeah. I like all those mysterious diseases. If I ever get sick, I mean, really sick, I hope it's from a mysterious disease."

"Why's that?"

"I've had a dull, dull life. If I'm going to go out, I want it to be with a little suspense." She tilted her head forward and moved closer, brushing her breasts against his chest.

May I lick your rash, ma'am? Just tell me something.

"Aren't you afraid Albert will come back?"

"Oh, he wouldn't mind."

"Sexually open?"

"Albert or me?"

"Albert."

She touched Hugh's lips. "Albert is a libertine. You know what that is?"

"Anything goes?"

"You got a Facebook page?" she asked.

The bedroom door opened and a breeze swept the cabin. The red sheet had fallen to the floor, fluttered under the draft. "No. I don't use that stuff."

"You're kidding."

"I avoided e-mail as long as I could."

"Why?"

Hugh shrugged. "Just not me, I guess."

She squinted. "You look like somebody. Eric Clapton. Anybody tell you that?"

"Once or twice." The rash was creeping up her neck. *Gonna take an ocean of calamine lotion . . .* "So with Albert anything goes?"

She pushed her index finger into Hugh's mouth. He tasted confectioner's sugar.

"Not anything. Not anything." She grinned. "No animals or that."

The fucking sheet billowed, grew wings. "Boys?"

"Boys?" She took her finger out of Hugh's mouth and pressed it to her tongue. She sucked for a second and then drew it out. "Am I wasting myself on you?" she asked.

"What makes you say that?"

"You into boys?"

"No. I was wondering if Albert was."

"It's an odd question."

"He's not, then?"

"No way, José. I suppose he'd be into young girls if he could get them, but he can't. He's stuck with me. But you could do worse." She put her hand against Hugh and kissed him. He held the kiss for a minute and then slipped his lips to her ear.

"Nakamura Reality," he whispered.

"Umm," she said.

"Mean anything?"

"Sure. That's where me and Albert met."

He eased her from him. "What?"

"Albert and me got together at NR."

"You worked there?"

"Sure. I was a clerk."

"And Albert?"

"A honcho—though he didn't know shit. That's what happens when your father runs the company. Nepotism, right?"

"Right—fuck. Mr. Abe was like the CEO?"

"I guess. Something like that."

"Does Albert still work at Nakamura?"

"Nope. They booted his ass out when his father died. Then they threw me out for good measure. Too bad, it was a fun job. I met Steven Spielberg once." She grabbed Hugh's ass and squeezed. "You a runner?"

"Yes. Yes I am."

Chapter 22

Fingal's Cave /28
A CLUE

For the next two years, Yuudai lived in despair. Sumiko, inconsolable, divorced Yuudai and returned to Japan to live with her father in double mourning. Yuudai quit his Hollywood job to spend his days stapling photos of his sons to telephone poles and bulletin boards throughout the lower Sierra. He followed up every lead, haunted police stations and hospitals. He visited the camping area a hundred times, stalking the paths in the most violent seasons, searching for a clue, a sign, the echo of a voice, but the forest was silent.

After two years, he gave up. His sons were dead. Either at the bottom of some remote canyon or in some shallow backyard grave.

For another ten years, he lived without solace.

At the end of that twelfth year, as winter turned to spring, he once more returned to the site of their disappearance. Not much had changed, and when he walked into the roadhouse—which he had avoided during his two years of searching—he half expected to see his old girlfriend sitting on her stool, her flannel shirt thin and faded. The seat was empty, but the bartender remembered Yuudai, and that sad night. Yuudai got drunk, cried and raged at the woman who tempted him. Where did she live? He wanted to put his hands to her throat. The bartender calmed him down, revealing that the woman was a stranger. He had seen her that night and never again.

It was as though her purpose was to draw Yuudai into his fate.

Yuudai set his chin on his fists, dispiritedly scanned the bottles of booze and promotional items, yellowed cartoon strips and shelf of dusty children's toys. The dinosaurs remained but one: the triceratops. Well . . . Yuudai closed his eyes. There was a tap on the bar. "She left these."

Yuudai looked down to see a pair of glasses.

"I tried to catch her to give them back but she was already burning rubber. A sweet little red Mustang."

Yuudai lifted the eyeglasses. "She's never been back?"

"Nope."

"If she ever does . . ."

"Not going to hurt her, are you?"

Yuudai shook his head. "I'd just like to ask her a question." Yuudai stared at the woman's glasses and then took off his own glasses. The wall of license plates blurred. He put on Demi's. The license plates still blurred without a degree of difference.

"Maybe this will help," said the bartender, setting a scrap of paper on the bar. Yuudai exchanged glasses and looked down at the paper.

"What's this?"

"Her license plate number. I caught it as she was taking off. I thought I might try to contact her to get her back the glasses. Never bothered."

"How—"

The bartender gestured to the wall. "My hobby. I dig license plates."

Yuudai read the letters: CSNDRA.

"Thank you."

Chapter 23

Hugh took an outside table. The temperature was 110 but the table was in the shade and the water mister functioning, rendering the heat bearable. He wiped cigar ash from the table and set down his coffee and Albert's manila envelope. He took the lid off the coffee, placed it on a brown napkin and sipped from the open cup. Hearing a familiar crackling sound, he looked up. At the trash can, an elderly, frail, sun-blasted woman crushed a can. She deposited it in a bloated bag in her rusty shopping cart, which squeaked like a mouse under each new weight. Dressed in a white toga of sorts, the woman was speckled with dust, but not dirty. Plagued by tremors and unhealed wounds, homeless and harmless, she pushed her cart along the boulevard and never begged, never asked for a penny or a smoke. It was to her that Hugh gave the heap of empty plastic bottles collected in the trunk of the Volvo. He would wait until he saw her wheeling her cart, hustle to the car, gather his plastic and set it in her path, as if God had placed it there for her to find. Today God had no empty bottles, but he smiled at her as she deposited another treasure in her bag, and she smiled back.

"Good luck," she mouthed to him.

"Thank you," Hugh said. He watched her push her cart away. Why had she said that? he wondered, but fearing a mundane response, let her disappear down the boulevard.

Turning on his computer, he then opened Albert's envelope, slipping out the contents, of which he expected little, but who knew . . . ?

Radiohead's "Paranoid Android" played. Hugh pulled out his cell phone.

"Hello?"

"Hugh Mcpherson?"

"Yes."

"Hey, this is Rob at San Diego News. I've got it."

"The paper? The *San Diego Sol*?"

"Mint condition."

"Goddamn, that's great."

"One hundred dollars, right?"

"Absolutely."

"Plus postage."

"Whatever. Can you send it right away?"

"I'd like to get paid first."

"I'll send you a check today. Cash if you like."

"You use PayPal?" asked Rob.

The mechanics of the transaction completed, Hugh hung up his phone. He should have asked Rob to describe the boat, but fuck it. He'd have the paper within a day.

He recalled the last of his conversation with Janet. To Hugh's questions about the company's operations, Janet told him that the company was pretty much like a dozen other special effects and fabrication companies that she'd worked for. Pretty ordinary. It was only their end product that people found amazing.

Was the end product ten years ago the kidnapping of his sons?

Hugh spread the envelope's contents across the table. There were a half-dozen glossy brochures, copies of maintenance records, copies of registrations and permits. He didn't know what he expected to find among the material, whose only purpose was to sell a boat. He leafed through the records, the registrations. Pointless. There were several brochures for the Tempter. He scanned the information and then pushed that group aside. Despite the woman he had encountered on Albert's boat, he wasn't convinced that Abe's predilections were confined to adult females, and who could know about his father? For sure such information wouldn't be found among brochures . . . He would have to go online, bring up those sites that disclosed the names of pedophiles. The last piece he opened was the most substantial and the least promising: the annual report of the Goto Corporation, the boat's manufacturer. He leafed through glossy color photographs of the company's boat manufacturing operations and detailed captions of the materials and processes that went into a Goto motor yacht. There were financial tables and earnings reports, messages from the director of this and predictions from the director of that. Toward the end of the report were smaller photographs depicting other branches of the corporation. They were impressive in their diversity: Pharmaceuticals, Agriculture, Restaurant Equipment, Newspaper Chains, Nursing Home Chains. On the inside cover of the brochure was a list of all Goto's holdings, with accompanying Internet addresses. Hugh scanned the list, not much surprised when he came across: *Nakamura Reality*. The next familiar name was less expected: High Meadow Mortuaries and Cemeteries USA, where Albert's father had been buried. At the end of the list in modest miniscule type was the address of the corporate headquarters: Kobe, Japan. He thought again of Gina.

The water mister came on. Hugh closed his eyes, tilted back his head and let the vapor cool his skin. Wet his eyelids. The pages of a calendar blew away like leaves, a device in an old movie. Gina had persisted with her solicitations until, until . . . He opened his eyes underwater.

He felt like a child who has been turned about a dozen times to induce dizziness. Giddy with the loss of balance, afraid but compelled to move. She stopped calling *when the boys died.*

Fetching his computer, he found a free table inside, plugged in and powered up, sitting with his back to the window. The Vista ringworm went round and round as if burrowing into a host.

Hugh typed in High Meadow's URL. The site came up. High Meadow Mortuaries and Cemeteries, the logo's graphics earth-toned, dignified and compassionate. Beneath the logo, a modest gravesite surrounded by brilliant flowers housed pull-down menus. Among the choices was one for locations. Hugh clicked to get the list, found Simi Valley, CA, and clicked again. The page that loaded was identical to the first except the logo now read High Meadow Mortuaries and Cemeteries of Simi Valley. The same large photo was used but the pull-down menus had changed. As he drew the cursor across the photo, a roll-over photo appeared revealing the entrance to High Meadow Simi Valley. The same wrought iron gates in Albert's photo opened to show an asphalt road winding through the inviting grounds. Broad fields of tall grasses, flowers and artificial brooks.

Hugh clicked on A Visual Tour of High Meadow. A dozen small photos appeared, each captioned with the name of particular sections of the cemetery: Oak Knoll, Sunrise, Little Pond . . . Clicking on the section took him to more photos of each section and further nested photos within these. He chose a section and surfed through its photos. He paused at one gravestone, whose dates surprised him: Born March 4, 1841. Died January 16, 1888. He wouldn't have supposed that the cemetery was that old, for it seemed like a modern corporate enterprise. No doubt Goto had acquired the original cemetery, expanding it exponentially. He thought he remembered reading that Forest Lawn had started that way. He considered the dates on other tombstones. That a life could be encompassed that way seemed to miss the point. Well . . . He clicked through to Little Pond. Here was a child whose life had not spanned three years. He doubled-clicked to enlarge the photo. Wantanabe, Asami, born August 27, 2006. Died June 7, 2009. In loving memory . . . He imagined the parents' sorrow, their hearts like brittle leaves. As he touched the mouse to escape, he pulled back his hand. He leaned closer to the screen, staring at the gravestone behind the child's. The name on it was *Mcpherson*. For a moment he couldn't remember if his sons had been buried: not buried of course, for there was nothing to bury. Had there been a service even? No, Setsuko would not agree to any sort of formal service. In her own way, she refused more than he did to believe they were dead. He moved the cursor over the gravestone and zoomed closer. H. Mcpherson. He slid the photo up to see the birthdate: Born: September 16, 1962. Hugh's birth date. He drew up the photo: Died July 15, 2000: the day his boys had drowned. The epitaph read: "In Loving Memory." It did not say whose memory. He right-clicked on the image, selected save target and stored the photo in his pictures folder, naming it High Meadow 1. There was a math problem that asked what was the probability of two people in a group of twenty-five—a classroom of students, let's say—being born on the same day? The math worked out that it was probable that two in thirty were born on the same day. It was counterintuitive, but the math was there. Surely there were numerous H. Mcphersons, and if there were more than thirty, many would have the same birthday; but it was not just the birthday, it was the year, the probability would drop with that. And then the same date of death as his sons. The coincidence seemed improbable, and yet, what other explanation?

Chapter 24

Hugh took Valley Circle to Box Canyon, driving the winding road at almost twice the speed limit, roaring down the grade that opened into Simi Valley.

He drove seven miles north on the 118 freeway and exited on the surface street that led to High Meadow. The mortuary and cemetery were at the end of the street, which intersected a road that extended several blocks and set the limits of the complex. The mortuary was to the left, adjacent to a parking lot, which was separated from the cemetery by a row of eucalyptus trees. The gate to the cemetery was a half block to the right. Hugh turned and drove through the gate, stopping at a booth where a guard smiled.

"Here you go," said the guard, handing him a folded map. "Are you here for a service?"

"No, I'm just . . . considering."

The guard smiled. "Take your time."

Hugh followed the one-way road that wound through the park, pulling to the roadside after passing the first section of graves. As he unfolded the map, a hearse cruised past. Fifty yards farther down the road, a number of cars were parked. The mourners were gathered around a priest reading from a Bible. Men were peeling back their jackets. Women fanning themselves with their programs. The priest looked up from his Bible. Several of the mourners followed his gaze. A dense white cumulus cloud formed the shape of an inverted mountain, which rendered the cemetery upside down, relocating the graves into the sky. A gravedigger was opening the ground with a shovel and the pitched dirt fell to the earth like dirty snow. Hugh returned to the map and located Little Pond. He drove past the mourners and continued for another quarter mile, pulling up behind a Prius. A few yards away a woman kneeled before a grave and arranged flowers. For a while the gravesites were unbothered except for the alighting birds and scampering squirrels.

He reached Little Pond and parked at the roadside. There were several hundred gravesites in the area, among them many Kobayashis, Saitous and Tanakas. The cemetery must have catered to the Japanese-American community. But the grave he sought stood out among all the Japanese surnames. As he approached, he saw that flowers had been left at H. Mcpherson's grave.

Hugh studied the stone's inscription for several minutes, but could draw nothing else from the engraving. He picked up one of the flowers and sniffed. The fragrance was gone.

"She *is* High Meadow," answered the guard when Hugh returned to the gate to inquire if Gina still worked at the cemetery.

"Where could I find her?"

"She's out showing some properties. You want me to call her?"

"No, that's all right. Where is she?"

"Oak Knoll." The guard pointed.

Following the guard's direction, Hugh walked toward the Oak Knoll section, in the center of which three people were standing. Two, apparently a husband and wife, faced him. The third was a tall, dark-haired woman in a pants suit. She gestured about her, touching the arms of the couple as she made her points. Hugh waited. The cloud mountain was dissipating, its peak rounding as if a million years had passed.

By the time Gina shook hands with the couple and turned them toward their car, the mountain in the sky had vanished.

As the couple drove off in their red Escalade, she snapped her notebook against her thigh. She turned toward Hugh as if she had known he was there all the time and walked toward him.

Gina was Asian-American, and likely Japanese-American. She was tall, though not as tall as Setsuko. Her stride reminded him of Setsuko's, like someone who could walk to the guillotine with self-possession.

"May I help you?" she asked.

"Gina?"

"Yes. And you are?"

Gina appeared no older than forty-five, which meant she couldn't have been more than twenty-five when he had first spoken with her, yet at the time he had thought her at least sixty years old. Rather than someone hawking gravesites, she looked more like an ex-ballerina. Her voice seemed feeble on the phone. Here it was strong, resonant. Her appearance was the antithesis of the telephone saleswoman.

"Pirie," he said.

"Hello, Pirie." She had a firm handshake. Her fingers were long and supple like Setsuko's.

"Are you looking for a wife?" she asked in a musical voice.

"Excuse me?"

"Are you looking for a site?"

"Oh, yes. I am . . . looking."

A loud clunk drew his glance in the direction of Little Pond. An indistinct figure drove a shovel into the earth. There was a second clunk.

"We're having problems with the backhoe. We have to do it the old-fashioned way."

"Is there another Gina here?" asked Hugh, unable to reconcile the voice.

"No."

"Perhaps fifteen or twenty years back?"

"No. I'm the only Gina that's been here. Why do you ask?"

"Many years ago you tried to sell me a site."

"I did?"

"You called many times. You were persistent."

She laughed. "I've heard less flattering descriptions."

Hugh smiled. "I imagine persistence is the most important quality of a salesperson."

"That and knowing what the customer wants, even if the customer doesn't know himself."

"I didn't recognize your voice. I recalled it much differently."

"Ah, well, I do have my little tactics." She cleared her throat. "He-hello, this is Gina from Hi-High Meadow," she said in the quavering voice that Hugh remembered.

"That's good."

"In this business it's a turn-off to sound too slick."

Hugh nodded and said, "In Little Pond, there's a grave with a headstone that says H. Mcpherson."

"Oh, then you're visiting."

"I'm Hugh Mcpherson."

She gazed at him. "Doesn't Pirie begin with a P?"

"Pirie's my middle name. I've been using it lately. My first name is Hugh."

"Ah," said Gina.

"Just a coincidence, I guess," said Hugh. "I mean about the names."

"I think we can assume that," said Gina, stretching her neck to one side as if getting out a kink.

"You called for eleven years, and then you stopped."

"Well, I guess I got my Mcpherson. I always get my man," she said, offering an innocent look that might offset her frivolity.

"You confused him with me?"

"I doubt that."

"But you stopped calling?"

"Coincidence, I suppose," said Gina.

"Could I get some information on H. Mcpherson?"

"Are you related?"

"It's possible. That's what I'm trying to find out."

"There are these great sites online—"

"I know, but I'm here now. I just want to know a couple of things."

"Like what?"

"Where he lived. What he did for a living."

"I'm quite busy. What are you trying to accomplish?" asked Gina, stretching her neck again but in the opposite direction.

"I want to fix a hole so the rain can't get in."

"And stop your mind from wandering?"

"Yes. That's it."

"*Where it will go.* This way." She turned sharply, took a step.

"Gina?"

"Yes?"

"What's your last name?"

"Goto. Gina Goto."

He followed her back to the mortuary where she had Hugh wait in the lobby while she went back to her office. Behind a solitary desk sat a small, expressionless man in a suit. On one coffee table, a half-dozen magazines were arranged in the shape of a cross. From the transverse, Hugh took a gardening magazine and leafed through it. He exchanged the gardening magazine for a consumer guide, thumbed through it and then set it back.

He walked about the lobby. There were a half-dozen closed doors, viewing rooms no doubt. He came to a door marked Display Room, tried the handle, which turned, and opened the door.

The room housed a dozen elevated caskets, arranged along a circular wall from least to most expensive—plain as a packing carton to elaborate as a king's crown. Hugh walked the circuit, noting that each had an individual tune that played while the viewer stood near the coffin. "Heaven, heaven is a place where nothing, nothing ever happens . . ." Was that really piping from a little speaker? He reached the last coffin, an ivory beauty with golden handles. He pulled up, but the casket barely budged.

"Be careful. That's $10,000."

A child stood at the entrance. A Beatles haircut and loose khaki painters' overalls rendered the child sexless. Perhaps nine or ten, the child had a lovely delicate face. He or she walked over to Hugh's side and, standing tiptoe, peered into the casket. She, for Hugh had determined it was a girl, stroked the silk lining.

"Silk. Very expensive."

"Yes."

"Do you know how silk is made?" she asked.

"I think so. But why don't you tell me," he suggested.

"They breed thousands of worms and then they mash them."

"Mash them? Are you sure?"

"Like mashed potatoes. Do you like mashed potatoes?"

"My favorite kind."

"I like the ones from the Stonefire Girl."

"Grill."

"That's what I said. They have garlic in them. Garlic is what you use to ward off vampires."

"Does it work?"

"I don't believe in vampires. There is—are certainly none here."

Hugh bared his teeth. She bared hers back.

"My name is Lily."

"Lily. What a pretty name. I'm Hugh."

"No you're not. You're yourself."

"H-u-g-h."

"Huge?"

Hugh respelled his name, but it was unnecessary. Lily smiled at his naïveté. She reminded him of Thelma, the little girl who had been misplaced in his English Learners class at the middle school. Thelma was ten years old, but her English was perfect and she was always a step ahead of his instruction.

"Do you know who my mother is?"

"Gina?" said Hugh.

"How did you know?"

"You look like her."

"I put letters in envelopes."

"I bet you're good at it."

"It's boring. Fold the paper in three, stick it in the envelope, damp the adhesive with a sponge and seal the envelope. That's it. Easy. But you try it two hundred times. What do you do?"

"I teach."

"What do you teach?"

"English."

"I speak English, Japanese and Spanish. English is the most difficult, but it's easy for me. Do you know any Japanese?"

"A little. I lived there once."

"Where?"

"Tokyo," he said, thinking the small suburb that he lived in wouldn't mean anything to her. To his surprise, she asked, "Where in Tokyo?"

"Edogawa."

"Aaargg," she growled, like a dog whose food was being taken away. "I hate Edogawa. It's boring. Nakano is much more interesting. We're going there in two weeks."

"Really?"

"We go back to Japan every summer. It's so hot. Almost worse than the valley. But nothing is worse than the valley."

"Do you have relatives in Japan?"

"Many. We have relatives in—"

Gina entered carrying a manila folder. "There you are, Lily. I looked all over for you. Your lunch is getting cold."

"I was talking to Hugh. Actually," she pointed, "I was talking to *him*, not *you*."

Gina said, "You shouldn't be in the display room without my permission."

"I heard a noise. I thought another bird had gotten in." Lily turned to Hugh. "We've had three birds get in since the New Year. Why a bird would want to be in here makes no sense. There's nothing to eat and nothing to drink. All they do is poop on the caskets. Very messy."

"Come on, Lily. Go back to the office and eat."

"Ahh, don't want to eat. It's boring."

"I wish she'd never learned that word."

"In English, boring. In Japanese, *taikutsuna*. In Spanish, *abburido*."

"If you're good, maybe we'll go see a movie, after work."

Lily grinned. "Goody. None of that G-rated stuff. I want to see the one in which the world ends."

"We'll see."

"We'll see, we'll see." Lily stomped toward the door and left.

"Bright child."

"She's a handful. Well, here's the file on Mr. Mcpherson. Death certificate from the county coroner. Contract for funeral arrangements. There's not much."

"Could I see it?"

"I can't do that, but ask me specific questions and I'll see if the answers are available."

Hugh nodded. "His occupation?"

"Mechanic."

"Car mechanic?"

"Yes, that must be."

Hugh took out a pen. He grabbed one of the spec sheets from the holder beside the casket. "Last employer?"

"Not available."

"Really."

"Sorry."

"Cause of death?"

Gina flicked an invisible speck from the glitzy casket. "Excuse me one second," she said, walking away. He watched her walk to the entrance, bend down and attend to something. She pressed a button and there was a whirring sound. She stood up. A round object about the height of a book moved back and forth across the carpet. It was a robotic vacuum cleaner.

"They work well. It will clean the entire carpet before its batteries run out. I can even turn off the lights. It works in the dark."

Hugh watched the little round robot shuttle around a casket.

"Myocardial infarction. Heart attack."

"He was young."

"It is not uncommon."

"The H. What does it stand for?"

Gina perused the papers. "No first name recorded. Just H. Mcpherson."

"Does it mention if they did an autopsy?"

"Let me check." Turning from Hugh, she pulled out the contents and leafed through them. "No, nothing mentioned. Perhaps he had a history of heart problems."

"Yes. That must be it. What about next of kin?"

"Now that poses a problem—"

The door opened and Lily entered, her mouth and chin bright red as if she'd been eating beets.

"It's doing it again," said the girl.

"Stay there, Lily," said Gina. "She gets nosebleeds all the time. It's so dry in Simi."

"Mama," moaned Lily.

Gina strode to her daughter, drawing out a large white handkerchief from her blouse and setting the manila folder inside the pine casket.

The robot vacuum cleaner buzzed about her feet. Gina kicked it away. The machine whined for a few seconds and then resumed its task.

"Let's attend to this," said the mother, leading her daughter out of the room.

Hugh waited until the door had closed. He walked to the casket and took out the folder. Had it all been done on purpose? The nosebleed a fake. The folder placed where he could browse through it. But more likely, a simple oversight. His father spoke sternly to him. *No different than stealing.* Hugh lifted the folder's edge, and then jumped as something knocked his foot. He looked down at the robot, bumping into his shoe. He waited until the thwarted machine retreated, the motor grumbling like Popeye. Hugh opened the folder and glanced at the papers, wishing he could press PrntScr and copy. He saw a name, an address. Lily was too pure to play a part. Or was there anyone too pure to play a part? He tried to memorize the information. At Coffee Bean, he would have to stare at the five-digit code for a full five seconds before he was sure of taking it back to his computer screen. Hugh felt his chest tighten as Mcpherson's might have done. No fuss here. Right into the casket. Hugh tucked the folder under his shirt and exited the display room.

On the lobby floor, Lily's blood still glistened.

Chapter 25

Hugh drove San Fernando Road past the auto salvage yards, cars stacked fifty feet high, tributes to "Ozymandias." The beast he tracked existed, though he could not yet say its shape . . .

Have you ever stolen anything? Hanna had asked.

When Hugh was eight years old, his father took his brother and him to a salvage yard, where they hoped to find a driver's side mirror for the family's Buick, hit by a watermelon on mischief night.

At the yard's entrance, big angry German shepherds stalked pens on either side of the gate, their saliva dripping down the chain link. Father and sons passed by towering pallets of radios and carburetors, a wall of hubcaps like a thousand-eyed monster, a fearsome mountain of slick black tires. Holding the broken mirror extended from his body like a flashlight, his father smoked his pipe as they walked along, but the scent of his cherry tobacco, which usually smelled of safety, was lost among the iron oxides and oil-soaked ground. Over rapid bursts of compressed air, a worker directed his father to the mirrors, where they spent an hour finding one that matched. On the way back, Hugh passed a shelf of gearshift knobs, beautiful chrome ones that ballooned his lips and nose. As his father waited in line to purchase the mirror, Hugh ran his hands over the knobs, picking them up and setting them down until he dropped one in his pocket, where it felt twice as heavy as in his hand. He waited with his brother, watching a worker dismantle a transmission, taking off a plate and exposing the oily gears inside. As Hugh stood there, a voice told him to empty his pocket.

He was an older man with a gray beard, smudged glasses and fierce eyes.

Hugh stared blankly, pretending not to understand. The man grunted, jerked his head back, reached into Hugh's pocket and yanked out Hugh's clenched hand, the ball not even half hidden. The man peeled back Hugh's fingers and took the knob. With his free hand, he smacked Hugh hard across the cheek. Hugh swung sideways from the blow, and his brother, watching, yelped. The man set the knob back on the shelf and walked away.

"Come on, baby," said the worker, wriggling the topmost gear, his fingers slicked with the green fluid, his forearm pulsing like a frog's throat.

"You okay?" asked Hugh's brother.

The heat spread from Hugh's cheek to his ear and the back of his neck, the hand's weight still upon him.

"You should tell Dad."

"Shut up," Hugh said as the worker with a grunt yanked out the gear. The worker held his hand palm up, relaxed his fingers and lifted the part toward his mouth as if he might consume it.

Metal screamed. The hard face of the employee or mere moral enforcer settled in.

As they exited the junkyard, Hugh walked on his father's right side, keeping his right cheek from his father's vision. He walked farther away than he usually did, for he did not want to brush against his father's body or to smell his father's smoke. As Hugh passed the shepherds' cages, he rapped his knuckles on the fencing, but still kept his distance.

When Takumi and Hitoshi were nine, Hugh had taken them on such an outing to find a rear light. He brought his own screwdriver and let his sons remove the part from the junked car. In the same car, he found a pair of dice and a hula doll. He handed them to his sons and told them to stuff the loot in their pockets.

The first street east of the last junkyard, Tuxford, was all informal salvage. Cannibalized cars and car parts spread across the dead lawns, guarded by listless dogs stretched out in the shade of fenders and engine blocks. The houses sat in disrepair, the lawns weedy or bare where not littered with iron, plastic and dog shit. Halfway down the block was 2409, the number he sought. Throwaway newspapers, shrunken and yellowed, were strewn across the walkway. He parked at the curb behind a beat-up Toyota pickup, its bed overflowing with gardening equipment. He shut off the engine and stepped out into the choking heat. Above the house, he saw the San Gabriel Mountains encased in a reddish brown haze.

Bent and dusty venetian blinds covered the windows. The mailbox beside the door held dozens of wilting flyers. But above the mailbox was a letter plate that said, "Mcpherson." And what if H. Mcpherson answered the door? H. Mcpherson alive, Hugh Mcpherson dead, tossed up on some distant shore, a banquet for the crabs, a nursery for the flies, and all this travail a mere dream.

He pressed the gummed-up bell. A bee buzzed. Something moved at the periphery of his vision. On the neighboring lawn, a brown pit bull with a huge tumor hanging from its belly looked at him mournfully. The price of consciousness is death, the dog whispered.

He pressed the button again.

He looked at the San Gabriels, where Hitoshi, Takumi and he had clambered over invisible rocks to fish in the swift flowing river in predawn darkness.

The door shivered.

"Who is that?" said a voice.

"Is this Mrs. Mcpherson?"

"Who are you?"

"I'm from High Meadow Cemetery."

"Where?"

"High Meadow Cemetery. It's about your son."

"My son is dead," she said.

"I'm from the cemetery where he's buried."

The door opened. A small wrinkled woman in a red jumpsuit peered up at him. "What do you want?"

"Your son is Hugh Mcpherson?"

"Harry. His name's Harry. That was his father's name."

"Ah."

"It's been twelve years since he's been gone. He wasn't an easy boy, but he never hurt anyone. Himself excepted, of course." A cat meowed at her feet, rubbing and burrowing between the red scaly ankles. The house smelled of kitty food, kitty litter and kitty piss. Deeper in the dim room several felines peered out from the underbrush. She would subscribe to *Cat Fancy*, and in the backyard there would be mounds the size of bread loaves topped with named stones. Beneath the mounds, plastic grocery bags would shroud the bone, fur and whiskers of beloved tabbies. One day a boy digging for worms would uncover the sanctified grocery bags, lay them out like dead soldiers on a battlefield and do the count.

"What's your cat's name?" asked Hugh.

"This one? Lily."

Hugh laughed. The woman tilted back her head and looked at him askance. "You think that's a funny name? I've named all my cats after flowers."

"Do you name all your flowers after cats?"

"I'm just an old woman, not a crazy one."

"There was a girl at the cemetery. Her name was Lily. I spoke with her minutes ago."

"I don't see—"

"My name is Mcpherson. H. But Hugh not Harry. I was born on the same day as your son, Harry."

She studied him. A second cat approached. Snowball white with penetrating green eyes. "I don't know what kind of scheme you have in mind. But I've told you, I'm not crazy. I have no money. I have only this house."

"Please, I'm just trying to understand why."

"You were born on the same day as my son?"

"The same day and year."

"You've had a hard life then."

"Why do you say that?"

"You look to be about fifty. Much older than Harry."

She remembered her son in his thirties. She'd forgotten that he would have aged. The dead stop aging. He was reluctant to remind her.

"He would be thirty-seven this September," she said.

"But he was born in 1962."

"1975. September 13, 1975."

"Not September 16?"

"I'd forget my son's birthday?"

"And this is the son that is buried at High Meadow?"

"Harry, yes."

"I saw the date on his tombstone."

"That was a mistake. They were supposed to change it."

Hugh took the paper out of his pocket and unfolded it. "But that's what it says on this."

"That's how it happened. The tombstone maker got the wrong information."

"And they didn't change it?"

"They were supposed to. But who was I to complain? They had him buried. It was a nice spot. Harry had no insurance, so I was glad they paid for it."

"Who paid for it? The mortuary?"

"Um, no. It wasn't the mortuary. A nice young man came to the house. He said his company was working with the cemetery. They were doing a promotion and would take care of everything. What was that company? McNamara?"

"McNamara?"

"'Oh, the drums go bang and the cymbals clang and the horns they blaze, um, away . . . a credit to old Ireland is McNamara's Band.'" She laughed. "Oh, that was a good one."

"McNamara or *Nakamura*?" asked Hugh.

"Oh, yes, that's it. Nakamura it was. Nakamura Realty."

Hugh sat in his car, engine and air-conditioning running. He could not drive yet, for his hands were trembling and his legs were like dead weight. He felt certain, but helpless. Takumi and Hitoshi didn't die that day. They were somewhere in the world. His job now was to find them. The awful thing that had been done to him would not give up its reason, its motive. His sons had been stolen, but why? This wasn't a crime of opportunity, but meticulous planning. Nakamura was the facilitator, but surely it was not running the game.

As he put the car into gear, he caught a whiff of carbon. He glanced down at the passenger seat on which he had set *Deadpan All the Way*. He lifted the book. In the bright light of Sun Valley one of the strings hanging out of the back cover shone like gold. Hugh plucked at it, but it didn't give. Smooth and shiny as copper. Did they weave wire into the fabric? Hugh tugged on the thread, which tore a path in the cover, exposing more metal. Hugh picked at the surrounding fabric, revealing a tapestry of metallic threads.

"Hello, Lily."

Lily kept her head down, bringing the mallet back a few inches, flicking her wrist, so that the mallet touched but did not hit the red ball. She took a full swing. With a crack, the ball shot across several gravesites, skirted a wall of rose bushes and then passed through a thin hoop, beyond which sat a blue ball. The second ball smacked the first, which rolled at an angle for several feet.

"Mama's mad at you," said Lily, raising her head to meet Hugh's eyes. "'He's a thief and a liar.' That's what she said." Lily set her mallet between her legs and tapped the earth. "Well, are you?"

"Yes, I suppose I am."

"You could be lying. Are you from Crete? 'Cretins always lie,' said the Cretin. That's a paradox all right. Do you play croquet?"

"I have."

"Would you like to play me? I'm getting very tired of competing with myself. If I win, I lose. If I lose, I win. It's not very satisfying. In fact, it's—" Raising her eyebrows, she waited.

"*Boring,*" said Hugh.

"How did you know?"

"How did you know I would know?"

"The little gray matter, monsieur," she said, tapping her head and smiling.

"I'm a cheat, too."

"Ha. That's a good one."

Hugh held out the folder. "I brought this back."

"Please set it down on Eli Pritchard." She pointed her mallet at the headstone with that name. They were in an older section of the cemetery behind the mortuary. As he'd gotten out of his car, the clack of the striking mallet drew his attention. "Do you know the rules?" Lily asked.

"I once played it with my sons."

"We play the six-wicket game here. Don't worry, I'll explain everything."

"I would love to play, Lily, but . . ."

She put the back of her hand to her nose.

"Are you all right? Is it another nosebleed?"

"I'm not a hemophiliac. Look."

She dropped her mallet and slapped her hand against a rose bush. Lifting her hand to him, she revealed a speck of blood on her palm.

"See."

"You told me that you visit Japan."

"If you're not going to play croquet with me, may I recite a poem?"

"Have you ever heard the name Kazuki?"

Lily cleared her throat.

> Pussycat, pussycat, where have you been?
> I've been to London to visit the Queen.
> Pussycat, pussycat, what did you do there?
> I frightened a little mouse under her chair.

To Hugh's applause, Lily curtsied.

"If you mean Kazuki, the famous novelist, certainly. He's my mother's second cousin, once removed, which is a very odd term."

Chapter 26

A FedEx package awaited Hugh in the lobby. As he walked back to the room, he tore open the envelope and extracted the newspaper.

He read the date and then opened to page three, where—if memory were to be trusted—the story took up half a page. His chest tightened as he prepared to view his sons' faces.

Instead, he saw a pickup wrapped around a California cypress.

He confirmed the date: *July 16* . . . He turned to pages four and five, six and seven. He went back to the front page, confirming that the page dates were not typos. He leafed through the entire newspaper, but found no coverage of the drowning. The family arrived at the Oceanside condo on July 14. He took the boys surfing the following morning, July 15. The boys died on July 15. The story was printed on the following day, July 16.

It took an hour to get through to the correct desk at the Oceanside Police Department.

"You're absolutely certain?" Hugh asked.

"There were four beach rescues on July 15, but no reported drownings."

"No one swept out to sea? Missing at sea?"

"No, nothing."

"Perhaps the Coast Guard has different—"

"We would have that also, sir."

Hugh turned off his phone and strode once again into that turbulent ocean seeking his sons. He was promptly swept back to shore.

The Irish bar on Sherman Way. The Irish bar with all the rules. No colors. No sleeveless shirts. No swearing. No baseball hats worn backward. No cell phone conversations. Strictly enforced. You didn't fuck with the old bartenders. They kept sawed-off shotguns behind the bar, which had never been robbed—successfully. Hugh sat and drank, staring into the tea leaf eyes of his sons. Not black holes. Not pennies. Not the ivory-framed windows of some opportunistic sea creature. The living eyes of his sons. If he had moved an inch, he would have danced a jig. But the only move he made was to slide another bill to the bartender and nod his head at his drink. To the others arranged like hogs at a trough, he was invisible. The visible invisible. The party's in my mind. Yet one white bearded Old Testament saint leaned into him and offered to take his burden. Facing the man, he reached between his thighs, drew up *Enrique the Freak* and slapped it on the bar. He halved the book and thumbed to page one thirty-seven. He placed his index finger on the highlighted text and in competition with Al Hirt's trumpet read, "He smeared the mechanical crayfish with butter." He smiled into the saint's beard.

"Poor light to read in," said the saint.

"Crayfish."

"Yeah?"

"I promised my sons crayfish."

"Like pets?"

"No, we . . . we were watching two crayfish in a tiny pool of water. My sons, Hitoshi and Takumi, wanted to catch one, but I said it was getting late." Hugh closed his eyes. " 'Your mother will be getting worried.' 'Can you eat crayfish?' Takumi asked me. 'Yes.' 'What do they taste like?' 'Crab.' 'Crayfish, yum,' Hitoshi said. I promised that in summer we would go camping at Big Bear Lake, where ten thousand crayfish lived. We would catch them and cook them." Hugh opened his eyes. "But we never did . . ."

"That's too bad."

"Like Aaron's grandfather."

"Excuse me?"

"Aaron's grandfather told him the story. My sons told Kazuki our story."

"Umm . . ."

"We'd seen the crayfish in the water that shouldn't have been there. Hitoshi and Takumi sipped from the honeysuckle . . . That moment, those moments . . . that's all there is and he stole it. He stole it and he put it right here." Hugh tapped the book.

"You're a little hard to follow."

"He stole my sons."

"Who did?"

Hugh tapped the book again, harder. "Kazuki Ono."

"Ah," said the saint, as if that made perfect sense.

"Kazuki and his daughter, my wife."

"Gotcha. A custody thing, huh?"

"In Japan they go back forever," muttered Hugh.

"They do, huh?"

"Tradition. When a couple divorces, the wife and children go back to her father's home and that's that."

"What's that?" asked the saint.

"The father never sees his children again. It's as if they don't exist."

"Sucks."

"Yeah, sucks."

"So Mr. Ono drowned them. Because let me tell you, I would have dug a tunnel. I would have parachuted down his chimney. I would have swallowed invisibility pills."

"No stopping you, man."

Hugh laughed. "But he killed me."

The saint grinned.

"You want to see my grave? I have it out in the car," said Hugh.

"Good luck, brother," said the saint, patting the lunatic on his back and turning to a new arrival.

Hugh shoved the book back under his legs and continued dream drinking.

His sons were alive and would reunite with him. There was no longer the insuperable barrier of life and death. They would be . . . twenty-three, *twenty-three!* How much would they remember? Some would be lost, of course, but there would be enough . . . the ecstatic adventures, the plunge into mystery. *The father comes back from the dead as well,* considered Hugh, gripping tightly his drink. Everything had to be carefully planned. Should he try to speak with them first by phone? Skype? Should he just hop on a plane and fly to Tokyo? Walk there on the water? Could this all be true? Was he in a delirium? Was he back in that Oceanside hospital room, staring vacantly at that newspaper?

He pushed off the stool. Steady. The Irish bar with all the rules. He walked to the juke box, pressed his hands against the warm glass. As he scanned the columns of song titles, Johnny Cash roared from the speakers.

"I hear the train a coming . . ."

Hugh tapped out the beat on the warm clear glass.

It was all real and he would have his sons back.

Hugh lifted his hand to reveal a fly walking upside down on the other side of the glass. Looking for a way out . . .

Chapter 27

Fingal's Cave /29
YUUDAI PLAYS DETECTIVE

A call to the California Department of Motor Vehicles got Yuudai nowhere. In the Stalking Age, numerous obstacles had been set up to prevent a citizen from tracking down someone through a license plate number. Yuudai suspected that even his preliminary phone call was being recorded. Before he took the step of falsely reporting a hit-and-run, he turned to Google.

CSNDRA was of course Cassandra. Demi was Cassandra.

"Cassandra California" produced 2,890,000 results.

"Cassandra's 1972 Mustang" produced 1,260,000

"Cassandra's 1972 Red Mustang" produced 105,000 results.

He closed his eyes and returned to that night. He was the one who had done most of the talking, but she had used an odd word . . . Bodacious? No. Delicious? No. Bitchin'? No. Hellacious. Hellacious. Yes.

He typed in "Cassandra's 1972 Red Mustang Hellacious California." 79 results.

Within an hour, he reduced the field to three candidates who had posted 1972 Mustangs for sale and described their cars as "hellacious fast." One Cassandra was in San Francisco. Two were in Los Angeles. That there might be dozens of 1972 Mustangs not for sale whose owners favored the word hellacious didn't dismay him, for he felt caught in a current that he neither wanted to nor could resist, and were he tossed up on some barren bank one hundred miles downstream, he would be no worse off than in his present state. He called the phone number of San Francisco's Cassandra Gissing. No, the Mustang, which had been her deceased husband's car—hellacious fast, he called it—hadn't been sold. She was retired, confined to a wheelchair and had no use for it. She offered to reduce the price by $300 if he bought the car within forty-eight hours. He thanked her and told her that he would consider.

Of the two remaining Cassandras, one was in North Hollywood, close to where Yuudai lived, and the other in Topanga Canyon. Neither listed a phone number, so he e-mailed both expressing his interest in the Mustang and asking for an appointment. The North Hollywood Cassandra responded within an hour with a phone number and address. He phoned her back, could not tell if her voice was Demi's, and so arranged to see the car. The North Hollywood Cassandra was the right age, but the wrong height—by a good six inches—and the wrong color. In ten minutes of conversation, he learned that she was a book-keeper, recently divorced—from a loud-mouthed drunken asshole—and unemployed. Yuudai agreed that the Mustang was cared for, a classic and a bargain at her price. Recognizing that she might have found a buyer, she stroked the car's hood, dabbed her eyes and offered him an iced tea. With misgiving, he promised to get back to her within a day. Unhappiness was well distributed.

When Topanga's Cassandra did not get back to him within forty-eight hours, he drove out to LA's rustic and close-knit community of artists, freethinkers and aging hippies, unfettered by even a traffic light until recent decades. Yuudai had commuted through the canyon for several years and knew well its few cafés and restaurants. The most popular was the Peace & Love Café, near the canyon's center, and always buzzing with left-of-center opinion, magical thinking and nonjudgmental gossip.

Kazuki ordered his coffee and took it to the café's deck. A few minutes before noon, it was a glorious day, the air so clean and clear as to be austere. He sat at a small table in the shade of a dollar tree. Vines threaded through a cedar lattice against which he laid his head to take in the rocky cliffs and dense green brush, a hawk circling lazily above. Dreamily, he turned from nature to observe the three people on the deck. Two were a young couple engaged in a fierce argument. The young man was shirtless and the woman wore a thin torn blouse. Head bobbing and weaving, screaming for her to be quiet, the shirtless man thrust his mouth at her face as if looking for the most paralyzing place to bite. The woman dug her fingers into the telling blue hair, bent her head almost to her knees and repeatedly asked him to leave her alone. A moment later, she jumped up, ran from the deck and strode south along the roadside. The bare-chested young man sprinted after her. Kazuki was tempted to follow them, to see how it would turn out. But the setting was now so peaceful. Not a car or motorcycle passed. The hawk circled. Quiet enveloped the deck. The only movement was when the other patron, a haggard man in worn flannel shirt, lifted his eyes to Kazuki, as if a question might be on his mind, as a question was certainly on Kazuki's mind. Would Hugh show up? He was a regular at the café, so it was not improbable. Kazuki chose to risk it. If it happened, it happened. With Gina's phone call, Kazuki suspected that Hugh would soon be seeking him out. But the prospect of the finished book had invigorated and strengthened Kazuki for the confrontation. Kazuki continued to think through the scene . . .

Yuudai would play it cool. He would drink his coffee until an opening appeared. He settled into a table on the deck and leafed through a latte-stained issue of the *Topangan Times* that had been left on a chair.

The other customer on the deck was an older man rocking on his bench, eyes closed, a cigarette clinging to his cracked lips, brittle white hairs springing from the open neck of his greasy green fatigue jacket. Yuudai took the lid off his coffee, set it on the napkin and sipped, gazing at the mountains and smelling the jasmine, occasionally returning the man's glance.

"Would you like to hear a poem?" asked the man.

"Of course," said Yuudai.

The poet glanced at Yuudai. "Uh, well . . ." The poet turned his head. "I charge a dime a poem."

"I'll take ten."

"That's all I got today."

"You won't use them up. You can say them again."

"That's right, I guess."

"I'll pay you for ten, but please just read six."

"Six, huh?" He pulled a dirty black notebook from his flannel pocket and removed the pen that had hitched a ride. He thumbed through it, notching pages.

"What you want to hear first? I got one about angels."

"No. No angels."

The poet cleared his throat. "Well, let's see . . ." He flipped through the pages. "I got one about flowers."

"What else?"

"The flower one is pretty good."

"All right. Flowers, then."

"What about the sea?"

"The sea? Sure."

The poet stood up, holding the notebook with two hands like a preacher with a Bible. He studied his words for a moment and his eyes danced around until they settled on the open page.

"The world is a pisser in many respects . . ."

Yuudai listened, applauding each time the poet looked up, which Yuudai supposed to be the end of each poem.

The poet's last poem was titled "Rock Pool," and Yuudai was surprised to find that it resonated with him.

> *A rock pool can be calm, but deep,*
> *A rock pool can be shallow and stormy.*
> *A rock pool can be cold as dry ice.*
> *A rock pool can be warm as shit.*

The poet repeated the stanza, the fourth line becoming the first line, the first line the second and so on. Using this formula he read the remaining stanzas, and then raised his glittering eyes to Yuudai's.

"I like that very much," said Yuudai.

"You got four more coming."

"Great. Hey, do you know a Cassandra?"

The poet grinned. "Damned straight. Calls my poetry hellacious, Cassy does."

Chapter 28

Fingal's Cave /30
CASSANDRA'S WARNING

Yuudai drove toward Cassandra's house, which the poet had described in detail. But the detail was not necessary, for when Yuudai came within fifty yards he saw the Mustang and the license plate.

Yuudai knocked on the door. There was no answer. He knocked again.

"Yeah, yeah, I'm coming," a woman shouted.

A half minute passed. A lock clicked, a chain rattled, a hinge squeaked. The door opened a sliver.

"You the guy who called about the Mustang?" the occupant asked as she drew back the door. Her face was bloated and splotchy, her soft green eyes rimmed with red and her dark hair now streaked with gray, but the ten years provided no disguise. Nor had the years so changed Yuudai, for her eyes went big with recognition. She slammed the door shut, but Yuudai had already stuck his foot in the jam. As he entered, she backed toward a table glowing with lit candles.

"What do you want?" she said, pulling the collar of her flannel shirt tighter.

"My sons!"

Cassandra backed toward the flames.

Yuudai dashed across the room and grabbed her shoulders. "Where are my sons?"

"I don't know hardly nothing about your sons. I was paid to get you to buy me a drink and talk."

"Did Katashi take them?"

"I don't know. I don't know."

"Where are they?"

"I told you—"

Yuudai pushed her against the table. A candle tumbled off, flickering on the floor.

"My house! You're going to burn down my house!"

"Did Katashi Ito hire you?"

"No. I don't know—"

Yuudai's hands slipped around her neck.

"Help!"

Yuudai smelled the melting wax. He kicked the table, knocking it over and spilling the remaining candles to the floor.

"Oh, my God," she rasped as his hands tightened.

"Katashi Ito?" asked Yuudai.

"Please, huh?" She coughed and her eyes brimmed with tears. "Yeah, yeah, it was the Chinese guy!"

"Japanese."

"Chinese, Japanese, whatever!"

Yuudai's hands fell. Cassandra dropped to the floor, crying with relief and snuffing out the candles.

Yuudai turned toward the door.

"You shouldn't fuck with him," said Cassandra. "I'm sorry about your sons, but you shouldn't fuck with him. You listen to me. Stay away from that boat."

Yuudai jerked around. "Boat?"

Chapter 29

Fingal's Cave/31
AN ALARMING PHONE CALL

Katashi watched the young woman draw the panties up her smooth legs. She turned her back to him. The thong settled between pink-hued cheeks. She had a small tattoo on her right shoulder, but without his glasses he was not sure if it was a flower or a face. He didn't want to see the woman clearly. He did not want to recognize her on the street. He wanted her to be no more substantial than a dream. He, himself, was not much more than a dream when the ferried women kneeled beside his bed and he touched them, pretending to paint them with his fingers, paint on a woman who had no resemblance to them, any more than to this woman who now removed the steel or marble or whatever the fuck it was at his request, though her lips were no less obdurate. She had no thought of him, this old man who paid more than was required, who offered her orange juice and goat cheese, who paused to write a note, to take a piss, to scratch a pimple on his sagging ass. Her clothes floated toward her. Shimmering. Shimmering.

"Is it a flower or a face?"

"Excuse me?"

"On your shoulder. Flower or face."

"A mole."

"Ah."

She kissed his lips, nose and ears. For an instant, he forgot whether she was leaving or arriving.

"Sayonara," she said, opening the door of the stateroom. Stepping into the passage, she stumbled, regained her balance, and called out, "Hey, how do I get back to Malibu?"

"Nigel's waiting for you on deck. He'll have a boat take you to the pier."

"Cool."

The woman gone, Katashi paced his room for ten minutes trying to remember a call he was supposed to make. The clear logic and steel-trap mental operations that had served Katashi so well in his various enterprises were starting to elude him. He was no longer sure what eight times seven or nine times six were. Not that he couldn't figure it out with a little concentration, but the answers didn't come to him instantaneously. The times tables weren't at the top of his head. Not to mention algorithms. Nor were all the words with which he once constructed pristine—what did the physicists call it? Damn, he couldn't remember!—arguments. Elephant—elegant! Elegant arguments that had penetrated his opponents' positions like armored bullets through flesh (*that* ultimate argument rarely called for). In certain circles, he remained Fuka, the shark, but would Fuka soon be toothless?

The ringtone played for thirty seconds before Katashi distinguished it from memory's melody. He almost failed to recognize the frantic female voice, but as his index finger touched the end button, the voice attached itself to a face and name that he'd sooner have forgotten.

"Slow down, slow down . . . I don't understand a word that you're saying, Cassandra."

Chapter 30

Among the gymnastic apparatus on Santa Monica Beach, three thick ropes hung from a horizontal steel bar twenty feet above the ground. As beachgoers, crimson-faced and drained of expression, trudged across the shadowy sand, Hugh gripped the rope and using only the strength of his arms ascended halfway. There he pinched the rope with his ankles to secure himself and caught his breath. Restored, Hugh continued to the top, twisting on the rope to view the rear façade of Kazuki's oceanfront hotel.

It hadn't been difficult to locate his ex-father-in-law's accommodations. A visit to the Pasadena bookstore where Hugh had heard Kazuki read weeks before, and the purchase there of several Ono novels, prompted the owner, Mr. Huddle, to share a few stories about his honored friend, and name-drop Ono's favorite restaurants, nightspots and hotels—*hotel*, for Ono stayed exclusively at the Santa Monica Olympic, on the oceanfront.

The villain's lair established, Hugh's first impulse was to visit the author unannounced and, without accusation, cold-cock him. When Ono regained consciousness, Hugh would present his indictment: twelve years ago, Ono had stolen his sons from that Oceanside Beach. Through some deception, perhaps involving Setsuko, his sons had been lured onto that waiting yacht. From there, Takumi and Hitoshi were taken to Japan, told that their mother would be joining them and given the tragic news that their father had died. In Japan, they would grow into manhood, removed from the dangerous paths their reckless and irresponsible father would have led them on.

Such a bullshit motive. At the heart of it all, Kazuki wanted his daughter and grandsons back.

Hugh balked at executing that measure for one reason: the risk that he would forever seal himself off from Hitoshi and Takumi, if not by incarceration then by alienation—for he could only guess what affection the twins might have developed for their grandfather, an affection that might trump their outrage at Kazuki's crime.

So for three days, Hugh simply had observed the facility. He spent his first hours outside the hotel entrance watching luxury vehicles discharge guests late from intercontinental flights, sleepy-eyed, confused and ill-tempered. In wondrously short time, these selfsame guests would emerge refreshed and ebullient, looking for the city's fabled sand, surf and sun. Transitioning to the lobby, Hugh read newspapers behind dark glasses and beneath the shadow of a lowered baseball cap. Feeling the eyes of hotel security on him, he removed to the hotel's lobby bar, where on a bank of high-definition televisions, he followed little green balls passing through a universe of angles, little white balls disappearing into holes in the earth and larger white balls soaring above a thousand hands reaching toward heaven. An ideal perch to watch the comings and goings of humanity. Of Takumi or Hitoshi, Hugh caught not a glimpse, but for two days in a row, Kazuki had emerged.

On both occasions, when Kazuki left the hotel it had been late afternoon. He had strolled the oceanfront to a pub along the walkway, into which he disappeared for an hour and then emerged to return to the hotel. Hoping that the outing was becoming a routine, Hugh saw this as the ideal environment in which to approach the author.

"Right on time," Hugh thought, spotting Kazuki exiting the hotel's rear entrance.

In his excitement, Hugh's grip slackened and he slipped down four feet. He regained his hold, lost it again and hit the ground hard. The jolt stunned and knocked the wind out of him, but he stayed on his feet, though he had lost sight of Kazuki. Hugh lumbered across the sand, but by the walkway caught his breath.

Laughter burst from the patio of the pub where a server dealt platters of fish and chips from her overladen arm, her body gliding effortlessly past bare muscular shoulders and outstretched legs.

Hugh shoved his hands into his pockets to stop their shaking. Kazuki had to be inside.

Crossing the patio, Hugh entered the pub through a screen door flocked with glitter flakes that smelled of fish. One hundred people or so occupied the L-shaped bar, two or three deep in hot spots. Its adjoining dining room, which held a half-dozen tables, was equally popular. Hugh edged through the crowd to the corner of the L, and stood next to a long-legged woman in a microskirt who was chatting it up with a Schwarzenegger lookalike rammed in next to her. Ordering a beer from a red-haired barmaid with huge green eyes and tattooed temples, Hugh took out his wallet and saw that the rope's friction had drawn blood to his palms. With a wad of bar napkins, he wiped himself clean, but a moment later, blood rose again. The barmaid brought him his beer, took his money, winced at his red palms.

Where was Kazuki?

Sipping his microbrew, Hugh looked around, pausing at a bookcase projecting from the wall, its shelves packed with rotting and discolored novels. On the jukebox, "I'm a

Believer" played. Carrying two immense plates of fish and chips, an agile server skirted Hugh to deliver the food to a couple arguing heatedly. It would sit there and go stone cold before the man and woman ate it.

"Penny Lane is in my ears and in my eyes . . ."

Hugh chugged his beer, ordered a second.

A high-pitched scream. In an alcove near the front of the bar, a young woman jumped up and down in front of a dart board, pointing to a flight lodged in the bull's-eye. Her other darts were all over the board. A second young woman clapped and hugged her companion. They wore bright summer dresses that clung to their bodies. They clinked their beer mugs and smiled at the joyful world.

The moment was broken when the woman arguing with her companion at the nearby table angrily shouted several obscenities. A shaft of light from the lowering sun struck her arm, setting her skin afire. A door slammed. Hugh saw Kazuki standing in front of the restroom.

Hugh gazed at his ex-father-in-law, who remained immobile. The author joined thumb to forefinger and seemed to dab an invisible canvas. Kazuki then took out a pair of glasses from the top pocket of his open-necked, white silk shirt. Fitting the glasses, he scanned the bar stiffly, like a myopic robot. Hugh lowered his head. Three brown bubbles in the bottom of his glass. Pop, pop, pop. A weight fell on his shoulder.

"Hugh."

Hugh looked up in unconvincing surprise, forced a smile and addressed his ex-father-in-law.

"How—how are you, Kazuki?"

"Oh, fine," said the author, studying him. "And yourself?"

"No complaints," said Hugh, his heart thunderous.

"I'm staying at a nearby hotel," said Kazuki. "Book tour."

"Of course," said Hugh, remembering his letter to Setsuko, which Kazuki would remember too. Already they were playing a game.

"I'm almost blind," said Kazuki. "Bear with me while my eyes adjust to the light. But if you would order for me?"

"Jack Daniel's?"

"Yes, neat. I envy your memory. The time bandits who have been plundering mine will soon have slim pickings. A melody or two. A few faces. A moonlit night in Ōsaka watching a beautiful young woman reddening her mouth."

Yes, yes, pretty shit. "Water back?"

"No, no water," said Kazuki, blinking.

Over the sliver of worn mahogany at their disposal, Hugh ordered the Jack Daniel's and another beer. While they waited for the drinks, they stared past each other, like shy strangers on a packed commuter train. A mediating third party had always separated them. Setsuko, Jack . . . The drinks arrived.

A surfing song by a band that didn't surf played on the jukebox. The harmonies held both men for a moment.

"You've been hanging around my hotel," Kazuki said. "Why didn't you just knock on my door if you wanted to see me?"

"It wasn't you I wanted to see," said Hugh.

Kazuki seemed not to have heard. He looked around, taking in the varied life like a common tourist. Spotting the bookshelf, Kazuki poked at the titles. Clucking, he drew a book out and thumped the garish cover.

"The dreaded *Vortex of Valtow!*"

Kazuki displayed the dust jacket to Hugh. "*Black Nebula* by Todd Ostermann. I read this book when I was a boy. It was one of dozens that were sent to me regularly by an American company—a book-of-the-month club, I suppose. Perhaps a two- or three-books-a-month club, for I recall many books arriving in their stiff resistant packaging." Kazuki leafed through the book as he spoke. "All were hard covers with bold, nightmarish dust jackets. I joined the club by tearing out a coupon in *Popular Mechanics* or perhaps it was *Popular Science*. The books were printed in English and each one science fiction, which I would discover was a very broad genre. They were defective books. They would come with chapters missing or reversed. Many typos. Paragraphs transposed. Some pages blank. Faint print on one page, out of register print on another. Characters' names changed from chapter to chapter. Those books had a great influence on my life and writing. I thought that was how books were supposed to be written. That in a nutshell is the secret of my style. Bad American science fiction."

Let him talk.

Kazuki continued, "Or do I just remember them that way? It seems that a publisher would go out of business if he published books like that, month after month. Unless these were printing press mistakes, defective books early in the run that publishers normally threw into the trash. Perhaps publishers realized there was a way to make money on these monstrosities by selling them at discount prices overseas, where the problems would be overlooked, especially if the readers were young boys and girls. Or perhaps the books were perfect and I have imposed my own flaws on them, which I've transposed to my own books."

Draining his glass, Hugh rocked its base on the wood. The bartender looked over.

"I'm here for Takumi and Hitoshi," said Hugh. "Are they with you?"

"No, Hugh, they are not with me."

"I'm begging you."

Kazuki's brow tightened with concern, but it was a tease, for he changed subjects. "You tried to take your own life?"

"Takumi and Hitoshi!" Hugh insisted.

"I put a knife to my belly," Kazuki said, pushing the book back into its place. "I got it in a quarter inch, spilled a fair amount of blood and then I remembered my responsibility, my daughter."

Kazuki sipped his drink.

"It was when my wife died," Kazuki said.

"Answer me," demanded Hugh, bringing his glass down hard on the bar. There was a crack, but the glass stayed intact. *Plastic.*

Jimi Hendrix's voice rose above the chatter. " 'There must be some kind of way out of here,' cried the joker to the thief . . ."

"Takumi and Hitoshi. I want to see them," said Hugh.

"If I thought that . . ." Kazuki's voice trailed off.

"Christ, man, just give me that moment."

"I want you to wait," said Kazuki.

"Wait? For what? Why the fuck should I have to wait?"

"For it to be finished."

"It? What?"

"My book."

"Your book? Fuck your book. My sons, Kazuki. I want my sons."

"You should have thought—" Kazuki cut himself off.

"I'm rotting in a Simi Valley graveyard. A little white fabrication, right?"

"A little white fiction."

Hugh slapped him lightly, but Kazuki's head jerked sideways as if from a boxer's leaden blow. Hugh's arm remained suspended, his open hand quivering. People had seen. People were closing in.

"You okay?" someone asked the old man.

"We were playing," responded Kazuki.

"My sons!" said Hugh.

Kazuki turned and walked toward the exit. Before Hugh could take a step, someone grabbed Hugh's arm, and then another.

"Motherfucker," Hugh screamed. But he was held, and it was for his own good and was kind of the strangers.

At the exit, Kazuki turned to mouth one two-syllable word to Hugh.

Patience.

Chapter 31

Fingal's Cave/32
YUUDAI BOARDS THE YACHT

Yuudai glanced at the Saab's digital clock. Almost one A.M.

He removed the stand-up paddleboard from the roof rack and leaned it against the car. Opening the trunk, he removed his shoes, shirt and pants, revealing his three-quarter length wet suit. He set his clothing neatly into the plastic tub in which he kept miscellany, including the sheathed knife. Slipping the knife out of the sheath and back in, satisfied it would be secure, he strapped the sheath to his right ankle. He next removed the paddle and quietly shut the trunk.

Balancing the stand-up-paddleboard on his head, he walked past the jungle gym and rings, the climbing ropes and parallel bars, across the bicycle path and shadowy sand, over the clumps of kelp and decaying sharks. He was little interested in the muttering loners and entangled lovers.

The yacht, as on previous nights, was moored two miles from shore, outlined by its running lights.

Yuudai strode waist deep into the water and slipped the SUP off his head. He walked the board through a few small waves, set his paddle on top and climbed aboard. A fog was creeping in, but Yuudai welcomed it.

Though paddling leisurely—nothing was to be rushed—and calmed by the gentle rise and fall of the sea, he was soon midway between the shore and the yacht.

But as he drew closer, his heart raced.

Now Yuudai thrust his paddle deeper into the blank ocean. If he could, he would have jammed the paddle to the ocean floor itself so that he could give one mighty push, propel the board from the sea and onto the very deck of the yacht.

"Slow down," he whispered to himself. "Take it easy. Don't let the sound of your own wheels . . ." He laughed and continued to sing as he paddled. The fog rolled in ever more rapidly.

Fifty yards from the vessel, Yuudai stopped paddling. As if a child gazing up from the base of a Christmas tree, he took in the configuration of lights, settling on the string that ran from the ship's bow and vanished into the fog-swept water.

Paddling noiselessly to the anchor chain, Yuudai lay down and unrolled the board's tether, tying it first to the paddle and then lashing it to one of the anchor chain's fat links. Getting up on his knees, Yuudai grasped the chain and slowly hauled himself to the bow, the chain's groan at his shifting weight no louder than what would be produced by the wash of a small passing boat. In less than two minutes, Yuudai was grabbing the bow rail and sliding under the polished steel to rest on the cool deck.

As he waited for his energy to return, he followed the approach of a sizeable wave. The enormous yacht took the impact dismissively, barely a quiver. Larger than any creature in the sea, a prehistoric beast of unimaginable size and power, a T. rex, a sauropod, a—

"Yuudai?" whispered his father on his death day.

"Yes, Dad?"

"The mother's hiding these little plastic dinosaurs on the café's patio."

"Stop, Dad," said Yuudai. "It means nothing."

"No, Yuudai. I saw them," said Herb, lifting his head from the pillow. "From the airplane. I saw them all that way. On the ground. The mother and daughter were there and they were playing and they were so joyful. It should have gone on forever. But then there was light and then they were gone . . ." His father's head fell back. Herb touched Yuudai's hand and whispered, "Mama hides the last toy, and yells, 'Iidesuyo.' Right? 'Iidesuyo!' The little girl jumps up, laughs . . ."

Chapter 32

It was eleven P.M. when Hugh stopped for the light on Pacific Coast Highway. On the radio the singer declared, "It's the edge of the world/And all of western civilization . . ." A line of midnight cyclists, glowing like bioluminescent jellyfish, streamed silently out of the canyon and turned with choreographed precision north on the highway, vanishing into the slipstream. Hugh glanced toward the Pacific, where six thousand miles away his sons might be sitting down to a lunch of sukiyaki or sashimi—or Big Macs for all he knew—and, too, they could be eating the same ten miles distant.

The car behind him honked. Hugh accelerated onto Topanga. Continuing to scold him, the car veered in front of oncoming traffic to rip past.

Tomorrow, despite the warning, Hugh would continue his surveillance. If he failed to find his sons in California, he would fly to Tokyo. He wouldn't leave Japan without finding Takumi and Hitoshi.

As he climbed the dirt road, he smelled the residues of the fire. His landlord had left a message on Hugh's cell phone. The insurance company had completed its inspection and would cover the damages. Preliminary repairs had been made to the house, and it was all right for Hugh to move back in.

Pulling up to his home, Hugh hoped that the car's headlights would find Hanna sitting in his backyard. He needed someone to lie with and listen to his story. He needed someone to hold and to wake up with in the night. Some-one to reassure him of his own existence.

He needed proof . . . of everything.

Under the hard white beams, the lounge chairs were empty and the scrawny blades of glass were still.

He took a sleeping pill, poured a glass of wine, downed another sleeping pill, and sat in bed reading *Barnaby Rudge*. But Dickens drifted . . . Costumed as a ballerina, Setsuko came to him, danced across his bed.

"I would have died with you," said Hugh.

Setsuko spun. "No jellybeans, no licorice, no cake."

Barnaby Rudge slipped down his chest.

Hitoshi and Takumi hung from Setsuko's elongated nip-ples, swaying gently as she rose from her bed . . .

"Mr. Maa-aac."

Hugh leaned over another woman, sliding his penis into her as Setsuko walked toward an open window through which wispy clouds pinwheeled across a deep blue sky. Peeking over Setsuko's shoulders Hitoshi and Takumi smiled and waved. On the horizon of the dream, a finger drained of blood pecked on a beating heart. Setsuko stepped through the open window. Hugh withdrew from the woman, running toward Setsuko. A skateboard screeched—

"Mr. Mac, wake up."

Tender down his cheek.

Light squeezing under his eyelids.

"What is?"

A soft quieting finger at his lips.

"Fuck, man, wake up. It's almost noon."

Hugh jerked up his head. The bits and pieces of dreams within dreams whirled around like food in the teeth of a garbage disposal. The pieces screeched as the steel teeth chewed them up to nothingness.

At the side of his bed, backlit through his window by blaz-ing sun, Anna posed with hand on hip, smiling sweetly and offering up her solemn brown eyes. Behind Anna stood Aaron.

"Sorry to disturb you," said Anna.

"How the hell—"

"You left your door open, man," said Aaron. "Smells like a campfire in here."

"Jesus Christ, you just walked in?"

"You live in the wilderness, Mr. Mcpherson. Walking up here, we saw a deer *and* a coyote."

"How did you find my house?"

"The plumber," Aaron replied.

Hugh pulled the sheet to his waist. "Why are you here?"

"You gave my picture to the cops," said Anna.

"Gave? They found your photo in my car when some asshole tried to burn down my house. Was that asshole you, Aaron?"

"Come on, chill," said Aaron.

"Chill?" Hugh jumped up, grabbed Aaron's shirt and yanked him close. For this alone he could be jailed. "Your sheet," said Anna, pointing to the floor.

Hugh shoved Aaron aside, recovered his sheet and dropped back on the bed.

"Man, that hurt," said Aaron, rubbing his neck. "What the fuck am I gonna torch your house for?"

"The police have been calling my house nonstop," said Anna.

"And?"

"I never answer, and when they come by, I hide. We can get in a lot of trouble."

"Yes," agreed Hugh. "They might take away your smartphone and laser printer."

"Ha, ha."

"How did your photo get in my car?"

"I don't know. Maybe it fell out of my bag," replied Anna.

"Fuck that photo," said Aaron. "Where's my story?"

"Your what?" Hugh asked, but he knew.

"Jesus Christ, you don't remember? I asked you for it. You were going to get it to me," said Aaron.

"Burned in the fire," said Hugh, gesturing.

"My grandpa's not going to believe that," said Aaron. "If it gets out what my grandfather did—I can't go home without it."

"I read it to Period Six," said Hugh.

"No fucking way!" said Aaron.

"I told you that the story was good. I wanted to let others hear it. I know you were embarrassed to have it read in front of our class."

"Embarrassed? You still don't get it. That shit was real."

"I do get it. I get it more than you can know. I'm sorry," said Hugh.

"I want the story back. Where is it? The school?"

"*Miseal,*" said Hugh, remembering.

"Who? What?"

"Miseal," repeated Hugh.

"Miseal Gonzalez?" asked Anna.

"Yes," said Hugh.

"Fuck you saying?" asked Aaron. "*Miseal Gonzalez?* Gonzalez is North Valley Locos. That fucking gang got ties all over Mexico. For sure they heard about my grandfather killing the boss's son. There's a price on grandpa's head, maestro."

"I gave Miseal the story."

"You *gave* him my story?"

"He was—excited about it. He asked for a copy, but I was on my way to a meeting. I gave him the original."

"*Gilipollas!*" said Aaron.

"He said he'd get it back to you."

But Aaron had already bolted for the door, Anna at his heels. "You were wrong, Mr. Mac," said Anna. "You told a story that wasn't yours to tell. That was a bad, bad thing to do." Hugh stood in his doorway, watching the indignant children disappear down the dark dirt road.

A gentle wind carried the Grateful Dead . . .

From the direction of the rock pool a white fluttering form slipped out of the bushes. Dressed in a wedding gown, Hanna bustled toward him, stumbling in the vintage costume.

Had he entered a theater with a revolving stage? Would it turn again to offer him a magician preparing to make an elephant vanish?

"God, what a mess," Hanna said, slapping at the burrs and leaves that had caught in the gossamer fabric. She grinned at Hugh. "Surprised, huh?"

"*Stunned.*"

"You want me to go away?"

"How did you . . . ?"

She looked over her shoulder, smoothed her dress. "There was a party." She pointed. "Just over the hill. Lasted all night—still going, I guess. I walked here on the path. Saw your car. You had visitors, huh?"

"They were students."

"Night school, huh?"

Hugh tightened his lips, but the laugh burst through.

"The kids—are they coming back?" asked Hanna.

"My students? No, I don't think so."

She tugged at the dress. "Does this look stupid? Like I just got married or something?"

"No. It's pretty."

"Goodwill," said Hanna. "It smells like the sixties. Come here. Smell." She took his arm and drew him closer. He breathed in no era but a woman's skin.

"Invite me inside, okay?" said Hanna.

In his living room, Hugh pulled off Hanna's wedding dress. His hands worked down her back and hips and he remembered to kiss her. His hand between her legs, his fingers soon swam in her liquid heat. He was inside her. No one spoke, and in the darkness, for a time, Hugh lost all yearnings but one. They slept for a while.

Later, Hanna lit a kettle as Hugh sat in his underwear and wondered. "*Karera wa hontoni ikite irudarouka.*"

"What?" asked Hanna as the kettle whistled.

"It's Japanese."

"You speak Japanese?"

"A little."

Hanna poured the boiling water into the two cups. She had brought the tea with her. Not a box, but six teabags, which she spread out over the kitchen table. It was rainbow tea, which she drank when coming down from cocaine.

"You were doing cocaine at the party?"

"No. But if I had, this is what I'd be taking." She squeezed Hugh's teabag with a spoon and then her own. She cupped her hands around the glass and blew on the tea. "I came down here last night before the party, but you weren't here. I was going to wait in the backyard, but it gets cold."

"I got back around midnight. When I came home, I hoped you were here."

"Did you? That's sweet."

He took her hand, caressed it. To give it all up. Almost as alluring as death. But he had to be moving.

"You sure are a restless sleeper," said Hanna.

"Bad dreams."

"Me too. If it wasn't for bad dreams, I wouldn't dream at all."

"Those are lyrics from an old blues song."

"That so? I never heard it."

"The lyrics are different but it's the same idea. If it wasn't for bad luck, I wouldn't have no luck at all."

"I like that. I'll have to download it," said Hanna, sipping her tea. "It's almost like I wrote a song . . . So, how did the fire start?"

"Kyle, I think."

Hanna licked her lip stud thoughtfully. "Yeah, that's Kyle."

Hanna lifted her legs and draped them over Hugh's knee. She wore one of his old shirts. Her skin calmed him. The feeling was too nice to disrupt. He sipped his tea and stroked her ankle, letting his fingers trail across her foot, blunt with sparkly toenails, little diamonds in the shell. "He's been following me," said Hanna. "Over hill and dale."

"*Gilipollas*," muttered Hugh.

"I don't know how I got mixed up with that loser in the first place. I guess it was because I started to lose my looks."

"You're a beautiful young woman."

"I'm almost twenty-eight. And that is almost thirty. I was pretty once, but that's long gone. I remember my skin was so tight and smooth, the way an angel fish's skin would feel if you could pet it without killing it." She mussed up her blonde, green-streaked hair.

"I have children almost your age."

"Knock me out. You're married?"

"I was."

"What happened?" she asked.

Hugh sipped the tea. He remembered Setsuko in this light. Frugal with her emotions at all times, in the morning her face expressed no more than an archaic statue's restraint.

"Did you love each other?" asked Hanna against his silence.

"I thought so, but it may have been an illusion. My illusion."

"Sounds like sour grapes to me."

"What are you doing, Hanna?"

"I'm cold."

Hugh lifted her foot from his thigh.

"Don't you like sex? An hour ago—"

"It's not a question of liking."

"It has to be like love?"

"I've got something to do."

"Maybe I'll just rape you."

"Hanna—"

"It's Joanna."

"Not Hanna?"

"Sometimes I just want it. Does that sound slutty? Stick out your tongue."

"No."

"If you stick out your tongue and pretend you're sprinkling salt on it, it will taste like salt."

"Oh, yeah?"

"Try it."

"I don't feel like it. I have high blood pressure. Salt's no good for me."

"It's imaginary salt, silly."

"What's so—all right. If it makes you happy."

He stuck out his tongue, held an imaginary salt shaker in his hand and sprinkled the salt on his tongue, knowing even as he did it the joke. Hanna buried her face in her hands.

"You get it?"

"Yes. I get it."

"You don't think it's funny?"

"I don't know."

"You're really a poop. Okay, tell me about your sons."

"What sons?"

"You said you had sons."

"I said I had children."

"Children then."

"Why did you say sons?"

"It's fifty-fifty, isn't it? Besides, you look like a man who would have sons."

Hanna too? *Fucking Hanna too.*

"Maybe you should go."

"Did I say something?"

"You know Kazuki."

"Who?"

"Kazuki Ono. You read his book. On the beach."

"Oh. Oh, no. Why should I know him?"

"You're lying, Hanna. Please get your dress and leave. Tell Kazuki he can't game me anymore."

He took her arm, ignored her pleas and led her outside.

Ten minutes later, he had dressed and powered up his cell phone to call the airlines when he heard Hanna's scream.

Chapter 33

Fingal's Cave /33
YUUDAI LEARNS THE TRUTH

Katashi opened his eyes, for he was the world's lightest sleeper. To ensure his unbroken rest, Katashi ordered the yacht's crew while at anchor to remain in their quarters from midnight until dawn, unless an emergency should arise. The crew member responsible for the disturbance outside Katashi's door would be summarily dismissed.

Rolling out of bed, Katashi checked the hour and scowled. Grumbling, he drew on a robe and walked to the door only to have it fly open in his face.

"I've come for my sons," said Yuudai.

"How did you get on my boat?"

"Thief! Liar!"

Katashi smiled, scratched his shoulder. Yuudai grabbed Katashi's robe, yanked him forward and pressed his knife to the man's throat. "Either I see my sons or your head comes off. Got it?"

"Yes, yes," said Katashi, "I understand."

His ex-father-in-law pushed away. The lines on his forehead deepened as he sat back on the bed. "Come here," Katashi said, patting the bed.

"I'll stand," said Yuudai.

As Katashi laid out his case, Yuudai scraped the knife against his own bare leg as if sharpening the blade on a whetstone.

"You went voluntarily to Cassandra's car. She didn't drag you there. She didn't take you at gunpoint."

"No, not at gunpoint," said Yuudai.

"She never struck me as being that attractive," said Katashi. "But I thought that would have been unfair. We all have a point where we can't resist."

"It seemed like—" Yuudai stopped. He looked down to see that his wet trunks were spreading a dark circle across the floor. He shifted, slapped the knife against his cheek as if in reprimand.

"You went to her car while your boys were back at camp alone."

Yuudai remembered how the night was warm and the stars brilliant. How far away Sumiko seemed, as if she were not in this world and all that attached to her could be set aside. Demi (for that was the name the woman gave) leaned into him, offering her breast beneath the flannel. How real it seemed and how like a dream Sumiko seemed.

"Yes," admitted Yuudai, "I walked the woman to her car."

"You left the food for your children at the bar."

"Yes . . ."

"Cooling on the bar while you swelled with heat."

"I didn't think . . . I had no intention . . . I wouldn't . . ."

Katashi continued. "Though the night was warm, the Mustang's windows were closed. When you got into the passenger seat, the smell of the marijuana filled your nose like a jungle essence. Cassandra lit up a joint and passed it to you. Next came the bottle of cheap burgundy. The goods traveled back and forth. You laughed at nothing, laughed at her stupid jokes, laughed at her suggestions. She had a cabin, she said, not far away. It had two bedrooms and a wonderful view. She liked you so much. She liked your strange name and your smell and your muscles and your eyes and the hardness of your leg as she contorted in the seat to put her legs over yours. 'Stay with me,' she said. 'I'll show you the wonders of the wilderness. I'll show you pure—'

" 'My sons are waiting for me,' you said."

" 'So, we'll get them,' said Cassandra. 'It will be much better at my place than that campsite. It's a real cabin with logs and a fireplace and outside a white owl lives in a cave. Deer are everywhere and red foxes—and sometimes a bear wanders by.' "

" 'I'm married,' " Yuudai muttered, echoing his faint resistance of ten years ago.

" 'But your wife isn't here. If you can't be with the one you love . . .' "

"She came over me then, crawled onto me in the passenger seat," said Yuudai.

"You didn't jump out?" asked Katashi.

"She unbuckled my belt . . ."

"You would tell your sons that it was an old friend you ran into. The boys would take the second bedroom. You would pretend to sleep on her couch, and then later after your sons had gone to sleep . . ."

"It didn't happen."

"But you—"

"She took my hand, put it down her jeans, put it into her . . ."

"It was always *them*, wasn't it, Yuudai?"

"It didn't seem . . ."

"No, it never seems."

"It was like a dream."

"Oh, always like a dream. As easy as a dream."

Katashi rose from the bed. "Do you think it was a dream for my daughter to hear that? To give me permission, even then, when I had proven your numerous infidelities?"

"Was Sumiko there?"

"Yes, Yuudai. She was there. The boys would not have gone without her."

"You took my sons to Japan?" Yuudai asked.

"Yes, and your father would have approved."

"What did—"

"You had been in a car accident. You'd had too many drinks at the bar. Their mother had to stay with you. The boys went back to Japan to stay with their grandfather until you recovered."

"But I never recovered."

"No, sadly. You died."

"I died . . ."

"They took it hard," said Katashi.

"I want to see my sons," said Yuudai.

"I know," said Katashi, scratching his cheek. He looked down at the floor, the puddle. Katashi's eyes welled.

"What is it?" asked Yuudai.

Then Katashi gave him the piece that would complete the puzzle and dissect Yuudai.

Chapter 34

Sitting on the bank of the rock pool, her dress sopping, Hanna stared into the clouded water and murmured, "Fucking shit . . ."

The stage had turned again.

"What's the matter?" asked Hugh.

Hanna rubbed her palms against her dark wet pant legs.

"I couldn't lift him."

"Lift who?"

She pointed to the water, but the sediment, perhaps stirred by Hanna's immersion, revealed nothing.

Hugh slid from the embankment into the water. Mud squished up through his toes. The water reaching his thighs, he took baby steps toward the center. He had not advanced two yards when his foot struck something resistant. He halted then, breathed in the familiar and comforting scents of a Topanga morning, the laurel sumac and jasmine, the black sage and buckwheat. He lowered himself until he crouched beneath the surface. He touched the timber, felt its contours and couldn't pretend it wasn't human. Before he remembered his own stale breath, he had his arms around the torso and was lifting his burden to the surface.

Hanna said nothing as Hugh dragged the body from the water, hoisted it on his shoulder and climbed the embankment. He set the body down slowly, gently. There was no rush. Kyle's face was gray, his eyes staring blankly. On his forehead was a dark indentation.

"I couldn't lift him," said Hanna. "I tried, really I tried."

"When? How—"

"I just saw him there at the bottom of the water."

"Was he at the party?"

"No, but I told you. He was following me."

"He may have just fallen. Hit his head on the stone. Was he on something?"

"Oh, sure, something. Bath salts, maybe. Drinking too, I suppose." She glanced at Kyle. "He stayed on the bottom. The sonofabitch stayed on the bottom. He was always going on about his muscle density. See what it got you?" She twitched, rubbed her thumb across the black lip stud. "They're gonna blame it on me, huh?"

"In the dark, Kyle slipped, hit his head on a rock and drowned," said Hugh. "Nobody's fault. Just bad luck."

"He's dead like that."

"Yes, like that."

"Kyle, you're an asshole," said Hanna, but she leaned sideways and touched his cheek. "Not gonna sell any newspapers to the Chinese now."

"I'll call the police, explain what happened."

"They won't believe you—me."

"It was an accident, that's all."

"Why couldn't he just leave me alone?" moaned Hanna.

"You can stay in my house until the police arrive."

"You're leaving?" asked Hanna.

"For a while . . ."

Hanna reached into the rock pool, scooped up a handful of water and splashed it on her face. Hugh stared into the pool. The sediment was settling, the water clarifying. A crayfish scuttled across the bottom and disappeared under a rock.

As Hugh waited for the crayfish to reappear, a red glow spread across the surface of the pool. Blood, Hugh wondered, glancing at Hanna, whose eyes had turned toward the house. An engine revved, and then died.

What else? What fucking else?

"Did you call them?" asked Hugh.

Hanna shook her head.

"Wait here," said Hugh.

The patrol car had parked behind the Volvo. The red light continued to flash as two officers exited the car. It was Escher and the other officer who had been there the night of the fire.

"Mr. Mcpherson?"

"Yes?" said Hugh, reaching the end of the path.

"I have a warrant for your arrest."

Hugh came to a dead stop. The sequence of events was wrong. They could not have a warrant if they hadn't discovered a crime. He finally managed, "My arrest?"

The two officers looked beyond Hugh. He followed their glance to Hanna. Rising to her waist like a Polynesian skirt, the brush hid Kyle's body.

"Excuse me, miss. Would you come here," Escher called out.

Hanna walked slowly up the path. A hesitant bride. Hugh met her eyes, uncertain of what he was warning. She stopped alongside Hugh. The cops looked her over.

"What's your name?" asked Escher.

"Hanna. Hanna Baker."

"You appear to be at least twenty-five years old."

"I'm twenty-eight," said Hanna. "I'll be thirty in November."

The cops exchanged looks. Escher shrugged.

"You know Mr. Mcpherson?"

"Sure," she said, almost brightly.

"What's your relationship?" asked the other officer, his hand on his holster.

Hanna shrugged. "He's my friend."

"You've slept together," said the officer.

Hanna looked at Hugh, who nodded.

"Maybe a little," said Hanna. "I mean, yes. There's nothing wrong with that, is there? Sleeping together isn't against the law."

"Not completely," said Escher's partner.

"You said you have a warrant. For what?" asked Hugh.

Escher ignored him. He took Hanna's wrist as if taking her pulse. "Do you know someone named Anna Mendez?"

"Nope," answered Hanna.

"You never saw Mr. Mcpherson with Anna Mendez?"

"I don't know her, so I wouldn't know. I mean, if I saw him with her."

"Anna is fifteen years old."

"Well, Mr. Mcpherson teaches."

"Yes, he does," agreed Escher. "But we're talking outside of school. Have you ever seen Mr. Mcpherson with girls who appeared younger than eighteen?"

"Is that illegal?" asked Hanna.

"Depends," said Wiseass.

"Would you please tell me what the warrant is for?" asked Hugh.

"You're being charged with the sexual exploitation of a minor."

"I gave a couple of students a ride. Jesus Christ, that's all—"

"Save it, Mr. Mcpherson."

The earth sunk, shifted.

Hugh was hardly aware of his arms being pulled behind him. The smooth cool metal and the soft jarring click.

They gave him one minute to say his good-byes to Hanna. He kissed her on the cheek and whispered for her to do nothing. Wait in the house. If she needed something— the trunk in the closet. Cash.

As they settled him in the backseat of the patrol car, Escher took pity on Hugh and informed him that they'd located Anna Mendez that morning. When asked about the photo, she said that her teacher, Mr. Mcpherson, had taken it.

At the station, Escher read him Miranda and allowed him to call his attorney.

Chapter 35

Fingal's Cave /34
THE ARROW

"... For their fifteenth birthday," said Katashi, "I presented Brent and James with mountain bikes and took them and my daughter on a holiday to a cousin's farm.

"For a day or two they were happy enough riding the bikes through fields and over hills, but on the third day, while exploring my cousin's barn, they found a store of sports equipment, including sets of bows and arrows. Brent sorted through the gear.

" 'We should leave it alone,' said James. 'Mom wouldn't—'

" 'Stop worrying,' said Brent. 'Pretend Dad is here.'

"A quarter mile from the house in an open field, they set down their bikes, shouldered their quivers and set their bows. Brent and James emptied their cases, but for one last arrow in Brent's: a hunting arrow. High above, a seagull floated."

" 'Bet I can hit it,' said Brent.

" 'No way.'

"Brent withdrew the arrow and gazed at the razor-sharp, blue-steel tip.

" 'Let's retrieve the arrows,' said James, darting away.

"Brent set the hunting arrow, drew the cord and aimed," said Katashi, miming the action of his grandson.

" 'Now,' Brent whispered, sliding his fingers from the bowstring. He watched the arrow climb. Closer. Closer. There! But no, the arrow passed before the bird, reached its apogee, turned, floated for an instant, and then gathered speed. The arrow would strike the ground at 150 mph.

" 'Did you see that?' asked Brent, glancing toward his brother, who had vanished. Brent's heart leaped as he saw James one hundred feet away, beneath the very spot where the hunting arrow would fall.

" 'James!' he screamed, and it was to that fearful cry that their mother, who had come out of the house to summon the boys to breakfast, responded.

"Brent dropped his bow and ran toward James, who plucked his arrows like a child picking dandelions.

" 'Get out of there!' screamed Brent. 'Arrow!'

"But James merely lifted his head to look toward his brother. Nor could he have seen the now-invisible arrow, racing through unavailable time.

" 'James, cover!' Brent shouted. The sound was hardly more than a handclap. Protruding from James's neck, the shaft was still vibrating as Brent took his brother's weight, and pulled the arrow from his brother's throat, which uncapped the artery. Brent screamed, as did Sumiko who ran toward them. Holding the arrow and drenched in his brother's blood, Brent looked up at his approaching mother and then plunged the shaft into his own heart.

"Screaming for help, Sumiko fell to her knees beside her dead and dying sons. She cradled their heads in her lap, tried to breathe life back into James, listened to Brent confess what had happened. She pressed her hands to their wounds, but with all her strength and all her great will, she could not save them. Unless—"

Katashi covered his mouth, breathed into his hand. He bent his head. His hand floated up as if weightless.

"When I came out, I found my grandsons alive and my daughter dead, an arrow through her heart. James and Brent were unwounded but swore to what had happened.

" 'She vanished, Grandfather. And then I saw above me the gull circling. There was the sound of an arrow flying and then the scream of the gull, the arrow in its breast. It fell, spun, but never landed. And then beside us was our mother with an arrow in her heart, and James and I unwounded.' "

Katashi put his fingers to his lips, tore out a smile. "Can one turn back time? Can one turn herself into another thing? Or was this an elaborate lie my grandsons had come up with to explain a terrible deed or mistake." The smile flickered, went out. "I only knew that my daughter was dead." Yuudai drove his hand through the stupid red locks, still wet from the sea. He had wanted to crush Katashi, but Yuudai was the one squeezed of life.

Katashi glanced down at the puddle, which appeared to be spreading across the floor and gaining depth. It's coming for me, he thought, the water wants me. Wants me back.

Katashi put his hand on Yuudai's, uncurled his fingers from the knife's handle. Katashi held the blade's hilt in two hands, centered the blade over his own midsection.

Someone knocked on the door. Yuudai turned.

"Dad?" asked a soft voice through the wood.

Fingal's Cave/Epilogue

The Italian historian Carlo Ginzburg hypothesized that narrative is rooted in hunting societies, derived from the hunter reading the clues of his invisible prey: scat, spittle, trails, fur, odors, entangled feathers, broken twigs. In deep forests or vast prairies, the hunter must instantaneously recognize and decipher from the track such subtleties as the trail's age, the animal's gender and even its emotional state. The hunter had to assemble the whole from the part, a complex and demanding process that the historian found traceable to "the narrative axis of metonymy." The hunter told a story based on the all-but-invisible signs, a sequence of causes and effects that was nothing less than a plot. In a nutshell, Ginzburg argued that the hunter's story told over the millenniums led to the invention of writing, which generated the myriad forms of the reading of shit, blood, piss, pus, guts, fur, feather and stink. From piss to Proust, but never escaping that old tale: No mystery, no narrative.

Chapter 36

Andy Benedict, Hugh's lawyer, took off his glasses, set them on the plastic table and dug his fingertips into the outer corners of his eyelids.

"Aaron Diaz," said Benedict.

"Yes," said Hugh.

"The grandfather is on the father's side? Not maternal?"

"I'm . . . not sure."

"We'll start out with Diaz." Benedict slipped on his glasses, took up his pen and made a few more notes.

"I didn't take the photo."

"Of course. Bad timing, that's all."

"I've got to get out of here," said Hugh.

"You understand that this," Benedict gestured, "is not a misdemeanor."

Hugh met Benedict's gaze. Hugh had been incarcerated for twenty-four hours, not a moment of which had he slept. He couldn't think clearly about the crime he was charged with, and he could not think at all about the implications of a dead body resting one hundred yards from his home. He wanted to blurt that out to Benedict too. But it would be too much. Too much of a shitstorm.

"You said you'd check on bail?" asked Hugh.

"Right now it's at a half million. I'll try to get it down." Benedict closed his notebook. "Never give a student a ride, right?"

Takumi and Hitoshi meant nothing to the attorney. Hugh was in the here and now. *Anna's photo.* Benedict shook Hugh's hand and told him not to worry.

Hugh worried.

Chapter 37

Kazuki couldn't drive slowly enough to neutralize the ruts. Even at ten miles per hour, the little rental car bounced unmercifully, setting his stomach on edge and loosening his bowels. On the passenger seat, the white box too was jittery, its cover popping up every two seconds to give the pages a peek at their destination.

With each completed novel, Kazuki experienced a day or two of inertia, but this time he felt different, as if every good system in him had gone bad and every bad had grown worse. Eyes, ears, kidneys, lungs, circulation—shot. "Small, old, empty man," he whispered, hearing his bones creak, his blood trickle, his heart hiss.

Beyond the hills, the sea was a blue tongue, licking itself clean.

Were I the sea . . .

Kazuki was relieved to see Hugh's cottage and car.

He parked behind the Volvo and waited a moment for his stomach to settle. It was only ten A.M., but the sun had already seeped into the hills and everything seemed to radiate warmth, from the blades of grass to the rocky outcroppings.

It was not an uncomfortable heat, like being in one's mother's kitchen on a winter day. How far away those days seemed!

Kazuki was confident that the charges against Hugh were false though he could not fathom how the circumstances unfolded. Not quite true. The world could throw nothing his way that Kazuki could not frame, but he didn't have the energy to imagine it. He was truly, as the English said, fagged out. Kazuki gazed jealously at the stands of scrub oak and eucalyptus, without hope but uncompromised.

The young woman was no doubt in the house, watching daytime talk and medicating herself. Kazuki walked up the path to the front door, but hesitated. The house smelled of carbons, an uneasy scent, hinting at the end. He held the white box in one hand, knocked with the other.

No response. He knocked again. Soft movements and a curtain drew back a centimeter.

"We don't want any," said a woman's voice.

"I'm a friend of Hugh's," said Kazuki.

"He's not here."

"I know."

"Then why are you looking for him?"

Kazuki held up the box.

"What's that?"

"Perhaps you could open the door?"

"Who are you?"

"I'm Hugh's ex-father-in-law. Kazuki Ono."

The eye stayed at the curtain a moment longer. Kazuki heard her footsteps. The latch clicked and the door opened.

He had seen her before, down at the P&L, in fact had let her play a small part in *Fingal's Cave*. It wasn't much more that a physical description. He did not bring the combative boyfriend into it.

"I've read your work," Hanna said stiffly.

"Are you a fan?"

"I wouldn't say that."

"How much have you read?"

"Um, ten pages maybe."

"Not bad."

"So what do you want me to do?" asked Hanna.

"I want to leave this for Hugh."

"What is it?"

"A book."

"Well, he's not here . . ."

"I'm leaving the country," explained Kazuki. He offered her the box, which she tentatively took. She stood on her toes and glanced over Ono's shoulder, fell flatfoot, and then averted her eyes.

"Thank you," said Kazuki.

"Sure, no problem."

As Kazuki turned, he heard the door slam.

Kazuki walked down the worn path to his car, but then, remembering Hanna's self-conscious glance, veered onto a descending path that led into thicker vegetation and rock outcroppings. Twenty yards down the path, he saw a stream, a rock pool and something else. At first, he failed to recognize the object as a body, thought it might have been a gnarled fallen tree trunk. But as he closed, he saw clearly what and who it was: the man whom Hanna had argued with at the café.

What had they done? Despite the heat, Kazuki dug his hands into his pockets and glanced back toward the house.

The body was a problem.

Kazuki noticed something scurrying in the rock pool. Reddish and a few inches long. It burrowed under a rock. Hunching, Kazuki untied his shoes, took off his socks and rolled up his pants. Wading into the water, he bent down, lifted the rock and grabbed the crayfish by its tail. As he did so, he saw several more of the little creatures scuttling about. Holding the crayfish, he walked out of the pool. There was a wound on the man's skull where the flesh looked tender, but the body was too far from the water. He shoved the wriggling crayfish into his pocket, grabbed the man's shirt and tugged the body until the head was floating in the pool.

He set the crayfish on the open wound. The creature froze for a moment, but then realizing its luck began to probe with its claws. As it dug into the flesh, the scent produced an immediate interest from other nearby crayfish, and soon a half dozen crawled out from the mud and rocks, mounted the body and were gnawing merrily away. The notice of the banquet went rapidly upstream and downstream. Among the advancing army of crayfish were several of different color: silver metallic. One crawled up the man's face and with its power claw rammed a hole in the man's skull. Soon numerous crayfish, the robotic well-represented, were disappearing the argumentative young man.

Taking out his cell phone, Kazuki dialed Nakamura Reality. The arrangements made to move the body, Kazuki sighed. He tugged at a lock of his thinning yellow hair and thought of the café poet.

> A rock pool can be calm, but deep.
> A rock pool can be shallow and stormy.
> A rock pool can be cold as dry ice.
> A rock pool can be warm as shit.

Not only was the rock pool deeper than Kazuki calculated, but contained much more shit than Hamlet's lecture to Horatio forewarned.

Which one of us was not in that pool? Struggling for a glimpse of the sky? Wiping the shit from our eyes. Sinking, sinking, sinking.

Alas, poor Yorick.

Alas, poor Yuudai.

The author turned back to the house.

Chapter 38

When Hugh awoke from a brief nightmarish sleep, someone was stretched out in the previously empty bunk across from him. The newcomer wore jeans and a long-sleeved white shirt. He had long straight black hair.

If Hugh were patient, the man would turn.

I'm just watching you, sir. That's all I'm doing.

The man's upper shoulder rolled back, as if he were about to turn face up, but the shoulder returned to its former position.

Hugh had no watch, no laptop, no cell phone to tell time. One Mississippi, two Mississippi . . .

The man didn't turn.

His cell mate might stay that way until the Mississippi ran dry.

Hugh rose from the bunk, stepped toward the man. Perhaps if he just bent over, he would see . . .

The man's hair all but covered his face.

. . . one thousand Mississippi—

Hugh touched the man's shoulder. The man coughed and turned, hair falling from his face, white shirt from his tattooed chest, a dense amalgamation of bird and beast.

"I don't go that way," said Jason.

"Who the fuck—" Hugh glanced beyond the bars to a guard walking a prisoner down the row. A cell door squealed open, another clanked shut. The guard having passed, Hugh hunched down, pressing his face toward the smiling Jason.

"Kazuki got you in here?" asked Hugh.

"I'm your guardian angel. Everyone needs a guardian angel."

"Where are my sons?"

"You eat anything?" Jason reached back on the bunk, grabbed a cloth bag and sat up. "Turkey sandwich?" He pulled a cellophane-wrapped sandwich out of the bag. Jason nipped the cellophane with his small, straight white teeth, unwrapped the sandwich and took a bite, chewing slowly and swallowing before he spoke. "I'm here to make sure nothing untoward happens to you. Child pornography is not a crowd pleaser in county."

"Then get me out of here," said Hugh. "If the all-powerful Ono can get you in here, he can get me out."

"First things first," said Jason, taking a bite of his sandwich. Another guard walked another inmate past Hugh's cell. Jason followed their progress. "Looked like Eric Clapton," said Jason, smiling to show the masticated food. "I shot the sheriff, but I did not shoot—"

"Is the objective to drive me insane?"

"—the deputy," sang Jason, then at the top of his lungs, "I swear it was in self-defense."

"Shut your motherfucking white hole up," someone shouted.

"May I ask you something?" said Hugh.

"Anything."

"Did he set this up?"

"Set what up?"

"Did he get Anna to lie?"

"Your student, you mean? Not the hippie chick?"

"That's *Hanna*. Or *Joanna*."

Jason raised one eyebrow.

"I can't hurt you, can I?" asked Hugh, digging his fingers into the worn mattress. "You're a tough guy, right? Martial arts or something?"

Jason sighed. "That pedophilia shit is troubling."

"I gave a student a ride."

"The way I hear it is that you told a story you shouldn't have told. You told somebody else's story."

Hugh ignored the apparently well-circulated point. "Has Kazuki left the country?"

"Not yet."

"Will he be gone when I get out of—this place?"

"You need some sleep."

"I don't want to sleep. I want my sons."

"I'm here to help you," said Jason. "Until we can get you out of here, you're in my care. You want a little something?" Jason reached into his bag, pulled out another sandwich and unwrapped it. "Pumpernickel," said Jason. "Look at all these caraway seeds." He plucked one from the bread, dropped it in his palm and then plucked a second. He held out his hand to Hugh. Hugh recognized the particular seeds as tablets of Fuguelle.

"Old school," said Jason. "No need to crush, wash and dry. You want?"

Hugh shook his head no.

"You need sleep. Your head needs to be clear."

"Kazuki wants me to forget."

"Kazuki wants you to remember. You need rest."

Jason waved the pills before Hugh.

Hugh recalled the comfort . . . if he didn't fight the drug. For a while the world tide-like would retreat. He would awake lucid. His saliva was copious as if he had sat down before some tantalizing feast.

"Yes. I want them."

"Good as done."

Hugh took two pills from the callused palm and swallowed it or them down.

Chapter 39

Ten minutes. Hugh waited on the dullness.

"Did you love her?" asked Jason.

"Setsuko?" Hugh replied.

"Who else would I be talking about?"

"Yes, I loved her."

"I don't mean in the beginning, I mean at the end."

Hugh imagined Setsuko at Mother's Beach. She wore a sleeveless white dress, tight across her tucked legs. Her black hair hung straight. With the exception of pale pink lipstick, she wore no makeup. She was sketching the bay, her lines no thicker than a spider's silk, but accumulating into recognizable detail: the half-buried piling, the dock with the kayaks, the masts and hulls. Hugh closed his eyes. He was against her and inside her. His mouth clung to her lips, slipped along her smooth neck to the swell of her breasts. His lungs filled with her scent, her sweet breath. Her pulse was the beat of the universe. If he could sit beside her and forget, forget his sons' voices—

Hugh's mind went blank for an instant, as if someone had snapped a switch up and down. "Forever, man, forever," said Hugh.

"Nice to hear," said Jason. "That day when you lost your sons—what happened to you?" asked Jason.

The light went out again. *Click.* Hugh yawned. "I spilled my coffee. I went back to the parking lot to find the mobile truck—"

"You're still singing that old song, huh?"

"I was gone five minutes," insisted Hugh.

"You remember those five minutes?"

"Of course—I . . ." The beach was sizzling. A man with a tripod snapped photos. A little girl in a black wet suit held an upright surfboard to her body. A glance back at the surfers. The boat named *Reality*. A boom box played an oddly affecting version of "Somewhere Over the Rainbow." Hugh wrapped his fingers around the Styrofoam cup that seemed to be dissolving. He went for a cup of coffee, that was all. Why was Jason—

"When I returned, my sons were gone. I dove into the ocean to find them. I didn't find them. The boat must have . . . taken them." *Blank.* No, don't go.

"The boat was there all right. The owner was a friend of Kazuki's. But it was only there to watch. To coordinate. How long did you say you were gone for?"

"Five minutes, maybe ten minutes."

"Yeah, Kazuki's gone to a lot of trouble to let you keep those five minutes. Let the man sleep. *Do not disturb.*"

"*My sons were gone,*" insisted Hugh, head falling.

"Come on, buddy, you need some rest," said Jason, taking Hugh by the arm and helping him from the floor. He eased Hugh into his bunk.

Chapter 40

Kazuki powered up his laptop. On the table was the printout of *Fingal's Cave* that he had taken back from Hugh's girlfriend. He had to add one, perhaps two sentences, which then might lead to three or four or, well, who knew? . . . but only then would it be truly finished.

Only after that could he leave this country.

Chapter 41

The cell door slid open.

Hugh jerked his head to the right. The opposite bunk was empty.

"Haven't got all day," said the guard.

The Valley Cab taxi merged into the left lane of Topanga Canyon Boulevard, the road ahead climbing into the mountains. On the first long curve, a deer emerged from a thicket. How wonderfully delicate its legs, yet as the taxi closed, it effortlessly bounded an almost vertical slope.

The taxi cruised into the village, slowed to a crawl in front of the Peace & Love. On the deck, the poet was performing for a shirtless man on whose shoulders balanced an iguana and a macaw.

The poet's words wafted through the taxi's rolled-down rear windows.

> *A rock pool can be cold as dry ice.*
> *A rock pool can be warm as shit . . .*

Inside the house, Hanna clung to Hugh.

"Where is he?" asked Hugh.

"Who?"

"Kyle."

"Kyle? He's out there, isn't he?"

"He's gone."

"Jesus, he's not dead?"

"No. He's dead all right."

"Then—maybe it was him," suggested Hanna.

"Who?"

"You know. *Mr. Ono.*"

"Kazuki was here?"

"Yesterday. I wasn't going to answer the knock, but I peeked through the curtain. He looked harmless, you know? He explained that he'd come to drop off a book for you, would I accept it? I figured why not? Damned if thirty minutes later, he didn't knock on the door again. He said he wanted the book back. 'It was never finished.' That's what he said."

Hanna and Hugh stood by the rock pool. Kyle's impression was still visible in the mud, but there were no signs that the body had been dragged away.

"Kyle wanted to be a zombie," said Hanna. "He was always saying how he'd rather be a zombie than go to heaven. Maybe he got his wish." Hanna laughed. "Any second now we might see him crashing through the window . . . Kyle, you stupid shit."

As Hugh turned back to the house, he noticed a swift movement at the base of the pool. Several fat crayfish scurrying for cover. The largest moved slowly, stiffly, its body an odd metallic color.

"Paranoid Android" played, and for a moment Hugh thought it came from the heavens. On the other end of the cell phone was Kazuki.

Chapter 42

Kazuki's choice of meeting place surprised Hugh. Hardly a tourist attraction, the archery range was little known even to Los Angelenos. But Hugh had momentarily forgotten the knowledge that his own odyssey bequeathed. For twelve years, his sons were in Kazuki's company. What had he not drawn out of them? What experience remained only Hugh's?

The boys were eight when Hugh had taken them to play basketball at the hilly and sprawling park, which sat adjacent to a golf course; but after shooting hoops for an hour, the boys became restless. Hugh suggested that they explore, see what else the park might offer. The archery range, an unexpected feature of the park, delighted them. There were a half-dozen colorful targets, and behind the targets a wall of stacked hay bales, which were backed up by a grassy hill.

As Hugh and the boys watched the archers, an older black man with a mysterious air came up to them. He laid his bow on a nearby picnic table shaded by a huge scrub oak and beckoned them to come closer. He showed them an unshelled peanut, which he then placed on the top of his baseball cap. A large blue jay darted out of the tree and alighted on the hat. Perched, the jay took the nut in its beak, cracked the shell and ate the peanut. When the bird had finished, the man put another peanut up there. He smiled at Hugh and the boys.

"I'm Francis," he said, extending his sinewy hand to the twins, and then to Hugh, who introduced Takumi and Hitoshi.

"And this is my friend, Bob," said Francis, pointing at the jay.

"Hi, Bob," said the boys, fascinated.

"Want to give him a peanut?"

"Sure."

Francis supplied the boys with peanuts, which they fed to the cooperative bird. For many minutes, Francis regaled the boys with the colorful history of archery. As one of the founders of the range, Francis saw himself as a spokesperson and recruiter for the sport. With Hugh's permission, Francis spent the next hour teaching the boys the rudiments of archery, allowing them to hold his bow and even insert the arrow, which had a blunt tip, the only kind of arrow used at the range. Hunting arrows had razor tips, explained Francis, which if shot skillfully could penetrate the hide of an elephant. Even the blunter-tipped target arrows could kill, a fact meant to impress. Francis said his bow was too strong for the boys, but there were some practice bows that he could find for them. But first they would have to take a safety class.

Soon after, Hugh bought them their own equipment, beginning another weekend ritual. But a year later, their initial passion cooled, and they were on to other things. When the twins gave up the sport, Setsuko was relieved, for the boys didn't confine their sport to the range, taking the bows into the hills and fields when Hugh was away at work, and despite their mother's denial of permission, Hugh thought it no big deal. They had only blunt arrows and they knew the safety rules. Setsuko wanted the bows locked up, but Hugh, though agreeing, postponed and sidetracked the action so many times that Setsuko stopped bringing up the subject.

In the end nothing happened, though one night Hugh came home and found all of the boys' arrows snapped in two. When Hugh asked what happened, Setsuko said she had broken them, but wouldn't explain why. Hugh bought more arrows.

Arriving at the range ten minutes before the appointed time, Hugh spotted Kazuki among a half-dozen archers on the shooting line. He wore a striped polo shirt, beige cargo pants and a Dodgers cap, his gray ponytail jutting up over the rear band like a rooster's comb. Hanging from a band around his neck were a pair of sports goggles, which Kazuki now set over his eyes.

Kazuki set his arrow and pulled back the compound bow, holding the string at the base of his ear for several seconds before he released. With a soft swoosh, the shaft flew true to its target, the yellow bull's-eye of the colored concentric circles. With the barest glance across his shoulder, Kazuki made eye contact with Hugh through the goggles' thick plastic lenses, acknowledging Hugh's presence, and then continued shooting until he'd emptied his quiver. Not every arrow found the yellow, but none were outside the red second circle. Three were grouped as if a single thick shaft. A whistle blew. The archers lowered their bows and retrieved their arrows, exchanging praise and consolation.

The whistle blew again.

Kazuki and the other archers set their shafts.

Don't hurry for me, you bastard.

When the round was done and he had returned his arrows to their quiver, Kazuki walked over to Hugh. He yanked off his goggles.

"Good morning, Hugh. Remember?"

"Yes, I remember."

Hugh had no sooner said that when Kazuki placed a peanut on his hat. Out of the tree a blue jay flew down, landed on Kazuki's hat and ate the peanut.

He'd extracted every detail from them, thought Hugh.

"The novel I've been writing is based on you," said Kazuki.

"I hope it's a success. I hope it gets one million readers."

"I want one reader."

"That's modest."

"You would have had the book already, but . . . I've had to make a few changes."

"Why don't you just tell me?"

Kazuki undid the band around his ponytail and let his hair unfurl. "Do you remember Setsuko breaking the arrows?"

"Yes."

"Why did she do that?"

"She wanted me to lock up their bows. The boys liked to go out on their own and shoot. She didn't think it was safe."

"But you did?"

"There's risk in crossing the street—with the light."

"In the book, the character that represents you," Kazuki smiled, "is named Yuudai, Yuudai O'Keefe. Yuudai's twin sons are named Brent and James, which correspond to Takumi and Hitoshi."

"I get it," said Hugh. Kazuki withdrew a tube of sunscreen from his back pocket. As Kazuki rubbed the sunscreen into his forehead, Hugh watched the archers, their precise movements taking him back fifteen years.

Takumi and Hitoshi dashed to the firing line. They stood arm's length apart and took identical poses, their slender fingers crooked over the strings as they drew back their arrows with such concentration that humanity's survival must depend on piercing that painted yellow foam.

A young pretty woman carrying a bow crossed their path. Kazuki followed her trajectory. Kazuki said, "You spoke with Gina."

"I saw my grave," said Hugh. "You kept tabs on me from the moment I left Japan with Setsuko and the twins."

"I wanted to protect them—and you."

"Me—ah."

"I protect you. You protect them."

"That was my responsibility," said Hugh.

"It broke her," said Kazuki. "Takumi almost killed Hitoshi with an arrow."

"It never fucking happened."

"Your mulish refusal to lock up the bows."

A shaft of sunlight broke through an opening in the branches above, gilding Kazuki's hair where it lay on his shoulder.

"When Setsuko told me, I knew my instincts were correct."

Someone was drawing Hugh's blood. Lighter and fainter. Soon the wind of the laughter would blow him away. He could not hold his ground against this little man who had written his life.

"My daughter was infatuated with you. You were open, joyous, innocent, self-deprecating, funny, a dreamer, yes, but not driven. You didn't want to fly to the sun. You didn't have dreams that would kill you. My daughter didn't know men like you. The young Japanese men of that time were intense. They were devoted to their jobs, their companies, their country. But you know, you've heard the stories. The sixteen-hour days. The seven-day work weeks. The after-work drinking parties with colleagues. The sleeping cubicles in train stations. Life was work or the celebration of work. Oh, not all, of course. But this was how Setsuko saw it. She was ready for an American, especially one that was tall, strong and handsome and cared nothing for conventional success. One who would be *true*. I thought it would pass, and then hoped it would pass and knew it would not pass. Setsuko loved like her mother loved, without limits." Kazuki paused. "My daughter and I were very close. My only child. My wife gone. I didn't want to lose her. You were the devil who would take her to the underworld and leave my world cold and barren. So, I did what I could."

"I want to see my sons," said Hugh. "You promised the truth."

"Do you remember a woman in Tokyo named Nanami?" asked Kazuki.

"Yes," said Hugh.

"You knew her before you met my daughter."

"That's right. But I told Setsuko—"

"That you would never see her again."

Hugh nodded.

"You kept your word?"

Hugh made a fist, smacked his thigh. "I want my sons."

"I need two more days. In two more days you'll see your sons."

"I need something now," said Hugh.

"Do you want it all?" asked Kazuki.

A shadow passed over the two men, but looking up, Hugh saw only empty sky. "Look here," said Kazuki, taking out his wallet. He withdrew a stiff square from the wallet and handed it to Hugh.

In the photo, their faces were at least a year older than the day they had disappeared. Their hair, which had fallen below their ears, was shorn.

"They cut each other's," said Kazuki. "Clipped it all off in protest, like the Irish singer. If that's not enough, you'll find it all at your former house."

"Hitoshi," whispered Hugh, eyes fixed on the image. "Takumi . . ."

"Two days. Two days to finish," said Kazuki.

Chapter 43

Without taking sleeping pills, Hugh slept well, waking with the energy of a ten-year-old boy. In the morning, he put on his sneakers and shorts and ran three miles. He ran through the hills and then on the roadside, and then back into the hills. It was his rule that when he ran, he never rested until he finished the distance. He pushed on, through watery legs and burning lungs. He ran with drink strapped to his hip and his ear leashed to an iPod, Radiohead playing at maximum volume. Today, Kazuki's promise replaced the lyrics of every song.

The last leg of his run was the most difficult. For seventy-five yards, the path climbed a bare hill, the slope increasingly steep toward the summit. During the final ten yards his breathing became pure pain, his heart a burnt-out motor, his legs leaden. But today he ran the uphill stretch as if he were bounding across the moon. By the end of his cool-down, it was seven A.M., and though there was plenty of light, the sun hadn't yet broken above the eastern crest. He uncapped the bottle and drank so thirstily that he choked. He spewed the green liquid over a listless lizard that vibrated for an instant and then returned to its torpor.

Sitting on the ground, Hugh assumed the yoga position that he had learned ten years before while sitting beside a woman with a serene face and breasts like half loops of rope.

Who had set him on the path to the truth? These were the things that God did, when God was around. He took out the picture of his sons in Japan. Their shorn heads made them look like Buddhist monks. How did they adapt to the Japanese language? How did they do in high school? What were their first girlfriends like? Did they play sports? But of course they played sports. Basketball, he supposed, although they were good baseball players, too. He envisioned a continuum of activities, and he saw them growing along the continuum. The sun broke over the hills behind him, its warmth on his back. Flashing across the hills to the sea, the sunlight exposed a wide white line advancing toward the shore. Did they ever surf again? He imagined of course that they would have. He traced their faces with his finger.

"All," Hugh murmured. Kazuki had said *all*. *You'll find it* all *at your former house.* Kazuki was not supposed to call him until late afternoon. He had plenty of time.

Hugh parked in front of the Studio City home. Was there an occupant to let Hugh inside the home? What was *all*?

Hugh got out of the car, walked to the front door and knocked.

No answer. No movement.

He knocked again, producing the same result.

As he unlatched the side gate, he heard a loud car engine. He glanced over his shoulder but saw nothing on the street.

He entered the backyard, pausing to examine the old valley oak. The crook of the tree was twenty feet from the ground and he couldn't see the planks.

He knocked on, and then tried the handle of, the back door.

He wouldn't break into the house. He knew a way in.

On the south side of the house, Hugh knelt before the crawl space. It was covered by wire mesh, along which several fat green caterpillars crawled. He pulled off the caterpillars, which spewed cool, electric-green juice over his fingers, and lined the insects at his feet, where they withered and darkened. A baby rat or mouse wobbled by, crying as if poisoned. Unhooking the mesh, Hugh poked his head into the opening and scanned. To his right was the bathroom, its copper pipes glowing. If he crawled straight forward, he'd be under the hallway. The outer wall of the third bedroom would start twenty feet forward. The closet would be six feet from the path below the hallway. He put one hand inside the crawl space and felt the cool coating. It wasn't dirt or dust, but a soft gray particulate, almost like powder, perhaps to tamp down the dry earth. He touched it like a cat testing water, his fingers curved so that the least amount of flesh would be polluted.

Hugh shimmied through the opening. He stretched his arm back to grab the flashlight, but his hand closed on air. He raked his fingers across the ground, but the flashlight had disappeared. He considered backing out and search- ing, but he noticed that light spilled into the crawl space from cracks in the floor and elsewhere. He wouldn't need the flashlight. He crept forward, his fingernails unearthing lumps of rat shit beneath the dust. As something scampered across his periphery, he lifted his head and rammed his skull on a cross beam, from which protruded a gleaming nail. He crawled another ten feet. The space went pitch black, as if a dense fog were rolling through. Hugh heard more scampering, longer flights. A sheet of light appeared a short distance away. Hugh scuttled toward it. Now four sheets of light, a rectangle of light outlining the trapdoor. He crawled beneath it. Turning on his back, he rested his head against the ground, bent his arms and raised his hands, fixing his palms on the wood. He pushed, but it held fast. Drawing up his knees, he shifted his position for leverage. He arched his back and exhaled as if on the last repetition of a bench press. The wood groaned and gave a little. He pushed harder. Above, something shifted, fell with a clunk. He pushed the panel higher until he saw a row of shirts and pants hanging above. He hooked his hands on the carpeted floor and pulled himself through the opening.

A large cardboard box lay on its side, its contents having spilled across the closet floor. Hugh picked up a tiny worn leather football from the heap of sports equipment. He pressed it to his lips, smelled the fragrant leather, inhaling forcefully to find the oil of his sons' fingerprints.

Clutching the ball, he crawled from the closet. The cedar bunk beds lay unmade, the pillows ruffled, the sheets tangled. Baseball bats, fishing poles and archery sets leaned against the walls, whose pale green surfaces were hardly visible beneath the dozens of glossy posters: gravity-defying skateboarders, berm-hugging dirt bikes, azure-tunneled surfers. Hugh picked up a shirt, pulled it to his face, found the scent of his sons, and within that, their freshly washed skin and hair.

Everything was back.

He got no farther than the living room when he had to stop and lean his back against the divider that had served as the family's bookcase. The air was filled with his sons' movements: the spurts on all fours, the great leaps from floor to couch, the thump of their elbows and knees as they wrestled on the carpet.

It was all there. Everything that Setsuko had purportedly given away: the skateboards, bicycles, radio-controlled cars, baseball bats, footballs and spinning rods.

At the end of the hall the door was closed on the small den that Setsuko had used as a studio. Hugh touched the handle. She liked him to knock first. He knocked and then opened the door. He did not expect to see her, and yet . . .

The easels, the brushes, the finished and unfinished work, all had been returned. Hugh picked up one painting, but set it down when he saw the one behind. He held up the watercolor, a seascape: "Mother's Beach."

Kazuki had gathered it all, as if it might restore what was taken away. Hugh set down the painting. He walked from the studio into the kitchen where he drew a glass of water. On the table was a key, unused a decade, but remembered.

Standing at the garage door, Hugh fit the key into the padlock, finessed the rusty tumblers and removed the lock from the latch. He raised the door, watched the spiders scramble as light filled the cluttered space that had never held one car, much less two. Tricycles and skateboards, deflated rubber pools, bassinets and mechanical rockers, model planes and punching bags, fire trucks and model train tracks. In the center of it all, open path around its perimeter, was a Plexiglas storage container the length and shape of a coffin. Hugh ran his hand along the slick surface, but like one of those crashed alien spaceships, it offered not a seam. Would it open by itself? A skeletal green hand slither out? But, wait, it was not strange at all. Why should it be strange? Hadn't he bought it?

Hugh hunched down, located a round indentation on the forward face and pushed. The top yawned as if awoken from a decade of sleep. Hugh peered at the container's contents.

He was fathoms below the water's surface, slowly rising toward the light, which was not the light of the sun, but a softer, ivory light.

Inside the Plexiglas box, fitted as if reversed forks whose tongs intertwined, were Hitoshi's and Takumi's surfboards. Hugh lifted the top one, Takumi's. He ran his hand along the smooth bottom, followed the curve of the fins and pulled the board to his lips. He then lifted Hitoshi's, pressed his hand to the painted palm tree bent under the wind. Holding the two boards to him as if they were his living sons, he gazed at the open traveling case. From this Kazuki had created Enrique's magical chamber, out of which Hugh had now escaped.

Chapter 44

As Hugh turned south on Pacific Coast Highway, the shadows of palms swept the Volvo's hood and the loose end of a nylon strap, lifted by the onshore breeze, tapped against the windshield as if counting the fleeting silhouettes. Tick, tick, tick.

Hugh bought the car rack at Val Surf on Ventura Boulevard. He was pleased to see that the surfboards on display hadn't changed in ten years, when last he and the twins had toured its rows of Roberts and Channel Islands boards, stroking the Rustys and Losts, debating the merits of each surfboard shaper, like wine enthusiasts judging vintages—still the same size, still the three fins.

In his backyard, Hanna watching, Hugh set his sons' surfboards on the ground and scraped off the dried wax, hard like an old man's stubble. He rubbed on the new, still sold under the brand name Sex Wax, which set him giggling like Scrooge on Christmas morning, free of the spirit world, back in the hurly-burly. Two hours later, he held the boards at arm's length and thought that his boys would appreciate his effort.

Was he not entitled to his whim?

He brought the surfboards into the house for the night and placed them on either side of his bed. Kazuki had called him as promised, and reiterated his promise to reunite him with his sons. Without a milligram of drug, Hugh fell asleep, for he had sailed into calm waters.

Yet whatever the mix of fiction and reality, it had led him to the truth. He may have wandered off on a fictional path, but its terminus was reality.

Hugh was to meet Kazuki at Mother's Beach at four o'clock, and his sons, Kazuki seemed to promise, would arrive subsequently.

Along the coast, it was a perfect afternoon. Hugh drove with the windows down, luxuriating in the cool breeze, drawn to the dazzling moves of the surfers at the endless breaks. Atop the rock seawall, departing beachgoers appeared, faces serene, sated, arms flecked with sea salt. Minutes later the Santa Monica Pier appeared like a sluggish barge, but soon sharpened, its thicket of amusements thinning until the Ferris wheel and roller coaster revealed their spokes and tracks and cars. He and the boys must have spent one hundred days on the pier, striding past the rides to the pier's farthest reaches, where they baited up and dropped their lines. These things they had done and would do again.

He exited PCH at the California Incline and continued south along Ocean Avenue, past the sleek hotels and restaurants, and soon into the Venice funk and flow. As he approached Marina del Rey, he glanced at the muddy canals where Takumi and Hitoshi had seined for bait, now bordered by a rainbow of exotic houses. Turning onto Via Marina, where dozens of sailboats glided across the wide expanse of the channel, he saw at the harbor's entrance the biggest yacht in the world. It looked as if it were stuck, heaving violently as it tried to break through the protective jetties.

At Mother's Beach, the car's clock read three forty-five as Hugh pulled into the same parking space as when he had met with Albert. As before, the seniors were cooking, perhaps dinner but not much different from what they had been cooking for lunch. Waves of smoke carried the rich odor of the charred meat and barbeque sauce. There were a few more visitors on the beach, more families. But it was so similar as to be the week before, and Hugh supposed, the week before that. He looked for Kazuki, but his ex-father-in-law was nowhere to be seen. Ten yards from the tide line, where Hugh, Setsuko and the twins had encamped, Hugh set down his gym bag and towel. He returned to the car, removed the surfboards and carrying one under each arm, walked back to his chosen spot.

"No surf here," said a boy of twelve or thirteen, sitting nearby with his mother, who was offering him a red pail and yellow shovel.

"It comes up later in the day," said Hugh with a wink.

Hugh stuck the boards in by their tails. He spread out his beach towel and sat cross-legged, facing the barbeques and parking lot. He didn't doubt that Kazuki would show up, just as he didn't doubt that his boys would follow. Minutes passed. If Kazuki were late, he would call. Hugh opened his gym bag, dug through the gear for his cell phone, and finally dumped the contents on the towel. He couldn't have been so careless as to leave the phone at home. No, must be in the car. It would take two minutes to run to the parking lot and get it. He rose, looked around. He considered whether he would take the surfboards with him or leave them by the blanket. He could walk backward: well, not backward, but he would turn from time to time to check on the boards. But if some swift-footed urchin grabbed one, well . . . This was the mistake he had made twelve years ago at Oceanside. He thought nothing would happen in his absence, and yet everything had happened. He had left his post. He looked toward the lifeguard stand. He stood up and called out.

"Hey, lifeguard!"

The lifeguard glanced at him. "Would you watch these boards for a minute? Just want to get my cell phone."

The lifeguard adjusted his sunglasses.

Hugh jogged past the seniors, the barbecues, and the Mother's Beach sign. As he reached the parking lot, "Paranoid Android" played softly. Someone was calling him. He reached his car in time to hear his recorded message, but by the time he opened the trunk and found the phone, the recording had stopped. The caller had hung up. As he checked his recent callers, a car pulled alongside him. Parked close. Bright red. Sports car. The call had been from an eight-hundred number. The sports car's driver's door opened. The door tapped the Volvo's body. Hugh closed his trunk.

"Sorry," the woman said, stepping out between the cars, bending to check Hugh's as if for damage. She turned and stepped toward him. "I try to be so careful." He glanced at her, saw that she was pretty and radiant in her summer dress. She was wearing a light, flowery fragrance that carried memories within its scent. He dismissed her concern with a shake of his head, but she smiled at him with glistening lips and asked him a question. He peered into the green eyes, so fixed on his, so interested in him. But it did not happen that way. It did not happen that way. Forgive me. But it did not happen that way. Forgive me. But it did not—he stepped back from the woman. He couldn't answer her question. He hadn't heard her question. He strode back past the Mother's Beach sign, the barbecues, the seniors. His feet sunk into the warm sand. The letters shimmered in his mind's eye like a heat wave.

Sandy.

Hugh envisioned the car coming toward him. The silver-framed license plate: CSNDRA, though he never addressed her, never thought of her—only the diminutive, Sandy, not Cassandra. Never Cassandra. He saw Sandy's face through the windshield. He should turn, run back to his sons, break the promise to meet one more time before he left with his family for Japan. She was visiting a cousin in San Diego. *Ten minutes, come on.* He knew what she hoped. One more chance to convince him of what he had drunkenly suggested. Fool. But Sandy smiled at him and the smile contained the promise that once more he would touch that lovely neck, the pearls of her spine, the slender waist and long thighs. Hear her silly giggle, taste the spearmint on her tongue, answer her bad riddles, submit to her insatiable desire. Unearth what he had buried for Setsuko.

Hugh walked down to the tide line, where he stopped before a weathered stanchion rising from the sand like a rotting arm in a horror movie. His arm snapped back. He smashed his fist into the inoffensive wood. His knuckles flecked with blood, Hugh screamed at nothing more substantial than the ghost of a memory. He could not summon her face, her frost-green eyes, her ever-parted lips, her aquiline nose and ears that stuck out tauntingly through the blonde strands. No, he could not recall—

I said it. Oh, I said it—so my fingers could rest there, so she would cry in relief, so she would laugh joyously. Yes, Sandy, we'll all run away. We'll live on an island with ceaseless waves for our boards and fruit that falls into our palms. Hitoshi and Takumi will grow to love you . . . forget, forget . . .

Setsuko had heard . . . It was only a fantasy, but it should not have been even that. It should not have been. An hour that he had lost, hidden from himself.

He couldn't see her again.

He didn't, or call her or think of her.

Hugh walked into the water, dipped his hand in the bay. When he looked back toward the blanket, the surfboards were gone.

But when he got within fifty feet of his towel, he saw the boards were there, lying flat, no doubt a breeze having knocked them down. He caught his breath. He brushed off the sand sticking to the fresh wax and restored the boards to their upright positions. It was then he noticed the box settled into the sand. He lifted the box, sat down on the towel and opened it. As he began to read, someone yelled.

The shout came from a woman, pulling a small child, thrashing through the water toward shore.

Behind the woman a dorsal fin appeared, and then a second and a third. Screaming children surged and stumbled through the water. A whistle blew. A dozen dorsal fins cut the surface, moving in a tightening circle. Hardly knowing he had taken a step, Hugh was thigh deep in the bay, his arms around a thrashing child.

"Wait! Don't panic!" said Hugh. "They're just leopard sharks. They're harmless. They show up every other summer."

"But they're sharks!" a woman protested.

"There's nothing to be afraid of!"

The lifeguard had jogged to the water's edge. He waved his hands above his head and grinned to allay the crowd's fear. "They're shy. Docile," explained the lifeguard. "They just eat worms and clams."

"What are they doing here?" asked a young mother with a baby strapped to her chest.

"They come with their young. It's safe for them here. Usually they don't come in these numbers, but they're harmless. Really. Harmless." The lifeguard waded out as in demonstration. He pointed. "There's one right there." A few yards from the shore a shadowy form rose to show a dorsal fin and then disappeared.

One man waded out. "Why, it's just like the Galapagos." He took a few more steps. "Hey, I see one."

Several more bathers returned to the water.

Leopard sharks.

Above their heads, a seagull circled.

Hugh returned to his blanket, opened the box and took out a manuscript with red covers. He turned back the cover.

Fingal's Cave by Kazuki Ono.

Hugh turned another page and read, "A few distant lights sputtered on as the plane neared its target, which from an altitude of thirty-two thousand feet was clearly visible beyond a few scattered cumulus clouds. Extraordinary only in its untouched landscape . . .

Two hours later, Hugh rose from his blanket and carrying the manuscript walked into the water. Amidst sharks, Hugh dug his feet into the bay's primordial mud, and let the appalling words seep into him.

He had never again contacted Sandy, but with more reason she had never again contacted Hugh. Kazuki had found her, paid her just as Katashi had paid Cassandra. But Hugh's resistance was negligible. Hugh did exactly what Kazuki planned for him to do. The job done, Kazuki paid Hugh's old girlfriend to disappear. Setsuko could not have known this. Setsuko knew only what she saw and heard.

Was he like Yuudai a danger to his children?

He was not Yuudai, but was he Yuudai in Setsuko's eyes?

Yes, or she would not have allowed her father's plan to unfold, his book to be written.

Surely Katashi had lied to Yuudai. For all her will Sumiko could not turn back time, could not become the bird that took the arrow. Besides, the voice behind Katashi's door called out *Dad*.

Chapter 45

Leaving Hanna in the car, Hugh entered the Olympic. The lobby was crowded. A three-piece jazz band played "Mood Indigo." Hugh waited in a line at the reservations desk behind a man in a short-sleeved pilot's uniform. The man's forearms were enormous. He was telling a joke to a woman in a cowboy hat. The woman laughed appreciatively.

Five minutes later the clerk smiled and asked, "Checking in?"

"No. I want to speak with Kazuki Ono. He's a guest here."

"Oh . . ."

"Is he in his room?"

"Are you a relative?"

"Yes. I'm his son-in-law."

The clerk's face tightened. "I'm surprised you haven't been notified."

"Notified?"

"Mr. Ono has passed."

"Passed? Passed as in died?"

"Yes. He passed."

"That's impossible."

"Were you out of the country?"

"No, I—how did he die?"

"Perhaps you should—"

"Please. It's okay."

"Natural causes," the clerk said carefully.

"Here at the hotel?"

"Oh, no, no. It was in the marina. There was a story in yesterday's paper. Wait . . ." The clerk strode to a door behind the desk. He came out a moment later and handed Hugh the paper. "It's in the Extra section."

On August 2, Kazuki Ono, a Japanese citizen, had died in Marina del Rey at Mother's Beach. There were paragraphs of information about Ono's writing career. How the English editions of his work sold very well . . . his literary prizes. Numerous ties to America . . . Nothing about children, grandchildren. Funeral services and burial were to be held at High Meadow Cemetery on August 5. As Hugh set down the paper, a small obituary caught his attention: *Valdez.*

"He's dead," said Hugh, getting into the car. "Is he dead?"

Chapter 46

Hugh ignored the flashers of the motorcycle closing on him. He had been over the speed limit, but not by much. If the police found Kyle's body, Hugh and Hanna would be the prime suspects. *Pass us,* Hugh prayed. *Be on your way to an accident.* But the cop remained on their tail. Hugh nudged the accelerator. If he kept driving, the cop couldn't physically stop him. It would be one of those slow pursuits, and if Hugh got to the cemetery . . .

"Better pull over," said Hanna.

"This fucking can't be," said Hugh. The motorcycle was on his ass now. Maybe ten feet away. Ignoring the insistent swirling light, Hugh sped up.

"There will be a million cops," said Hanna. "Please, Hugh?"

"I'll slow down, let you out."

"You don't—you can't." Hanna clapped her hand over his, squeezed.

Hugh groaned and pulled over.

The helmeted CHP officer waited by his motorcycle for a few moments, recording the Volvo's license plate and calling in the information. These steps finished, he approached Hugh's car.

"Sir, may I see your license and registration," said the officer.

Hugh nodded. The officer bent his head, glanced at Hanna, and then removed his sunglasses. Hugh gazed at the cop.

"Sir, license and registration?"

"Oh, yes."

It had been almost ten years, but as Hugh extracted his driver's license and looked up, he recognized the young officer, who simultaneously recognized him.

"Hey, Mr. Mac!" said the surprised officer.

"Arash, right?" responded Hugh.

"Yes, *Arash*. Man, you've got a memory."

"Cause and effect," said Hugh.

" 'Cause and effect?' "

"Arash talks without permission. Arash gets paper pick-up. Arash changes chairs without permission. Arash gets paper pick-up."

The young officer threw back his head, laughed and clapped Hugh's shoulder. "So how have you been? Still teaching?"

"Yes, same school, same classroom. And look at you. A policeman."

"Rookie year. Can you believe it?"

Hugh turned to Hanna. "One of my former students: Arash. I had him in my class the first year I taught."

"Cool," said Hanna.

"Man, we gave you trouble," said Arash.

"Ah, it was nothing."

"No matter how pissed off you got, you never yelled."

"Sure, I yelled."

"I don't remember."

Hugh nodded. "I yelled."

"Ah, a little, maybe." Arash looked away, put his hand to his mouth as if he were about to cough. He met Hugh's eyes, released his words. "You were my favorite teacher, Mr. Mac. You pushed us, but we learned a lot. I learned stuff I didn't think I could."

"That means a great deal to me," said Hugh.

Arash nodded. "Yeah, yeah. So what are you doing in Simi?"

"A funeral. High Meadow."

"Oh, I'm sorry, Mr. Mac. Family?"

The police radio crackled. Arash excused himself and walked back to the motorcycle. In his rearview, Hugh watched Arash converse for several minutes on his radio. Arash was expressionless as he walked back to Hugh's car. If they had found Kyle's body and were looking for Hugh and Hanna, Arash would quickly put memories of middle school behind. Hugh pressed the clutch to the floor, started the engine and shifted to first.

"Hey," said Arash as he came within an arm's length of the car, "are you running late?"

"Excuse me?"

"For the funeral?"

"Well, yes, actually."

"That's why—" Arash grinned and put away his ticket book. "Need an escort?"

"Oh, you don't have to—"

"Glad to. Where did you say?"

"High Meadow," replied Hugh.

"Cause: Late for a funeral. Effect: CHP Escort," said Arash with a grin. He returned to his bike, mounted and shot in front of the Volvo.

Hugh followed the motorcycle, siren blaring and lights flashing, as they continued into Simi.

"Wow, you lucked out," said Hanna.

At the cemetery gates, Hugh shook Arash's hand. "You're about the same age as my sons," said Hugh.

"You got sons? Never knew. Great."

As Arash mounted his motorcycle he called out, "Watch your speed. We don't mess around in Simi."

"Back again?" asked the gate guard.

Hugh nodded. "The Kazuki Ono services?"

"Oak Knoll section. Just drive—"

"Thanks. I know . . ."

Dozens of cars had parked roadside. Hugh pulled up behind a Lexus with a license plate frame reading *Japanese Consulate*.

As Hugh exited his car, a hearse drove up, braked, and then slowly backed into the space behind Hugh. The hearse's license plate frame read *Nakamura Reality: Funerals for all Occasions*. Hugh glanced up. The hearse's driver, wearing sunglasses and a cap, nodded twice and then smiled pleasantly at Hugh.

Hanna and Hugh walked swiftly on the path leading into Oak Knoll, perhaps one hundred yards distant, where the mourners gathered. On the approach, they passed several smaller services, white placards identifying the loved one. On the second placard, written in large Gothic letters, was the name *Juan Valdez*. A black arrow pointed to the ceremony, already in progress. Among the handful of attendees, Hugh recognized Anna and Aaron. Anna turned her head, caught sight of Hugh, nodded solemnly and then, her arm discreetly at her side, spread her index and middle fingers to make the peace sign. Looking back toward the gravesite, she shook her head ever so slightly.

What pauper was going into that grave?

Hugh moved on.

Above an open grave, High Meadow's most expensive casket swayed. None of the mourners looked familiar. Hugh feared he was at the wrong service until the crowd under pressure from the rear ranks reshaped itself, propelling forward Mr. Huddle, the bookstore proprietor, who met Hugh's eyes and smiled sadly. Now Hugh saw others whom he recognized: Gina and her daughter, Lily; Kazuki's confidant, Jack. Lily waved her hand at Hugh and mouthed *boring*. Hugh glanced at Hanna who clung to his side, the weight and solidity of her body comforting. Like tall grasses parting daintily at the passage of a snake, the mourners separated to permit the late arrival of a cassocked priest.

"I'm Father Maloney," said the priest, edging his way to the coffin. "Please accept my apologies for being late, and when the collection plate for my speeding ticket is passed around, give freely." The remark drawing no laughs, Father Maloney cleared his throat and raised his arms above his head. In his left hand, he held a Bible.

"Kazuki Ono was a latecomer to the Catholic Church, accepting its graces within the last beat of his heart, the last snap of synapse, the last metamorphosis of light into corneal impulse . . ."

A shadow fell upon the mourners. Hugh glanced up to see a raggedy cloud rushing north, so swiftly that blue sky returned before his eyes could turn away.

". . . let us commend Kazuki Ono to the mercy of God . . ."

Tracing a circle in the blue, a solitary gull alternately dipped and climbed.

A motor droned.

"We therefore commit Kazuki Ono's body to the ground; earth to earth, ashes to ashes . . . dust to dust . . . in the sure and certain hope of the resurrection to eternal life."

The hoist whined loudly at the heavy casket, as if complaining.

Above, the gull screeched in reply.

Hugh was hardly aware that the service had ended. The house lights had come up, the concert was finished. Mourners broke past Hugh, stripping their jackets, returning to their cars, talking of dinner.

Someone had taken his hand. "Should we go?" asked Hanna.

The gull squawked again.

Hugh slipped his hand from Hanna's. "Would you wait here a moment?" he asked.

Hanna shrugged, lowered herself to the grass, smiled up at the bright blue sky.

As Hugh came in sight of H. Mcpherson's grave, the ground sunk beneath him as if freshly shoveled.

At the gravesite, two tall young men with long black hair set bouquets of flowers on the grass beneath the stone.

"Sons?"

The two men turned. The one who had retained his bouquet let it fall, scattering the flowers.

"Dad?" asked Hitoshi—for though twelve years had passed, Hugh was certain which twin addressed him. Takumi stepped back, clutching the gravestone.

"Are you a ghost?" asked Hitoshi.

"It's not possible," said Takumi. "Where—"

Hitoshi moved toward Hugh then stopped and jerked his head back as if to take in his father's scent. His eyes grew big, liquid. Hugh touched his son's smooth bare throat, and Hitoshi's hand slipped over his.

"You're all right, then?" asked Hugh.

"How are you alive, Dad?"

The giving earth now seemed to drop out entirely. Hugh reached up, but there was no ledge to grasp. Without purchase, he sank. Oh, how fucking black and cold it was. He gazed up, saw only nothingness. He had not come out of the sea then. But what was that sound? A shadow? A lighter shade of black? The clap of a hand against water. Swimmers. Someone swimming over him. The swimmers drew closer: Hitoshi and Takumi. He heard their voices and felt their strong arms around him, pulling him to the surface.

Beneath Mcpherson's headstone, Hugh lay. Above him were his sons. He trembled, fought back a trickle of bile, dug his fingers into the soft grass and laughed.

He watched his sons study him in disbelief. Finally, Hitoshi bent and touched him. Assuring himself of his father's flesh, Hitoshi said, "Then—then our mother is coming back too, from—"

Takumi let out a breath. "—the dead?"

"Your mother?"

Hitoshi looked toward Takumi, who pushed away from the stone. Takumi stood tall and threw back his shoulders. "Our mother is gone."

Above them, the circling gull squawked. Hugh rose to his knees, followed the gull's path.

"Gone Mama," said Hitoshi.

"Dead? Setsuko's dead?" asked Hugh.

Neither son said a word.

"But how?"

Takumi and Hitoshi exchanged glances. They would not tell him, for he would not believe it. But Hugh already knew and believed. *Anyone or anything that tries to take what I love.*

As his two sons lifted him to his feet, Hugh looked up toward the circling gull. But she too was gone.